Secret Royal

S. C. Wise

CENA Publishing
Flower Mound, TX

ISBN: 0615359531
ISBN-13: 978-0615359533

CENA Publishing, December 2012

Other books written as Stephanie Amox:
Painfully Ordinary
Family Secrets
New Beginnings
Rushing Calm

ACKNOWLEDGMENTS

To my family who exhibits an epic level of patience with me when I'm writing. Love you guys more than you'll ever know.

My editor Julie – thank you for never being afraid to challenge me and reminding me that not everyone can read my mind. Working with you has made me a better writer and all the years I've called you friend have made me   a   better   person!

PLAYLIST

1. Between the Raindrops – Lifehouse
2. Breaking The Girl – Red Hot Chili Peppers
3. Breathe – Taylor Swift
4. The Call – Regina Spektor
5. Come Away With Me – Norah Jones
6. Crystal – Stevie Nicks
7. Don't Know Why –Norah Jones
8. Fearless – Taylor Swift
9. I'm Not The Only One – Sam Smith
10. It was Always You – Maroon 5
11. Just The Way You Are – Bruno Mars
12. Leave The Pieces – The Wreckers
13. Set Fire to the Rain – Adele
14. Stay With Me – Sam Smith
15. Take Me to Church – Hozier
16. Under The Bridge – Red Hot Chili Peppers
17. The Way I Loved You – Taylor Swift
18. White Horse – Taylor Swift
19. Thinking Out Loud – Ed Sheeran
20. Carry on Wayward Son - Kansas

1 EMORY

"Did you want to talk to me?" Evie toyed with her necklace as she stood in the doorway of her boss's office.

"Yes, we need to come up with a new email format for our monthly shareholder newsletters. I need you to get updates from each of the functional groups and put it together," Sean instructed without ever even looking up at her.

Evie's heart raced. Finally, here was her big chance. "No problem. I'll start working on it now and see how much I can get done before I leave. I'll send it out to the usual distribution list as soon as it's done after I get back on Tuesday."

Sean waved his hand dismissively. "No, that won't be necessary. Just send it to me as soon as you're done and I'll send it out from my email account."

Evie's face fell and her grip tightened on the doorframe. *Of course you will,* she thought. *Why should this time be any different?* Sean always had Evie do all the work and took all the credit. She even suspected he had sabotaged the couple of times she'd applied for other positions within the company. He wanted to keep her right where she was – firmly under his thumb. Thankfully Monday was Labor Day and she would have a three-day weekend to unwind. It was at times like this that she was grateful she lived in Texas. She was heading to the small town of Emory for the weekend to visit her favorite aunt. Evie knew the trees would still be green and the weather would be warm enough to enjoy the lake if she wanted.

"Evie?" Sean's voice broke into her daydream. "Do you think you could have this ready by Tuesday morning?"

Leave it to him to add insult to injury – he was actually asking her to work on his project over a holiday weekend while, she suspected, he spent his time at the lake.

Evie felt a spark of anger flicker to life within her chest; she'd finally had enough. "I'm sorry, Sean, but that just won't be possible. I'm going out of town this weekend to spend some time with my family." She wasn't sorry at all. In fact, she was enjoying watching him squirm. She had never stood up to him before, and he was having a very hard time maintaining his composure.

His eyes darted around the room and he picked at the eraser on his pencil. "But... It needs to be done by then and I have plans at the lake."

Evie shrugged her shoulders. "I don't know what to tell you, Sean. I'm driving my mom out to visit her sister in the country and we won't be back until late Monday night."

His face brightened. "I know! You can take one of the laptops and work on it while you're there. You can dial in from your aunt's house."

Evie realized she was enjoying herself. "No can do, Sean. There's hardly even cell coverage down there – finding Wi-Fi would be unheard of. Sorry; either you'll have to handle it on your own, or wait until everyone gets back to the office on Tuesday." She turned on her heel and headed back to her desk, leaving him sputtering.

He'll probably fire me for that, but I just don't care anymore. Hell, it's already 5:30; I might as well go home now. Everyone else left almost an hour ago, she thought. She slammed her desk drawer after grabbing her purse and keys, stalked out of the building, and jumped into the car. Her phone rang as she locked the doors.

"Hey, Mom. What's up?"

"Hi, baby. Are you out of the office yet?" Her mother, Colleen, had always had a voice like a warm, comforting blanket.

"Just leaving now. Sean was trying to get me to work on a project for him this weekend so he could go to the lake. He actually suggested I connect through Wi-Fi from Emory." She dissolved into giggles.

Colleen chuckled. "Did you educate him on why that's a stupid idea?"

"Oh yeah. I wish you could've seen him. He looked so confused."

The display on Evie's phone flashed an incoming call from Sean.

"Oh, nice. Hang on, Mom, Sean's calling. Why am I not surprised?" She switched calls. "Hello?"

"Evie, thank goodness I caught you." Sean breathed a sigh of relief. "I wanted to see if you could come back to the office and we can try to knock out some of the framework before you go out of town tomorrow."

Evie thrust her chin out defiantly. "I'm terribly sorry, but I'm picking my mom up right now."

"But... I thought you weren't leaving until tomorrow." He wailed.

"We changed our plans and are leaving tonight." She said unsympathetically. "Sean, I hate to cut you off, but I need to get out of the car and help my mom. See you Tuesday." She grinned to herself and hung up the phone. It wasn't like her to push back, and she liked it.

"Mom?"

"I'm still here, baby. What did he want?"

"He wanted me to come back to work tonight since you and I weren't supposed to leave until tomorrow morning."

"You are kidding me!" Colleen was appalled.

"Nope. Get your stuff together, Mom; we're leaving tonight. We'll drive through somewhere for a bite to eat and some caffeine. I just want to get out of here. Will you call Aunt Winnie and tell her we'll be there tonight?"

"I can be ready in five minutes." Evie could imagine her mother's beaming smile. "I'll call her right now. See you in just a little bit."

Evie hung up the phone and smiled to herself. She was really looking forward to their trip to Emory and the tranquility she knew she would find there. She found Colleen waiting in the driveway with her bag sitting at her feet. They headed for their favorite drive-through for crispy chicken sandwiches and iced tea. They had just settled in for their long drive when her mother turned to her and crossed her arms.

"Why do you let him take advantage of you like that?" Colleen demanded with a frown.

Evie sighed. "It's just not worth the fight most of the time. I need the job and haven't had any luck the few times I've tried to find something else. No one seems willing to take a chance on me, neither at work, nor in my personal life. They all want me to make their lives easier and to 'know my place.' They could care less how I feel about things." She said sadly.

"Oh, sweetie, you just haven't found the right one yet." Colleen said reassuringly.

"Clearly." Evie replied sarcastically and rolled her eyes.

They sat in silence for a few minutes before Evie clenched her jaw. "Never again," she swore. "I'll never let another man exhibit that kind of control over me ever again. I'm ready to be in charge of my own life for a while."

Her mother patted her hand and gave her a smile of encouragement. "Now that's more like it."

They drove in silence until they reached the Emory city limits. Evie exhaled a huge sigh of relief as a giant weight lifted off her shoulders. The silence of the car was momentarily shattered by the shrill ring of Colleen's cell phone.

"Hell-oooo." Colleen sang into the phone.

"Hi. Are you guys close?" asked Aunt Winnie.

"We sure are. We just passed the city limits."

How does she DO that? Evie mouthed at her mother. Her mother shrugged her shoulders and focused her attention on her call.

"Why don't you two make a quick stop at the liquor store and we'll make some cocktails? I already whipped up a pan of brownies." Winnie said.

"You bet." Mom said with a smile as she hung up.

Evie grinned. "Let me guess – we're making a small side trip? What kind of dessert did she make this time?"

Her mom chuckled. "Brownies."

"Hmm, I think that calls for mimosas." Evie said as she pulled into Big Daddy's Liquor Store.

They pulled into Aunt Winnie's narrow gravel driveway about 15 minutes later. Aunt Winnie's small frame appeared in the doorway of her little yellow house, which was dwarfed by the trees surrounding it. She was a tiny woman with a larger-than-life personality. Actually, all the women in their family were tiny. Their hair was the one major thing that differentiated them from one another. Winnie had short, curly, salt-and-pepper hair that framed her elfin face. Colleen had fine hair the color of caramel, which she wore in a pixie cut. Evie's hair was her crowning glory; it fell in a cascade of strawberry-blonde waves down her back. People frequently commented on its beauty.

Winnie's blue eyes met emerald in deep understanding. "Hard day, Evie-girl?" She asked knowingly.

"Nothing some homemade brownies and three or four mimosas can't fix." Evie said with a grin.

Evie helped her mother grab the bags and they stepped up on the porch. A wave of tranquility swept over Evie as she crossed the threshold and looked around at the familiar surroundings. She followed the smell of freshly baked brownies into the kitchen. Winnie pulled three large glasses out of the cabinet and set them on the breakfast bar alongside the gallon of orange juice and several champagne bottles.

"Who's mixing tonight?" asked Colleen.

"I vote for Evie. Mimosas are her specialty." grinned Winnie.

"OK, OK. You two always end up getting your way anyway. It's my fault – I've spoiled you." Evie waved her hands in mock defeat.

The three women spent several hours sitting in Winnie's cozy little kitchen reminiscing over old family stories.

"Oh my God! Mom, tell me she is kidding! Did Pawpaw and his brothers really break each other out of jail by using a horse-drawn carriage to pull the cell bars out of the wall? No *wonder* I have such issues with authority in my personal life – it's in my genetic makeup." Evie dissolved into laughter. Her mother and Winnie joined in her laughter and soon they all had flushed cheeks.

"It is awfully warm in here; shall we continue this party out on the back porch?" asked Winnie while fanning her face.

Evie was already heading toward the back door with a champagne bottle under one arm and her empty glass and a jug of orange juice in the other. She looked back long enough to call over her shoulder. "Come on, Mom, there isn't anything to worry about out here."

"No way; you know how I feel about being outside at night. I just feel too exposed. You ladies go ahead, and I'm going to grab a long, hot shower." Colleen grinned.

Evie shrugged. "Your loss. Come on, Aunt Winnie, I can't wait to get outside in the breeze." She held the door and waited for her beloved aunt to pass through. She refreshed both drinks and handed one to her aunt. They sat on the porch and watched Winnie's kitten pounce on a cricket that had found its way up to the house.

"Evie, you seem overly tense. What is wrong, baby-girl?" Winnie's blue eyes were deep with concern.

Evie took a large swallow of her mimosa. "Aunt Winnie, it's just the same old story. My boss is a jerk; he has me do all the work and then he takes all the credit. Then there's my personal life... or lack thereof." Evie sighed deeply. "I can't seem to find anyone who can love me for who I am. They all want to control me in one way or another. I've just about given up hope of finding someone who likes me for me... not what they think they can turn me into." Evie allowed her chin to drop to her chest.

"Darlin', maybe you're just looking in the wrong places. I think a couple of days here in the country may be just what you need."

"You know what, Aunt Winnie? I think you're right." Evie said with a smile.

They sipped their mimosas, both lost in thought. Evie noticed a flashing out of the corner of her eyes and gasped. "Fire flies!" She exclaimed and pointed at the grove of trees growing at the back of the property. Her smile stretched from one ear to another.

Winnie turned in the direction Evie was pointing. "Well, would you look at that? It's the fairy-flies. It's been a while since they've been around." She returned Evie's grin.

Evie leaned over and gave her a quick squeeze. "The fairies; I had almost forgotten!"

Winnie had always told Evie stories about the local fairies when she had visited as a child. There were two types of fairies, the Tuatha De and the Shadow Fairies. Even as a very young girl, Evie had known the basic rules of Tuatha De, or the fairy realm: do not approach a fairy circle at midnight, or the fairies might make you dance until you die of exhaustion; never fall asleep in a fairy circle, or the fairies might carry you away to Tuatha De; and if you ever found yourself in the fairy realm, you must never eat or drink anything – to do so would make you forget your life in the human world and you would be trapped forever. Evie had always loved the stories about the Tuatha fairies with their tall, statuesque grace and heartbreaking beauty. They were everything she had always dreamed of being. They were tall and lean, while she was petite and curvy; she had a tiny waist with toned legs from years of dance classes. She stared at the dancing points of light in the distance and let her imagination take flight.

"Evie? Hello?" Winnie was snapping her fingers in front of Evie's face, trying to pull her out of her daydream.

"Oh, I'm sorry." Evie said, startled. "What's up?"

"I was asking where you wanted to sleep. We can go inside or we can sleep out here in the hammocks, but I'm too wiped out to drag out the tents."

Evie smiled. They had frequently slept outdoors during her visits as a child. She had always loved the feel of the cool night breeze and the soft light of the moon against the sparkling backdrop of the night sky.

"Definitely the hammocks." Evie said emphatically. "Let me go tell Mom, 'cause you know *she* isn't about to sleep outside. Why's she so paranoid about being outside at night? It's so incredibly peaceful. I've never understood that at all."

Winnie shook her head. "She has her reasons, but that's a story for another time and place." She said softly.

Evie looked at her with a raised eyebrow before walking into the house to talk to her mom.

"Be careful out there." Her mom said, nervously picking at the edge of a blanket.

"Mom, relax. I'm going to be in a hammock, not three feet from Winnie's hammock, and they're both just steps from the back door. We'll be fine. The fairy-flies are out tonight." Evie said excitedly.

"Somehow that doesn't make me feel any better." Her mom said dryly.

Evie caught her tiny mother in a bear hug. "Get a good night's sleep. We'll see you in the morning for breakfast."

Her mother gave her a loving smile. "You two take care of each other out there." She said over her shoulder as she retreated to the bedroom.

Evie grabbed a couple of pillows and blankets and lightly ran down the back porch steps to the hammocks nestled between two ancient pine trees.

"Here you go." Evie said tossing a pillow and blanket to her aunt. "I grabbed these since it cooled off quite a bit tonight."

"Good idea. It might get a little chilly with the breeze tonight." Winnie agreed.

The two women snuggled under the blankets and let the cool breeze gently rock the hammocks. Evie watched the tiny lights flicker in the distant trees as she drifted off into dreams of a mighty fairy warrior.

A small ball of light emerged from the trees and circled the hammocks before slowly shimmering into the shape of a heavily muscled man. He soundlessly walked over to the two sleeping women and stood over the younger one in awe.

She was back. He had seen her once before several years before. *Could this really be a descendant of Beauford Adair?* Aulis wondered to himself. *She has the same small build of the Adair women, but she's far more curvaceous than the others,* he noticed with a smile. He reached out and gently touched a lock of her hair. *She would be the first Guardian with red hair in many centuries. It's the color of molten lava and falls in waves like the ocean rises to meet the sea.* Without thinking, he placed a seed in the palm of his hand and muttered a few words over his closed fist. When he opened his hand, a beautiful purple lily blossom lay in his palm; he tucked the blossom behind one of Evie's ears. The purple flower was a striking contrast to her red-gold hair. He ran his hand over her shoulder and down her side to where her tiny waist dipped in before meeting her hips. Evie stirred and moaned softly in her sleep.

"Well, puss, you crave to be petted, do you?" He murmured wickedly. He licked his lips in anticipation. "I think I can accommodate you." He pushed aside the blanket and ran one hand down her toned thigh to cup a firm calf and massage it.

Evie squirmed in her sleep as she slipped deeper into her erotic dream. *The fairy warrior loomed over her, the soft moonlight catching the slabs of muscle on his chest and stomach. His dark hair hung to his shoulders in thick curtains on either side of his face. His eyes burned with raw need as he ran his callused hand down her leg while he devoured her with his eyes, and she felt herself drowning in her own desire. When he leaned down, she could feel his warm breath against her ear, sending shivers through her body. "You are mine." He whispered against her ear. His voice sent a delicious shudder all the way to her very soul. She lifted her face to his, and he consumed her lips in a kiss that caused them both to go up in flames. Evie kissed him greedily until her lips were swollen from the intensity. He pulled back reluctantly, his eyes wistfully memorizing the planes of her face. "I must go, but know this – we'll meet again very soon." He kissed her deeply one last time and then disappeared in a flash of golden light.*

2 THE FLOWER

Evie awoke with a start and sat up so quickly she almost flipped out of the hammock. She looked over and saw Aunt Winnie was already up – probably cooking breakfast. *What an amazing dream,* she thought. She raised her arms above her head and stretched with the grace of a cat. She sighed happily, still caught in the memory of a perfectly delicious dream. She reached up to brush her thick hair back from her face and found something caught up in her hair; she stared in shock at the purple lily now lying in her trembling palm. Evie shook her head back and forth in an effort to clear her mind. She looked back down at the all-too-tangible evidence of her dream and scrambled out of the hammock, sprinting toward the house when her bare feet touched the soft grass like a fox during a hunt.

She burst through the back door breathlessly, allowing the screen door to crash shut behind her. She looked at her aunt with wild eyes. "Aunt Winnie?" She asked tentatively while holding the flower in an outstretched palm like an offering.

Winnie paused from moving freshly cooked bacon out of her old iron skillet and stood with the tongs in the air. "Evie, what's wrong? Where on earth did you find a lily this time of year?"

Evie's voice barely rose above a whisper. "It was in my hair."

Winnie took several steps toward her, bacon forgotten. "Evie... did something happen after I fell asleep last night?" She suddenly grabbed Evie's upper arms. "Tell me you didn't go into the woods last night to chase the fairy-flies!"

Evie shook her head. "No, I haven't done that since the last time I was here and I ran off in a tequila-sunrise-induced haze. As a matter of fact, I haven't drunk one of those since that night. Ugh, what a hangover."

"Child, do you remember what you dreamt of last night?" Winnie asked casually.

Evie blushed to the roots of her hair.

Winnie chuckled. "I can see that you do remember. Can you tell me what it was about? I don't need a lot of detail, just a basic idea."

"Um… yeah, sure." Evie stammered. "It had a big, beefy fairy warrior in it and he put a flower in my hair."

"That is all?" Winnie asked in disbelief.

"Well, yes – without going into a lot of detail." Evie said, still blushing.

Understanding lit in Winnie's eyes and her mouth formed an O. "I see. Darlin', looks to me like you have a fairy admirer."

Evie stared at her, eyes wide in disbelief. "You have got to be kidding, right?"

"Not in the least. I've told you all the stories about our family's connection with the Fae. You always believed before; why the sudden change?"

Evie fought desperately to maintain a tight grip on her sanity. *Why? Probably because I'm almost 30 years old – that's why.* She shook her head, trying to sort her thoughts.

"Because we were always talking about someone else. Besides, the warrior in my dream was *way* too perfect to be real." She gave a small smile as she recalled some of the details from her dream. Perfect wasn't nearly a strong enough word to describe him.

Winnie patted her arm gently. "Describe him for me. This is very important." She said seriously.

"OK." Evie shrugged. "He was really big. Not just tall, but heavily muscled… and I stress heavily. He had thick hair that fell down either side of his face and went just past his shoulders. The only light came from the moon, so I couldn't tell the exact color – only that it was dark. He didn't really say much except 'You're mine' and 'We will meet again, very soon,' and then I woke up."

Winnie inhaled sharply. "Wow, Evie-girl. Sounds like you hit the fairy jackpot. If I am not mistaken, you have grabbed the attention of one of the most important fairies in the entire realm – Aulis. He and his twin brother, Ari, are the two most feared warriors in the human and fairy realms."

Evie gulped audibly. "Dear God – you mean there are two of them?"

Winnie laughed. "Oh yes, but Ari married many years ago, so it had to have been Aulis." She fanned herself with a crocheted potholder. "That one's reputation as a lover is positively legendary. Women of all races have thrown themselves at his feet for centuries. However, he's never been known to pursue a woman; they've always come to him."

"Lovely. Just what the world needs – another cocky jerk." Evie sneered.

"Evie! Do you understand the significance of that flower in your hand?" Winnie slapped one palm down on the breakfast bar.

Evie shook her head. "No. How would I?"

Winnie sighed softly. "By leaving that flower in your hair as a gift, he has branded you as his. It also serves as a warning to other magical folk to stay away as you're under his protection." She put her soft, withered hands on either side of Evie's face. "My child, he's never done that before, not in all these centuries. I've heard many stories of him, but they all had one recurring theme – he never found a woman who could hold his attention. Believe me, many tried... and failed. This is an incredible honor he has bestowed upon you."

But Evie hadn't gotten past Winnie's first sentence. "He's *branded* me? I refuse to let *any* man have control over me. I swore after my last boyfriend that I'd never lose control in a relationship again. I'm tired of having someone barking orders and trying to change who I am." Evie was vehement.

Winnie clapped a hand over Evie's mouth. "Shhh. You must not offend him. Show him the respect he's due. For now, we need to put the flower in water and display it in the window. Don't get wound up just yet. I strongly suspect he'll be making another appearance soon. We'll play it by ear – but you'll have to keep your tongue folded behind your teeth and show respect. Fairies are easily offended."

Evie nodded with wide eyes. "OK." Now her aunt had her worried. *What kind of man is he? Would he really cause us trouble?*

Colleen breezed into the kitchen. "Who'll be making another appearance soon?" She asked as she grabbed a piece of bacon off a plate and popped it into her mouth.

Evie didn't notice her aunt shaking her head and mouthing "No" until it was too late. "Aulis." She said simply.

The color drained from her mother's face and her eyes became huge pools of chocolate. Evie could tell she was struggling to remain calm. "Did you say Aulis? Winnie, tell me she means someone else! Please?"

Winnie patted her arm gently. "You know exactly who she means. Colleen, they are back." She said softly.

Colleen began to shake. "No, not now. Winnie – if they have returned it can only mean one thing."

Winnie nodded. "War." She replied.

Evie waved her hands in the air. "Whoa, whoa, whoa... War? What the hell are you two talking about? War with whom?"

Winnie looked at Colleen in frustration. "Didn't you ever tell her any of our history?" Winnie sighed. "Evie, all the fairy stories I told you when you were little are true. If Aulis has come out into the open, it means the Shadow Fairies and Dark Trolls are threatening Tuatha De again. The Shadow Fairies were once Tuatha until they switched sides in order to embrace the darkness and obtain powers that weren't normally available to them. The two factions have been at war with one another for millennia. The Dark Kingdom includes all the Shadow Fairies and Dark Trolls, and their leader has been attempting to take control of both kingdoms and rule them all. The King of Tuatha will send Aulis to us, looking for the Relic. The whole point of leaving the Relic here instead of in Tuatha was to keep it safe from the Shadow Fairies. Whoever holds the Relic during a time of war is damn near invincible. There are very few things more powerful than the power of suggestion. In the right hands it has immense power."

Evie looked at her questioningly. "Wait. From what I remember of the stories, I thought no one knew where the Relic is, or even what it looks like, for that matter."

Winnie nodded. "Yes, you're right; unfortunately, the description was lost in our verbal history generations ago. Hopefully they can tell us what it is so we can find it. Because clearly we're going to need it."

Colleen suddenly froze in her tracks as she pointed at the flower in the kitchen windowsill with an unsteady hand. "Where. Did. That. Come. From?" She enunciated each word very clearly.

Winnie looked at Evie helplessly. The truth was always the best policy. "It was in Evie's hair this morning." She said quietly.

"Wha... wha..." Colleen stammered and fell back in a faint. Evie caught her tiny mother before she could hit the floor.

"Now what do we do?" Evie asked.

"Let's move her to the couch, and we'll figure something out together when she wakes up." Winnie said determinedly.

3 A WARNING

"So where were *you* last night?" Ari asked, thumping Aulis between the shoulders as he lay face down on his massive bed.

"Go away and let me sleep." Aulis grumbled.

"Oh, come on!" Ari was insistent. "I'm dying to know what was interesting enough to keep you out until dawn. It couldn't have been a woman, or she would still be here recovering from your formidable skills in bed... which, by the way, run in the family. If you don't believe me, you can ask Kimbra." He said with a smirk.

Aulis involuntarily grinned. Kimbra was Ari's wife; she was good for him and kept him grounded. Ari absolutely worshipped her and their baby daughter, Lizbeth. Aulis couldn't blame him. Kimbra was like a sister to him, and Lizbeth had her uncle firmly wrapped around her tiny pudgy fingers.

He thought back to the events of the night before, shaking his head. What possessed him to Mark her with the lily? He had never done that before. He groaned and rubbed his hand through his silky black hair.

"By Oberon!" Ari shouted, grabbing Aulis' left hand. "You bear the Mark!" He pointed at an intricate red and black tattoo-like mark on the back of his hand in the shape of the ancient flame. "Who were you with last night?" He demanded.

"Ugh." Aulis grunted. "Back up and let me sit up for a minute – and stop acting like some old woman." He growled.

Ari took a step back, crossing his massive arms. "OK, brother. Out with it. Who is she?"

Aulis stretched, raising his arms over his head, then rubbed his face. There was no way around this; his brother would never let it go. "She is an Adair." He mumbled.

Ari doubled over in laughter. "A *human*? Really? After all these years, you Marked a human?"

15

Aulis grabbed a silken pillow from the pile on his bed and hurled it at his twin, hitting him directly between the eyes and knocking him to the floor.

Ari lay on the floor, his body still shaking with laughter. "Hey, don't get me wrong, brother. I was beginning to think you were going to forever roam the world alone. I'm just so grateful you finally chose someone! She could be a gnome for all I care." He winked at his twin. "Besides, it'll get Kimbra off my case about 'finding someone' for you. She's always afraid you are secretly lonely."

Aulis grunted and rolled his eyes.

Ari sat up and began plucking at the tassels on the rug where he sat. "So, tell me. What does she look like, and how did she feel about being Marked by a giant of a fairy? A good-looking one, if I do say so myself." He chuckled as he stared at his mirror-image twin.

Aulis sighed. "It's complicated."

Ari looked at him, concerned. "What's wrong? What did she say?"

"No, that's just it – she never uttered a single word. She was asleep the entire time." Aulis said quietly.

Ari shook his head. "Wait a minute. Are you telling me you Marked this human without having even spoken to her?" He narrowed his eyes. "What was so different about her that it made you act so impulsively? She won't understand the significance of the flower, you know."

"Yes, she will." Aulis met his brother's gaze.

Ari looked at him quizzically. "Why do you say that?"

Aulis paused momentarily before answering his twin. "Because… she was with Winnie Adair."

Aulis heard a sharp intake of breath from his brother. "Do you think she's the current Guardian?" Ari asked with wide eyes.

Aulis shrugged. "I have no idea. Not that it really matters – she *will* be mine." He said definitively.

Ari raised an eyebrow at the possessive note in his twin's tone; it was something he had never heard before. He was dying to meet the human who had elicited this type of response from his normally stoic brother. He was broken out of his daydream by the sound of tiny bare feet slapping against the glossy mahogany floor.

"Unca Owie, Unca Owie!" cried a tiny, high-pitched voice.

Both men turned to see baby Lizbeth running toward her beloved uncle with outstretched arms.

A wide grin split Aulis' face as he cried out. "Hey there, my Lizzie!" He reached down, sweeping her up in his powerful arms and nuzzling the soft skin just below her ear. He rubbed his whiskers against her tiny cheek and she burst into a peal of silvery laughter.

She grabbed his cheeks with her chubby hands. "I wuv ew, Unca Owie." She said in a sing-song voice before kissing his cheek.

He smoothed back her baby-soft platinum hair. "I love you too, Lizzie girl."

Ari's lovely wife, Kimbra, watched this exchange from the doorway, and her heart ached at the sight. Her brother-in-law was such an incredible person and truly deserved to be happy. If his relationship with Lizbeth was any indication, he would make an amazing father. She watched as Lizbeth rested her head on his wide shoulder, and he reached up with his left hand to stroke the back of her head.

The contrast between their hair matched their personalities: Aulis with his black hair and serious demeanor and Lizbeth with her platinum curls and sunshine smile. At that moment, she couldn't tell which one of them was more euphoric. Then she saw something that made her entire body stiffen, and she let out a shriek.

"No *way*! Aulis!" she screamed. "You *Marked* someone!" She ran toward him, grabbed him by the shoulders, and shook him. "Who is it? Who?" She demanded.

"Momma, no!" squealed Lizbeth. "No shake my Unca Owie!"

Ari sputtered with laughter as he gathered his daughter in his arms so his wife could continue to shake and question his twin. Ari was thoroughly enjoying every second of it.

Aulis picked Kimbra up by her upper arms and set her down about a foot away.

"Woman, stop shaking me." He smiled at his sister-in-law. "You can't manhandle me like you do him. You may have him on apron strings, but not me."

Kimbra crossed her arms over her chest and glared at Aulis. "You're not going to change the subject. I'm not leaving until you tell me who finally captured your attention enough to Mark them!"

Aulis grinned and tweaked the end of her nose. "Since when do I report to you? Ari and I may look alike, but we don't come as a matched set." He winked at Lizbeth, who was squirming in her father's arms.

Ari pleaded with his brother with wide eyes. "Aulis, quit teasing her. Poor Lizzie and I will ultimately be the ones to suffer." He winked at his wife to show he was kidding.

Kimbra stuck her tongue out at him, and Ari waggled his eyebrows at her. "Later, my love." He said with a chuckle.

Aulis decided it was time to take pity on them. "Kimbra, there really isn't anything to tell. The whole situation is rather bizarre. I wasn't planning on doing it... Things just sort of happened." He dropped his hands at his side.

She frowned, drawing her eyebrows together. "There must be something special about her for you to have graced her with the Mark so readily. The Fae have been chasing you for *centuries* and you have hardly looked at any of them twice. Why this one?"

Aulis gave her a small smile. "Kimmie, she's human."

Kimbra looked at him with wide eyes and gasped. "Really? A human? Where did you get involved with a human, and how long has this been going on?" She asked worriedly.

Aulis gave her a half-smile. "Well, it's complicated."

Ari stifled a laugh. There was no way Kimbra was going to let it go at that.

She narrowed her eyes. "Humor me. I'm sure I can keep up."

He took a deep breath. "She's an Adair. I first saw her a few years ago. She was wandering around Winnie's property chasing what she thought were fire flies." He grinned at the memory. "She had imbibed a few too many drinks and was running barefoot through the grass, her long red hair flowing out behind her. At the time, I wasn't really sure what her connection was with the Adairs."

Kimbra gave him an affectionate smile and motioned for him to continue.

Aulis looked slightly embarrassed. "Well, after she returned home, I wanted to know more about her. It was very simple to do when she would take walks outside, which she did often. The scrying pools were able to lock onto her spirit quite easily."

Kimbra looked at her husband, then back to Aulis in astonishment. "You mean to tell me you have been watching her all this time, but you still don't know exactly who she is, or even her name?"

"Kimmie, it's not like the scrying pools have sound, only pictures and emotions." Ari replied.

She wrinkled her nose at him. "I know. I guess I'm just surprised he would've taken such an interest with so little information."

Aulis waved his hand dismissively. "Look, it all boils down to one thing: I sensed her as soon as she arrived last night. I waited until she fell asleep before approaching her and saw her sleeping in the hammock. Each time my mind pictured her with another, I felt a blinding rage. My entire being could not bear for her to belong to anyone else. She *is* mine." He finished through clenched teeth.

Kimbra threw her arms around Aulis' neck as tears began streaming down her face. "I despaired of you ever finding someone to make you happy. I'm so excited for you, and I can't wait to meet her!"

Ari reached out and helped Aulis disentangle himself from Kimbra's iron grip. "Kimbra, darling, there'll be time enough for that. We need to let Aulis sort things out. We don't even know how his human is going to react to her present situation. I seriously doubt having a bunch of fairies descend on her is going to help things."

Kimbra gathered their squirming daughter into her arms. "OK, OK. I know when I'm outnumbered. I'll wait... for now." She threw a smile at both men over her shoulder, and Lizbeth grinned happily and frantically waved goodbye.

Ari looked back at his twin and saw the conflict written plainly on his face. "Aulis, why don't you get some fresh air? You look like you could use it. You and I can catch up when you get back. It looks like we will have some preparations to make for Oberon's visit to the Adair place, now that we need the Relic."

Aulis nodded his head. "Maybe you're right. A walk in the forest could help me clear my head." He stood up and trailed his twin out the door.

4 A WARNING

Colleen mumbled incoherently as her head tossed from side to side on the wide couch.

"Mom?" Evie asked, concern heavy in her voice as she held the cool washcloth to her mother's forehead.

"Evie?" Her mom replied, sounding dazed. She started looking around the room. "Winnie?"

"Right here. Are you feeling better now?"

Colleen slowly sat up and swung her legs over the edge of the couch. "I guess I'm feeling as well as I can under the circumstances."

Evie bit her bottom lip and glanced at Winnie. Her mom's face was still so ashen. She didn't look like she was in any shape to talk about the fairies.

Winnie sat next to Colleen on the couch. "So, what are we going to do?"

Colleen put her face in her hands. "Winnie, we are out of our league. If the war is beginning again, we have to get away from here. All we know about the Relic is from old stories. We have no clue what it looks like, or where it is hidden."

"Colleen, remember who we're dealing with here." Winnie said quickly. "We cannot afford to anger the king. Oberon has been incredibly good to this family in innumerable ways. Our family was entrusted with the secret eons ago. Running away isn't an option – it's our sacred duty to do what we can. We'll work through this together."

"What has this King Oberon done for us? I've never even heard of him before today." Evie's forehead creased.

"Evie dear, that story will have to wait for later. I promise to tell you everything when the time is right." Winnie shook her head.

Colleen looked at her feet. "You're right. I can't allow my personal fears to get in our way."

Winnie nodded. "Exactly. I think we'll have a visit from Aulis and the king's guard very shortly. We need to make the necessary arrangements and assume they'll show up tonight. We also need to make sure Evie has the proper attire for a visit from the king. I have great-grandmother Adair's dress, but we'll need to do some quick alterations to accommodate Evie's, um… generous bust line."

Evie rolled her eyes skyward; *leave it to Aunt Winnie to make breast references in times of stress.* "Great, so exactly what do we need to do?"

Winnie looked at the ceiling thoughtfully. "We'll need to gather several herbs, along with fresh fruits and vegetables. Fortunately, we'll be able to get those things from my garden. However, we'll also need some wildflowers to put out as an offering. Someone will need to go into the woods and gather the flowers."

Evie jumped up. "I'll do it." She grabbed a basket off the kitchen counter and headed toward the back door.

"Only the blue ones and yellow ones, as those represent the sun and moon." warned Winnie.

"OK, yellow and blue. Got it." She called over her shoulder as she let the screen door slam shut. She seriously needed some time to think, and a walk through the forest sounded like a good place to start.

Colleen turned to Winnie. "Do you really think she's been Marked, and by Aulis of all people?"

Winnie nodded. "I can't see any other explanation, Colleen. She found a purple lily in her hair after dreaming of a visit from a mighty fairy warrior. She painted a vivid picture of Aulis – right down to the last detail. Honestly, the way I see this, if Aulis is truly the one who has Marked her, she's extremely fortunate. I can't imagine anyone else being able to keep her safe the way he can. However, we'll know soon enough."

Colleen nodded silently, deeply worried about her daughter.

Evie walked to the back of the yard, entering the woods while swinging her empty basket. She deeply inhaled the sweet moist air and shook out her long, wavy red hair, thoroughly enjoying the freedom that walking in the woods always allowed her.

From his perch high up in the branches, Aulis knew the exact moment Evie entered the forest. He felt an unfamiliar tightening in his pants as he watched her shake out her glorious hair in the gentle breeze. She affected him in a way no other woman ever had, but why? He leaned back against the tree trunk, allowing his growing erection free rein as he watched her pass by below.

Evie felt a tingling sensation run through her entire body. She lifted her face skyward and breathed in deeply. Aulis watched her avidly, knowing she would never see him unless he allowed it. She gracefully flitted across the moss-covered floor of the forest, gathering flowers as she went; he smiled as he noticed she was picking only blue and yellow ones.

She stopped suddenly. *Isn't this where we saw the fairy-flies last night?* She mused to herself. She saw a shaft of light breaking through the canopy above. She followed the path of light to where it ended in a ring of flowers on the forest floor. As she drew closer to the ring, she gave a gasp of recognition.

"Those flowers! They're the same as the one in my hair this morning!" She exclaimed to no one in particular.

Aulis held his breath in anticipation. She could see the fairy ring and acknowledged the flower he had Marked her with the night before. Evie lay down her basket and stepped into the ring of flowers. She sat in the lotus position within the center of the circle and took several deep breaths. She sat that way for the better part of an hour before she began to yawn. She lay on her back, reveling in the warm rays of sun on her face. She fought to keep her eyes open but eventually lost the battle and fell into a peaceful sleep.

Aulis smiled and dropped from his hiding place in the canopy. He stepped into the welcoming fragrance that came from within the circle. The air surrounding them began to shimmer and formed into an invisible wall.

Aulis knelt down beside Evie and ran his hands through her silken hair. Evie moaned softly. He felt his pants tighten further in response. He reached down and shifted his colossal erection, trying to ease his discomfort. He ran his hand down her shoulder and lightly caressed her arms, following their path to her small waist. Evie whimpered and squirmed in her sleep. His breath caught in his throat as he pushed one strap of her emerald camisole down her arm, exposing the rosy tip of one generous breast. She groaned and arched her back into his hand, firmly caught up in what she thought was the beginning of another deeply erotic dream.

Aulis felt the last shreds of his self-control fall away, and he quickly covered Evie with his massive body. He rested on his forearms to ensure he didn't crush her with his weight as he devoured her lips. Her entire body responded like it was going up in flames, and that fire soon engulfed Aulis as well. His rough cheek rubbed down her silken neck, and he caught the tip of one breast in his mouth and began to suckle. Evie's emerald eyes flew open and looked at Aulis in shock. Aulis held her in his smoldering gaze, and she soon found she was incapable of coherent thought. His kiss ravaged her mouth as his hands roamed from her shoulders to her calves. He alternated between nibbling her full bottom lip and then taking it in his lips and sucking on it. Just when she began to think again, Aulis ran his hand up the soft skin of her thigh and under her shorts. He reached between their bodies, gently parted her nether lips and was rewarded with the moisture he was hoping to find. Evie reared up and gasped as Aulis covered her mouth with his. He took her woman's jewel between two fingers and began gently rolling it back and forth. Her whole body convulsed in ecstasy as she felt something glorious building inside her. Aulis pressed himself more firmly against her and rolled his hips in response. Pulse racing, her entire body shattered into a million points of light as she arched into the pleasure he brought her with his hand. She had very little experience with men and had never experienced a true climax. She closed her eyes, equal parts utterly sated and embarrassed. Sometime later she opened her eyes shyly, only to find herself alone.

Was it another dream? It seemed so incredibly real. I must be slowly losing my mind. She sat up and realized she still had one bared breast. Did it just slide off her shoulder in her sleep, or did she really have another run-in with her fairy warrior? She fanned her face. *No one that perfect could really exist. Who am I kidding?* She reached up to brush her hair away from her face and pulled back another purple blossom with shaking hands. Without another thought, she grabbed her basket of flowers and ran headlong through the woods toward her aunt's little white house.

Aulis watched her silently from his perch in the trees, still in a state of semi-arousal. So much for his quiet walk through the woods so he could sort out his thoughts.

"Losing your touch, Aulis? I thought women usually ran toward you – not away from you like a canary fleeing a cat." A tall, blonde, well-muscled fairy materialized on the branch next to Aulis.

"Shut up, Niklas. I don't remember asking for your opinion, or your company, for that matter. What do you want?" Aulis growled.

Niklas let a smile spread slowly across his face. "Aulis, you must learn to relax." He purred. "I was just curious to see this human who's caught your interest." He arched an eyebrow and looked for Aulis' reaction out of the corner of his eye. "She's quite lovely, I'll give you that – all womanly curves and that thick waterfall of red hair. I would venture to say she *might* even be worthy of a fairy."

"Leave this one alone." Aulis warned through gritted teeth, the cords of his neck straining with the effort it took to control his temper.

"Is that a challenge?" Niklas asked with a sly smile and a glint in his violet eyes.

"Not this time, Niklas. This isn't a joking matter." Aulis said with steel in his voice.

Niklas laughed. "It's not as if you've Marked her or anything."

Aulis unconsciously looked down at his hands.

Niklas followed Aulis' gaze to the tattoo on his left hand. "By the gods! You did Mark her, didn't you? What was her reaction? Did she accept your claim?"

"It's complicated." Aulis grumbled, realizing he'd said that far too often that day.

"She doesn't even know she was Marked, does she?" Niklas laughed knowingly. "You know it's not binding until she understands the customs. Right now she's ripe for the picking."

"Stay away from her." Aulis warned.

"I say let the best man win... and I intend to. I haven't faced a challenge this appealing in centuries. But I do admit I'm curious what Dahlia's reaction will be to this news." Niklas shrugged.

Aulis looked at him, puzzled. "Dahlia? What does she have to do with this?"

The other fairy rolled his eyes and smiled wryly. "Aulis, can you really be so clueless? Dahlia has been going around for more than a century scheming to become your wife. She's chased off anyone who's shown a serious interest in you. It'll be interesting to see how your human fares against her."

Niklas dropped from the branch onto the moss-covered ground below, leaving Aulis with clenched fists and gritted teeth.

5 PREPARATIONS

Evie burst through the woods into the clearing where Aunt Winnie's house rested. She didn't stop running until she reached the back door, and then paused momentarily to catch her breath. She eased the back door open and faced her mother and aunt with what she hoped was a serene smile.

"What's wrong, Evie-girl? Did breakfast not agree with you?" joked Winnie.

Her mother took a step toward her with narrowed eyes. "Evie, what's wrong? Something happened, didn't it?"

Winnie looked at Evie with a sly smile. "So… Evie, had a visitor in my woods, did ya?"

Evie blushed to the roots of her hair. "I didn't say that." She mumbled.

Winnie chuckled. "You didn't have to, baby doll." She said with a knowing smile.

Colleen looked from her sister to her daughter and back again, clearly confused.

Winnie patted the back of Colleen's hand. "Let's try Great-Gran's dress on Evie and see what kind of alterations it's going to need."

Colleen smiled brightly. There was nothing she liked more than beautiful clothes. "I'll go get it." She called over her shoulder as she headed to the back bedroom.

Winnie turned to Evie. "Evie, prepare yourself. I fully expect your mystery man to make an appearance here tonight and formally introduce himself. Remember what I told you about refraining from insulting him."

"Don't worry, Aunt Winnie; I'll be on my best behavior. I just don't know if I'll be able to make eye contact with him. I'm so embarrassed." Evie said, her face flushed.

"I told you his reputation was legendary." Winnie giggled quietly and patted her on the back.

Colleen came down the hallway with a bright yellow garment bag. She hung it on the door frame leading into the kitchen and, with a dramatic tug of the zipper, opened the bag to reveal a dress that took Evie's breath away.

"Wow. I've never seen anything like it. It's exquisite." Evie said in a hushed voice.

The dress was a stunning midnight blue, the bodice sprinkled liberally with diamonds and yellow topaz. The dress had a plunging neckline and a slit up one leg to mid-thigh; it would cling dramatically to each and every one of Evie's curves. She reached out absentmindedly and stroked the silken material.

"Beautiful, isn't it?" Her mom asked with a gentle smile.

Evie simply nodded, still not trusting her voice.

"That dress on you will look almost illegal." Winnie said with a wicked grin. "The color will set off your eyes and make your hair positively shine. Every eye in the room will be on you."

Evie gulped nervously. That was exactly the type of attention she normally hated.

Winnie took pity on her, patted her on the back and handed her the dress. "Go try it on, and let's get to work before we run out of time."

Evie hesitantly took the dress and headed to the guest bedroom to change. She stepped into the dress, carefully pulled it up over her bust, and slid her arms through the straps. She tentatively turned around to look at herself in the mirror. She met her own emerald gaze in the mirror and gasped. The dress was truly spectacular. The color made her glow, and the gems caught the light and threw off a reflection that made it look as though she was surrounded by a cloud of pixie dust. The neckline plunged so low it barely covered the rosiness of her nipples, and the material hugged every rounded curve, fell softly to the floor and pooled around her bare feet. *If they can raise the neckline a bit, this dress will truly be a sight to behold. I have never felt sexier or more secure in my femininity.*

Then she put her face in her hands and groaned. How would she ever be able to face him after the intimacy they had shared in the forest? He may have centuries of experience, but she had none. She straightened her back and stared at her reflection once more.

"I'll endure the embarrassment if it means maintaining our family honor and not shaming my mother and aunt." She assured her reflection in the mirror, then shook her head and laughed. She sounded like something from a soap opera. She gathered the hem of the dress in her hands and headed back to her mother and Winnie.

"Oh, Evie!" exclaimed her mother. "You look breathtaking." She

26

narrowed her eyes at the amount of décolleté the dress revealed. "Of course, we'll have to alter the bust."

Winnie let out a low whistle. "Wow! You take that dress to a whole new level."

Evie gave her a small smile and blushed furiously.

"However," Winnie continued, "your mom is right. The length isn't bad, so you can wear any shoes you want... or simply go barefoot." Winnie smiled at her niece. She knew Evie went barefoot every chance she got, and she wanted Evie to be as comfortable as possible when Aulis and the king arrived.

The three women worked on the dress for the next couple of hours before they allowed Evie to change back into her shorts and camisole.

"Well, it looks like we have all the preparations ready. We all have time for a quick nap before we have to start getting dressed. It's gearing up to be a very busy night." Colleen said.

Winnie reached out and took Evie by the elbow. "Come on, Evie. Let's go out back and let the breeze rock us to sleep in our hammocks. I always do my best napping outside." Winnie grinned.

Evie gave her a tentative smile, as she wasn't sure she would be able to sleep outside for fear of another close encounter with the man her aunt called Aulis.

"I... I'm not sure." Evie stammered. "Maybe I'll just lie down on the couch for a while."

Winnie placed her hands on her hips and cocked her head to one side.

Oh no. Evie thought. She had seen that stance many times growing up. It meant her aunt was determined to get her way.

"Evie." Winnie purred. "Come outside and spend some time with me. I don't get to see you very often these days, and I'm not getting any younger, you know." She looked at Evie meaningfully.

Evie sighed. She knew when to admit defeat. "OK, you big bully – you win." She gave her aunt a quick hug as she went out the back door.

The screen door had barely closed when she felt her tiny aunt's withered hands on the tops of her arms. "What's wrong, child? You seem overly nervous. What exactly happened when you went to gather flowers?" Her blue eyes were soft and kind.

Evie gave her aunt a loving smile. Winnie had always been able to pick up on her moods. Evie had never successfully hidden any emotion from her – her clear blue eyes saw right through it.

"Winnie, I'm so confused. So much has happened in the past couple of days. I don't know what's real and what's fantasy." Evie said quietly. She rubbed her face with her palms before continuing. "Yesterday, I was angry with my jerk of a boss, and today we're preparing for a visit from the king of the Fairies and his guard! Can this really be happening? On top of that, there's the issue of my complicated run-ins with Aulis."

She blushed furiously and continued. "I have very little experience with men and when I think of our encounters, it makes me blush. I can't even imagine what my *mother* would think."

Winnie looked at her in disbelief. "Do you mean to tell me you are still a maiden?"

Evie burst into peals of laughter. "Oh, Winnie, stop! You make it sound positively medieval. I just never found anyone I cared about enough to make me want to get that intimate."

Winnie continued to stare at her in shock. Evie's face began to redden. "Winnie? Please say something. You're embarrassing me and making me feel like a freak."

Winnie was instantly apologetic. "I'm sorry, sweet pea. It just came as a surprise. Of course, this changes everything. Aulis will just have to keep his damn hands to himself for now. It's against all the laws pertaining to relationships between fairies and humans for them to lie with a maiden without a marriage or handfasting first."

"Handfasting? Are you serious? I thought that was only something that existed in romance novels. What does it mean in the real world?"

Winnie chuckled. "You do have a flair for the dramatic, don't you? Have you been reading your mom's books again? Handfasting is an ancient tradition. It involves a written agreement, witnessed by both families, that states the two parties must live together as man and wife for a year and a day. If a child is conceived before the end of their year together, then they agree to marry."

Evie growled. "It's exactly like the books. The woman lives with some guy as his legal whore, and then if she happens to get knocked up in the process, the guy will finally agree to marry her. Why isn't the woman good enough to marry in the first place? It's so unfair!"

Winnie squeezed her shoulders. "Evie, look at it this way, baby – it also gives the woman a way out if she isn't happy. She won't end up forever trapped in a loveless marriage."

"You always did have a talent for looking at the bright side of things, Winnie." Evie smiled. "Maybe handfastings should happen more often – the divorce rate might actually decrease."

Winnie wrinkled her petite nose at Evie, but her crystal blue eyes flashed with laughter as she sat gracefully on her hammock.

Evie plopped down on her hammock with enough force to swing it wildly from side to side, almost pitching her to the ground. As the movement quieted, she laid down and tried to sleep.

6 A NEW SUCCESSOR

Aulis dropped from the branch where he had been sitting and slowly walked back to the circle of flowers where he and Evie had lain earlier. He continued to shake his head. What exactly had Niklas meant? Had Dahlia been manipulating things behind his back? He had no intention of ever marrying her, and he had been quite clear about that fact… or so he had thought.

He stepped into the circle of flowers and spread his arms wide with his palms facing the sky, causing the muscles in his arms to ripple. He began calling the portal to go home. The vivid purple blooms rapidly expanded toward the heavens in a symphony of green and purple as the blooms and vines twisted together to form a doorway. A light shimmered at its center and exploded outward from the doorway, showering Aulis with a fine dust that sparkled in the light. He stepped through and found himself in the main audience chamber of the royal palace. It was humming with activity as the entire kingdom prepared for the king's visit to the human world and the introduction to the current Guardian. Aulis scanned the vast expanse of white marble for any sign of his twin. He was so engrossed in his search, he was startled by a voice at his right elbow.

"Aulis, you wicked thing. Where have you been? I have not seen you in days," purred a tall blonde woman with cold grey eyes.

"Hello, Dahlia." Aulis sighed. "I've been very busy with preparations for the king." Although he needed to investigate Niklas' claims regarding Dahlia, it would have to wait. He simply didn't have the time right now. How was he going to get rid of her?

His answer took the unexpected form of Taarmo, a longtime member of the king's guard and one of Aulis' direct reports. He couldn't help but like the blonde giant, who was extremely loyal and followed orders without question and without causing problems. Taarmo lumbered up and clapped a meaty hand on Aulis' shoulder.

"Aulis!" He boomed. "I just heard the good news."

Dahlia raised one manicured eyebrow and turned a bright smile toward Aulis. "Oh! What good news? What are we celebrating?"

Taarmo chuckled. He had never liked Dahlia. She put on one face around Aulis, but when he wasn't around, her true colors came out – and they weren't pretty. She made everyone's life a living hell and loved to play the part of Aulis' wife behind his back. However, she was smart enough never to do it when Aulis was around. He was going to enjoy making her squirm for a change.

"Oh, Dahlia, haven't you heard? Aulis finally Marked someone, after all these centuries!" Taarmo looked at her with wide innocent eyes and a brilliant smile.

Aulis ran his left hand through his hair in frustration. Dahlia caught sight of the intricate black and red Mark on the back of his hand, and her smile faltered slightly before her happy mask slipped back into place.

"Marked?" She asked Aulis. "Really! When did this happen?"

"Last night, apparently," laughed Taarmo.

She narrowed her eyes at him before turning back to Aulis with a smile frozen in place. "Then this surely is a day for celebrating. So, who's the lucky fairy?" She asked.

"Lucky *human*." Taarmo corrected.

"Human?" Dahlia parroted in disbelief.

"Yep." Taarmo grinned. "Who would've thought when Aulis finally Marked someone, it would be a human?"

Dahlia was visibly stunned, like a bird that's flown into a wall, and Taarmo was enjoying every second of it.

Aulis continued to scan the room and gave a dismissive wave of his hand. "It's a long story. If you two will excuse me, I need to find Ari. Taarmo, have the team assembled and ready to go within the hour." He called over his shoulder as he strode from the main hall.

Dahlia stared open-mouthed at his retreating form, while Taarmo stifled a chuckle. She looked back at him, completely bewildered.

"A human? I don't understand. After all this time, why would he choose a human? What could she possibly have to offer him?"

Taarmo shook his head in disdain. "She's an Adair, Dahlia – and from what I heard, she's most likely the current Guardian."

Her shoulders slumped. "The Guardian?" she wailed.

"Yep." Taarmo replied as he walked away to begin making the preparations that Aulis had requested.

She stood frozen in place like a lost child. *This must be a bad dream.* She thought. *This can't really be happening.* She began to feel sick to her stomach. Suddenly she felt a warm arm sneak around her shoulders.

"Hello, my beauty," said a low voice.

Dahlia turned toward the voice in daze. "Niklas, go away. I am not in the mood for you; it has been a rough morning."

"I heard. That's why I'm here. I think we can help each other."

She eyed him suspiciously. "Why would you want to help me?" Niklas had pursued her many times, and she'd always rebuffed his advances in favor of Aulis.

Niklas pulled her closer and spoke softly into her ear. "Because we both have the same goal in mind."

Her eyebrows shot up. "Really?"

Niklas let a slow smile spread across his face. "We both want the human away from Aulis."

She looked at him, stunned. "What reason could you have for wanting them separated?"

Niklas chuckled. "Ahh, I take it you haven't seen her yet? She's extremely beautiful – even worthy of a fairy."

Dahlia felt a white hot hatred bloom in her chest for this yet-unseen competition. Niklas saw the hatred combust in her eyes and smiled; he had her right where he wanted her.

"There isn't anything you can do. It's too late – he's already Marked her." She spat.

"Wait, my dear, allow me to explain. She's human and cannot fully understand the meaning behind the Mark. If she doesn't understand and accept it, then the Mark isn't binding." He smiled brightly.

Understanding lit her eyes. "Niklas, you're a genius." She linked her arm in his. "Let's go find somewhere quieter so you can explain what you have in mind."

They walked out of the hall, whispering animatedly.

Kimbra stepped out into the hall and watched the couple with narrowed eyes. They were definitely up to something and, whatever it was, she was sure it didn't bode well for her brother-in-law. She would have to keep a close eye on them.

Aulis finally found Ari with Oberon in the king's private war room. "Aulis, my boy," boomed Oberon. The king was a tall, muscular man whose salt and pepper hair did nothing to detract from his commanding presence. His very presence screamed royalty. "I just sent a page to find you. I want to go over tonight's preparations with the two of you. How go things with your men?"

Aulis relaxed slightly; here was a subject he was comfortable with. "All is well, Your Highness. Taarmo is gathering my men as we speak. They'll be ready and assembled within the hour."

"Excellent. I can always depend on you two to get things done."

Oberon beamed.

Ari bowed his head slightly. "It's our honor to be of service."

Oberon raised one eyebrow. "My arse will be chapped from your lips on it before long if you keep that up. Where did you pick that up?"

Ari looked at his twin, who was desperately trying to stifle his laughter, and back to the king with a sheepish smile. Aulis' lips were quivering with the massive effort he was exhibiting. He finally lost the battle and dissolved into laughter. Aulis wiped the tears from his eyes before turning back to the king.

"Kimbra." They both said in unison.

Ari scratched the back of his head uncomfortably. "I believe her exact words were, 'You should show him the respect that his position is due.'"

Aulis and Oberon were holding onto each other for support as they laughed, their bodies two enormous columns of quivering muscle.

"Begod, boy. I was there when you were born. I wouldn't admit it to just anyone, but I even changed a diaper or two. That's about as close as two men can get." Oberon replied, still laughing.

Ari snickered. "OK, but you have to tell Kimbra, or I'll never hear the end of it."

Aulis wiped the tears from his eyes again. "I think I'll tell Kimbra of your outrageous behavior in front of our beloved King."

Ari looked momentarily frightened. "You wouldn't! I swear I would get you back. Your human would be terrified of you forever once I got done with her."

Aulis raised his hands in mock defeat. "OK, OK. I know when I'm beat."

The King turned to Aulis and studied him thoughtfully. "Yes, Aulis, I've heard the rumors as well. You have my entire castle buzzing like a beehive. Tell me what's going on."

Aulis sighed. "It's complicated."

The King gave him a small smile. "So I've heard." He looked pointedly at the Mark on the back of Aulis' hand. "I can also see for myself that some of the stories are, in fact, true."

Aulis told Oberon of the events to date. Oberon stroked his graying goatee thoughtfully.

"An Adair? I guess we'll know tonight if she's truly this generation's Guardian. If that is the case, I can't say I have a problem with you pursuing the relationship further. It's a little unorthodox, but I can't imagine anyone better suited to protect her. However, it must be a true Marking." Oberon looked at Aulis pointedly.

Aulis looked directly into his eyes as he rubbed the Mark. "Oberon,

I'd renounce my immortality for her at this point."

Oberon widened his eyes. "Such a strong reaction, considering you've known her such a short time. I wonder. What has happened to make you feel thus?"

Aulis shook his head. "Nothing really. It sounds strange, but I felt something awaken in me when I saw her. Something I didn't even know existed… like hearing someone else sing a song out loud, but it's one you created in your own mind." Aulis felt his cheeks redden. Oberon would understand his embarrassment better than anyone; he was more comfortable discussing strategy than matters between men and women.

Oberon looked stunned, yet impressed. "The *Anum Amhrán*, the Soul Song. Could it really be possible?" He whispered.

Aulis and Ari looked at him, confused. It was Ari who spoke up first. "The Soul Song? What is that?"

"I need to do additional research first." Oberon pointed at both men as his face became very serious. "Do not speak of this to anyone but me! Understood? This is for your own protection as well as hers."

They nodded in unison, as only twins can do. Before Aulis was able to question Oberon further, Taarmo came into the room and bowed.

"All is ready. We may depart any time you are ready, sir." He said to Aulis.

Aulis nodded in response. "Well done. I knew I could depend on you."

Taarmo beamed under his praise. Oberon watched with overwhelming pride. Aulis had grown into a fine leader – firm, but fair, and his men would willingly follow him to the ends of the universe.

Oberon waved a hand at Taarmo and Ari. "Would you two leave us for a moment? I need to speak with Aulis privately."

Both men nodded and bowed.

"Oh, Ari?" Oberon said quickly. "When you find Kimbra, will you please let her know I'd like to speak with her?"

Ari grinned at him. "Yes, sir, I sure will." He said as he closed the door behind him.

"Oberon, what's wrong?" Aulis asked, concerned.

Oberon smiled at him like a proud father would. "Relax, Aulis. I've had something on my mind for quite some time now. I was still undecided until I heard the truth of you Marking your human from your own lips."

Aulis looked at him, confused. "I'm not sure I understand."

Oberon clasped Aulis' forearm with his large wrinkled hand. Aulis' eyes went wide with understanding.

"Aulis, my child, I name you as my successor. You will be forever more Prince Aulis of the Tuatha De."

Aulis looked at him speechless for several moments before he recovered any semblance of control. "But... but... Are you sure? There are others with royal bloodlines."

The King grimaced. "You would have me put Niklas and his ilk on the throne?"

"No!" Aulis shouted, and then regained his usually calm demeanor. "I accept the position with honor and pride. I only hope I can live up to your expectations." He grinned.

Oberon patted his back. "I have no doubts you'll not only live up to them, but surpass them as well. I will make the announcement at the banquet tonight." He grinned mischievously. "I want your human to hear the good news directly from me. I want to see her face when she realizes she'll be the next fairy queen. I understand the phrase 'fairy queen' has another meaning altogether in her world."

Both men dissolved into laughter that rang joyously throughout the war room.

7 COLLEEN'S STORY

Evie sat cross-legged in the backyard while she allowed her hair to dry in the breeze. Her mother had insisted on giving her a manicure and pedicure. However, as the day wore on, Evie grew restless indoors; she had already informed her mother that, if she had plans to do makeup or anything else, she would have to come outside. Evie looked at her shaking hands, the nails now covered in a pale peach lacquer. She closed her eyes and turned her face skyward, enjoying the warmth of the last rays of sun before it completely sank below the horizon.

Niklas watched her avidly from the trees. Normally he wouldn't bother with a human, aside from the occasional tumble. However, she was beautiful, even by fairy standards. If the rumors were true, and she was the current Guardian, that just made her all the more desirable. Niklas looked forward to winning her from Aulis. It would be his greatest victory.

His attention was drawn away from Evie by the sound of the screen door slamming shut. Evie's mother headed out the door with a handful of baby's breath in one hand and a large makeup bag in the other.

Here we go, thought Evie.

Colleen sat cross-legged behind her daughter, taking long strands of hair and wrapping them around her finger.

"Oh, Mom, it's curly enough already. What are you doing?" Evie grumbled.

Colleen lightly smacked Evie on the back of her head. "Hush, child, there's too much at risk here. Our family has a huge responsibility to the fairies, and I'm afraid of what their reaction will be when they learn that, not only do we not know where the Relic is, we don't even know what we should be looking for."

Evie turned, facing her mother. "Mom, you have to relax." She threw her hands up in exasperation. "Why can't we just explain the situation?"

Colleen shook her head violently. "No, we simply couldn't."

Evie grabbed both of her mother's hands. "There's something you aren't telling me. What is your story with the fairies? You seem to have a very real fear where they're concerned. On the other hand, Aunt Winnie is quite taken with them."

A shudder ran through Colleen's body as her eyes darkened with fear. "I guess I should've told you a long time ago. You know there's been a member of our family living on this land for centuries. Your grandmother always warned Winnie and me about going into the forest at night and to stay away from the 'fairy-flies,' as you call them. We always thought they were only stories, until the night we followed the lights into the forest."

Evie's green eyes widened as she motioned for her mother to continue.

"Your aunt and I got separated. The sound of a twig snapping behind me made me spin around, and I was face-to-face with the most exquisite man I had ever seen. He was tall and blonde with an athletic build...." Colleen's voice trailed off in memory; then she shook herself and continued. "I knew what he was, as well as the fact I was in danger. But I completely took leave of my senses. How could anyone with such an angelic face be bad? Unfortunately, I was about to find out.

"He approached me like a panther stalking his prey, and my body shook in anticipation as he drew closer. He gathered me in his arms and kissed me passionately. I was extremely innocent then, and had no experience with men, and certainly no man like this – he excited me and scared me all at the same time. I felt a warm breeze blow through my hair, and it quickly built in intensity. As the wind roared in my ears, I saw Winnie emerge through the trees and call out my name. The next thing I knew, I was in the middle of a large room made of stone, and I was completely surrounded by strange, frightening creatures I later learned were Dark Trolls and Shadow Fairies.

"The fairy who had abducted me was named Stanis. For three days he was my constant companion and jailer, constantly grilling me about the location of the Relic. I was terrified and had no idea what he was talking about. At the end of that time, Oberon, the king, and his brother, Lyrr, appeared with the entire royal guard to rescue me. Lyrr himself was assigned as my protector. He whisked me away to Sanctuary to hide until the battle had ended. Sanctuary is a secret place where only royalty can enter, and we were safe until things quieted down and Oberon was able to set the protective spell around our house. The spell stops Shadow Fairies and Dark Trolls from ever being able to set foot on our property again. That was when I learned how the Tuatha owe our family for protecting the Relic and how tightly we are all tied."

Her soft brown eyes met her daughter's emerald green gaze. She blushed as she continued. "Lyrr and I grew quite close during our time together, brief though it was." She cleared her throat nervously.

Evie narrowed her eyes suspiciously. "Mom, what are you trying to say?"

Colleen refused to meet Evie's eyes and wrung her hands together. Her voice dropped to a whisper. "Evie, Lyrr was your father."

"What?" Evie's cry echoed through the trees.

Niklas winced at the sudden volume of Evie's voice. What had her mother said to garner such a reaction? If only he was a little closer and could hear.

Winnie burst through the screen door, raced to where they were sitting, and quickly clapped her hand over Evie's mouth.

"Shh, child. Even the trees have ears. Only four people know this secret: your mom, me, Oberon, and now you. It must remain that way; your safety depends on it."

Evie struggled out of her aunt's iron grasp and jumped to her feet.

"Have you two lost your minds? What the hell is going on around here?"

"Evie, sit down!" Winnie said sharply.

Evie's eyes went wide as she slowly sank back to the ground.

Winnie's tone gentled. "Child, there are many dark elements at play here. Didn't you ever wonder why you've never met your father? Shortly after your mother was brought home, Lyrr disappeared."

"What do you mean, disappeared?" Evie whispered.

Winnie leaned in close. "Disappeared – as in gone without a trace. By the time we learned he was missing, your mother had already discovered she was carrying you. We kept you a secret for several months out of fear, not knowing what else to do. We finally contacted Oberon and told him of your existence. He was overjoyed at the prospect of a niece, but still heartbroken over his missing brother. They've never stopped looking for him. To this day, they still search. It's widely suspected he was taken by the same Dark Trolls and Shadow Fairies he saved your mother from."

Evie raised a shaking hand to her mouth. "Is he dead?"

"No!" Her mother said emphatically.

Evie looked at her in shock. "How do you know for sure?"

"I just know. He is alive, but definitely held against his will. Otherwise, he would have come back to me." Colleen said forcefully.

Evie stared into the tree line trying to absorb her new knowledge, when a flash of movement caught her eye. "What was that?" she asked absentmindedly.

Winnie's head snapped around, eyes scanning the trees. "We should move inside. I think this conversation would be safer if continued indoors. I'm afraid we have attracted an audience."

The three women scrambled to their feet and headed inside as Niklas watched their disappearing backs and wondered what they were up to.

Aulis leaned in the doorway of the king's private chambers, arms crossed and foot tapping impatiently. Dahlia watched him from behind a colossal white-marble pillar with narrowed eyes. Was he really in such a hurry to see that human again? What was so extraordinary about her to make two powerful fairies act like boys? She felt the white-hot rage fester deep inside.

Ari hurried down the adjacent hallway with Kimbra close on his heels.

"Ari, slow down." Kimbra wailed.

Ari sighed deeply and slowed down. "Woman, you are killing me. I'm already running late to meet up with Aulis. I'm dying to see the human who made such an impression on my normally borderline-emotionless twin."

Kimbra giggled, giving Ari a playful push in the chest before she took off running and calling over her shoulder. "Me too."

Ari gave her a mock growl before chasing her down the hall. She flew down the hall, skidded around the corner, and careened into Aulis. He caught her in his massive arms, saving her from crashing to the unforgiving marble floor.

"Nice one, Kimbra. You know, if you'd been watching where you were going instead of watching Ari…." His voice trailed off.

She grimaced at him. "Yeah, yeah – thanks, Mom." She grumbled. Ari came around the corner, saw Aulis' immense arms suspending Kimbra a couple feet off the floor, and burst into laughter.

"Let me guess." He paused, gasping for air. "You were too busy watching for me, and Aulis ended up saving you from yet another concussion."

Kimbra shot him a dirty look. "You make it sound like I'm constantly slamming my head into things."

Ari pulled her into his equally strong arms. "I wouldn't have you any other way." He kissed her thoroughly before putting her feet back on the floor.

Kimbra looked over Ari's shoulder just in time to see Dahlia's head duck behind a pillar. Kimbra narrowed her eyes. What was Dahlia doing here? Internal alarms went off, and Kimbra was aware of a cold certainty falling over her: There was no way she was going to let Dahlia come between Aulis and his chance for real happiness; she had waited too many years to see him happy. She looked back at her brother-in-law as he resumed pacing in front of the king's door.

Dahlia peeked around the pillar again, only to find Kimbra's gaze fixed firmly on her. She abruptly stood up and scurried down the hall, back toward the main chamber. Kimbra gave her husband a kiss and smiled broadly at Aulis before subtly turning in the direction Dahlia had headed.

8 MORE THAN COINCIDENCE

Evie sat cross-legged on the cool wooden floor in front of the worn leather couch that now held her aunt and mother.

"You realize if anyone overheard this conversation they would put the two of you away somewhere?" Evie looked at them pointedly.

Winnie snickered at the exasperated expression her sister wore. Her mother's tone perfectly matched the expression on her face. "Evie, you aren't taking this nearly seriously enough. Why do you always have to be so cynical?"

Evie waved her hand dismissively in the air. "Oh, I don't know. Maybe it's because things have gone so smoothly in my life up to this point?" She grimaced. "Seriously, Mom, any normal person would exhibit more than a little disbelief at the story you've laid at my feet today."

Winnie patted her sister's shoulder soothingly. "Colleen, you have to give her credit. She's handling it a whole lot better than we initially did all those years ago. We used to scoff at Gran's stories, and look where it landed us."

Evie's voice dripped with sarcasm. "Yeah, it landed you with me."

Winnie grimaced. "You know what I mean."

Colleen sat staring into space like a lost child. Obviously, she wasn't going to be of any help. Winnie straightened her shoulders and focused her attention back on Evie.

"Evie girl, it boils down to this: all signs point to you being the next Guardian. You're going to have to choke back the sarcasm, as well as your pride, and follow the rules and protocol set forth by our ancestors and the fairies. You and Aulis will need to sort out your relationship, but it'll have to take a backseat to the Relic. Does that make sense?"

Evie looked properly chastised. "Yes, I understand. It's just really hard for me to believe all this is really happening." To her horror, she felt tears gather in the corners of her eyes. She took a deep breath and gathered her courage. "OK, Winnie, what next?"

Winnie beamed her approval. "That's my girl. Listen carefully and I'll explain exactly what you need to do."

Evie nodded for her to continue.

"The first thing is to take the flowers you gathered and create a bouquet. Flowers are very important to them symbolically because they are such an integral part of nature; this is the same reason your mother tucked sprigs of baby's breath into your curls. The blue flowers represent the moon and the yellow represent the sun. We will add white roses for purity and purple lily to symbolize the fairies themselves. Now, you will hold these in your left hand until you pass them to his successor."

Evie's eyebrows drew together. "His successor? How many people are involved in this dog and pony show?"

Winnie sighed. "Let me take a step back. We will be waiting outside for the king's arrival. You will be standing slightly in front of your mother and me. You will hold the bouquet in your left hand and a glass of wine in your right. When Oberon approaches, you will offer him the wine. When Oberon takes the wine, you'll turn and present the bouquet to the man standing at his right, who will be his eventual successor. It's a gesture showing our family's loyalty to his court. At that point, we'll be able to talk to Oberon about the Relic and our lack of knowledge where it's concerned."

Colleen gasped. "Winnie, we can't do that! What will he do when he learns we don't know where it is?"

Winnie grunted at her. "Colleen, really, you're being oversensitive about all this. Or have you forgotten how quickly he came to your rescue once before?"

Colleen looked at her feet. "No, you're right."

Evie walked into the kitchen and mixed three large mimosas. She handed one to Winnie and an especially potent one to her mother before tossing her own back with shaking hands. As the combination of champagne and orange juice soothed her frazzled nerves, she let her mind wander to Aulis.

Aulis paced the floor outside Oberon's chamber, lost in thought. Evie filled his every thought. He imagined the silken texture of her hair, her soft curves, and her wondrously sensual response to his touch – like she was made just for him.

Oberon emerged in his ceremonial robes to find Aulis pacing and chuckled to himself at Aulis' impatience. It was a rare sight. Aulis' self-control was legendary; it is what had helped him remain single for so long.

"Aulis, my boy," Oberon's voice boomed, "is everything ready for our departure?"

Aulis snapped to attention. "Yes, sir, the men should be joining us shortly."

"Excellent." Oberon pointed to a marble bench loaded with silken cushions just outside his door. "Let's have a seat and talk while we wait."

Aulis walked over and sat on the edge of the bench. "What did you want to discuss?"

Oberon chuckled as he sat comfortably. "Always one to get right to the point, aren't you?"

Aulis smiled guiltily. "Touché, sir."

"Aulis, I plan to make the announcement tonight about naming you as my successor. However, I am going to need you to stand with me during the ceremony at the Adair homestead."

Aulis looked at him in surprise.

Oberon shook his head ruefully. "I know, I know. The gossip is bound to spread like wildfire long before the feast begins. I want to make sure you're prepared to deal with all the attention that is bound to come with the announcement. I have no reservations about having you eventually take my place. You will be a strong leader, and our people will flourish under you. However, there will also be those who resent my decision." He let his voice trail off.

Aulis' eyes narrowed. "You mean Niklas? I think we both know he's the last thing this kingdom needs." His hands slapped the top of his muscled thighs. "He won't honor our agreements with the Adair clan, and any human who enters our woods will be in danger."

Oberon clapped him on the back. "Very shrewd. I knew you would understand. So tell me more about this human you have Marked. What does she look like, and what is her relationship with the Adair clan?"

A slow smile spread across Aulis' face. "You know, I don't really understand it myself. I saw her for the first time several years ago. Almost every time I've seen her, she has been with Winnie."

"Almost every time?" The King echoed with a wicked smile.

Aulis blushed before clearing his throat. "Well, um… Yes, almost every time."

Oberon threw his head back laughing heartily and motioned for Aulis to continue. "Carry on, my boy. I can hardly wait to hear the rest."

Aulis absentmindedly stroked the black and red mark on the back of his hand. "She is tiny yet voluptuous with no sense of her own beauty." He shook his head in disbelief. "She believes there's nothing special about her, but something about her called out to me the very first time I saw her. I felt drawn to her, quite frankly, against my will. She has thick, luxurious hair that hangs down her back in a strawberry-blonde cascade."

Oberon's head snapped in his direction. "Strawberry blonde hair? What are the color of her eyes?"

Aulis spoke softly, as if in a daydream. "They are a brilliant emerald. I can't remember the last time I saw that color."

Oberon looked off into the distance. "I have known only one person with eyes like that." He mused to himself.

Both men were briefly lost in their own thoughts until their attention was caught by the sound of footsteps rapidly approaching. Taarmo stopped in front of Oberon and bowed before turning to Aulis. "Sir, all is ready for our immediate departure. We have the portal called up, and the entire guard is awaiting your arrival."

Aulis nodded. "Thank you, Taarmo. Well done." He turned to Oberon. "Whenever you are ready, sire."

Oberon stood, smoothing out his robes. "Well, let's not keep everyone waiting. I'm very anxious to meet this human of yours."

The three men walked briskly down the hallway until they reached the main chamber. Oberon's guard was surrounding the iridescent light of the glowing portal. Aulis scanned the room and quickly made eye contact with Ari, who nodded his head slightly to his left. Aulis' eyes followed the movement to find Niklas standing with the guard. Aulis raised his eyebrows in surprise and looked pointedly at the king. Oberon leaned in close and whispered.

"Easy, my boy. There's too much at stake here. Don't antagonize him before the announcement is made, or you're only going to cause yourself more grief. Have Taarmo and Ari watch over him, but make sure he's not aware they're watching him."

Aulis nodded and quickly motioned for Ari to join them. Aulis leaned over, whispering instructions to him as a broad smile spread across Ari's face. He was definitely going to enjoy this particular mission. Aulis shook his head and chuckled to himself. He motioned to Taarmo and spoke quietly.

"Taarmo, I have a special task for you and Ari. Apparently Niklas is planning on joining the king's party to the human world. I need you and Ari to watch him very closely and intervene if needed. However, we need to make sure he has no idea he's being watched. Understood?"

Taarmo smiled brilliantly. "Absolutely, sir. You know you can count on me. Ari and I will have no trouble keeping it all under control."

Aulis looked at Oberon, who was shaking his head and stifling a laugh. Aulis' voice boomed through the main chamber. "All is ready, Your Highness. Whenever you are ready, we will depart."

Oberon motioned to the portal. "Let us not keep them waiting any longer."

"Yes, sir!" His men answered from all corners of the hall. Ari and Taarmo stepped through the portal and quickly scanned the area for any danger.

Ari looked at Taarmo and smiled as they awaited the arrival of Aulis, Oberon, and finally the rest of the king's entourage. "Maybe we'll get lucky, and Niklas will be stupid enough to try something and we'll get to smack him around a little?"

Taarmo laughed. "We can only hope, right?"

Their conversation was brought up short by the arrival of the king and Aulis, who moved quickly toward the edge of the forest.

Oberon snickered. "Aulis, my boy, you must have patience. Let's at least wait for the rest of the men to get through the portal."

Ari laughed heartily as Aulis shot him a look that would have withered a lesser man. Finally the rest of the entourage were ready to head out. Aulis set a brisk pace as they headed for Winnie's house.

Winnie sensed the portal, looked out the window to see a faint glow in the trees, and quickly stood up. Colleen looked like she was going to be physically ill; Winnie could see how hard she was struggling with this visit. Winnie handed Evie the bouquet, which she accepted with trembling hands. Winnie gave her a comforting smile, and Evie relaxed slightly.

"OK, ladies, here we go." Winnie said as they headed out the screen door to the backyard.

9 ROYAL VISITOR

Aulis was the first one to clear the tree line. He saw Evie and inhaled sharply. She was an absolute vision in the ceremonial dress with tiny white flowers tucked throughout her hair; she looked like a fairy princess. He chuckled to himself when he realized that, since he had Marked her and Oberon had named him successor, she now was, in fact, a fairy princess. He couldn't wait to see her face when she realized that. He snapped to attention when he realized the king and his entourage had caught up to him.

Oberon followed Aulis' gaze to Evie and froze momentarily when he realized Winnie and Colleen were standing just behind her. What did Colleen's presence here mean? Who was this child? How did she fit into the larger picture? *But these questions will be answered later,* he thought. He squared his shoulders and moved regally across the clearing.

Evie's hands shook violently. She prayed she wouldn't spill the wine all over the king. She watched him stride across the clearing. He was definitely a powerful man, but it was the man just behind him who made her entire body quiver. This was the man from her dreams, or what she'd been thinking of as dreams. She turned slightly to look at her mother and aunt. Her mother looked positively green and was shaking like a leaf. Winnie looked at her and mouthed "Aulis." Evie nodded, understanding her immediately.

Evie took a steadying breath as the king approached, giving him a brilliant smile as he stopped only a couple of feet in front of her. She extended her right hand, offering him the glass of wine she held. Oberon took the glass and drained it quickly. Evie turned to Oberon's right and offered the bouquet to Aulis with trembling hands. He took the bouquet and held it close to his chest, his smile reaching all the way to his eyes.

Winnie was beaming at Oberon, and he felt his heart skip a beat. It has been far too long since he had seen her. She was just as he remembered, all the way down to the mischievous gleam in her crystal blue eyes.

Oberon took a step forward and searched Evie's face, immediately recognizing the familiar sparkle in her eyes. He raised his eyebrows at Colleen in a silent question; she silently nodded once as tears streamed down her face. Then Oberon reached out and crushed Evie to his chest, stroking her hair like a child. Aulis and the entire entourage looked on in shock. Ari cleared his throat, and Oberon snapped out of his reverie, quickly releasing Evie and letting her step back.

"We accept your offerings and embrace you as the Guardian of the Relic." Oberon said formally and turned to his men. "Men, make yourselves comfortable while we move indoors to conduct our business. Aulis, you are with me. Ari, Taarmo, you are both stationed at the door. No one is to enter without my express permission."

"Yes, sir."

Winnie took a step closer to Oberon. "Your Highness, I've prepared plenty of food for your guard. If you can spare a couple of men to assist me, I'll have it brought outside."

Oberon smiled. "Of course. I would expect nothing less from you, Winnie. Aulis and Ari, will you please assist her?"

"Of course," they replied in unison, following Winnie into the small house. Colleen and Winnie understood the significance of Oberon sending Ari and Aulis to assist. He was establishing the women's status, clearly notifying everyone these women were under his direct protection. Winnie handed the various trays to the men and caught Aulis by the elbow before he headed out to the door.

"Please do not think me disrespectful, but I need to make sure you understand my niece is a maiden. I think we're both clear on the rules surrounding that, yes?" She spoke quickly in a low voice.

Aulis bowed to her before running one hand through his hair. "Of course; my honor would allow nothing less."

Winnie stared at the flame on his hand and whistled low. "So it's true. You did Mark her, didn't you? Aulis, you're going to have to be very patient with her. She's still having some trouble absorbing everything that's happened to her in the past two days. She hasn't had good luck with men in the past and is very unsure of herself. She's more special than you know."

He couldn't believe she was going to help him. She wanted him to be with Evie. He gave her a brilliant smile. "Winnie, I promise I'll do my very best."

She met his smile with one of her own. "I know you will. Oberon, Colleen, and I are depending on it."

She held the door open for him, and they carried the rest of the food to the troops. The men were astounded at the reception they were receiving from Winnie; they never expected the humans to be so accommodating. They dug into the spread with gusto as the king and Aulis followed the women back into the house.

Oberon walked into the den and sat on the couch, indicating for the women to join him. Winnie sat to his right while Colleen slowly sunk into one of the large club chairs. Evie stood in the middle of the den, shifting uncomfortably from one bare foot to the other. Aulis leaned on the doorframe, his very presence making Evie extremely nervous.

Oberon took Winnie's hand in his, kissing it gallantly. "Evie," he said softly, "do you know who I am?"

Evie fought to keep her voice level. "Yes, sir; you are Oberon, king of the Tuatha De."

He studied her carefully. "Come now, child, you know that's not what I meant."

Aulis watched them, deeply confused.

Evie sighed deeply and sank to her knees. Aulis instinctively moved to catch her until he realized she hadn't fallen.

"I know what you meant. You are Oberon, my uncle – brother to my father, Lyrr." She said quietly while a single tear ran down her cheek.

Aulis looked at the king in shock. Lyrr had a child? There had not been a single whisper of this during Lyrr's disappearance. Now he understood why Oberon insisted they move inside to have this conversation. He rubbed the Mark on his hand.

Oberon looked at Aulis pointedly. "I'm sure you are wondering where this leaves you since obviously Lyrr has an heir?"

Aulis shook his head. "No, sir. I will protect her just as I've served you all these years."

Oberon sighed. "No, you won't."

"What do you mean?" Aulis asked carefully. Was Oberon going to negate his claim on this woman?

Oberon motioned for Aulis to move closer until he stood at Evie's side. He reached out and helped Evie stand, then put Evie's trembling hand in Aulis'. "Aulis, this changes nothing. I'm entrusting you not only with my kingdom, but with the only child of my beloved brother. I recognize your Mark, and we'll announce it at the banquet tonight." He turned to Winnie and Colleen. "Will you ladies be my guests at the palace tonight? I will have rooms prepared for each of you."

Colleen sat stunned, but Winnie grinned impishly. "Of course we will. I'm anxious to hear what's been going on since we were there last."

"Then it's settled." Oberon said with an all-encompassing smile.

Aulis stared at Evie in wonder. She was half-fairy. He would have to watch her like a hawk after this was announced at the banquet. Niklas already saw her as a prize to be won; when he learned of her birthright, he would also see her as a means to take the throne. She would be in extreme danger.

Evie felt the heat rising in her cheeks. Had the king really just *handed* her over to Aulis like some sort of possession? This was exactly what she didn't want.

Oberon stood up, slowly stretching. "Now, if you ladies will pack a bag, we can be off."

Winnie pulled Colleen to her feet and motioned for Evie to follow. "We'll be ready in just a moment." They walked down the hallway to the master bedroom, where Winnie pulled out an overnight bag and set it next to the bags Colleen and Evie had brought. "Quickly, grab your things. The sooner we get to the palace, the safer we'll be. We may also be able to get some information about Lyrr and see if they have any new leads."

Colleen quickly forgot her fear at the prospect of being reunited with Lyrr, and even Evie stopped being mad at the world long enough to consider the possibility. They threw everything into their bags and rejoined the men within the span of 10 minutes. Oberon held the door for the women, then followed with Aulis. As soon as the women emerged from the house, Aulis and Oberon stopped to give new instructions to Taarmo and Ari. Ari looked over his shoulder at Evie, wide-eyed in disbelief. He turned back to Oberon for the remainder of their instructions.

Niklas sauntered over to Evie with a bright smile. "Hi. I'm Niklas. I'm very pleased to meet you."

Evie studied him with guarded eyes. He was a blonde giant with sparkling violet eyes and an open, friendly face. She quickly felt herself begin to relax.

"Um, hi. I'm Evie. It's nice to meet you." She smiled back at him.

He gestured around the backyard with one arm. "It's probably all a little overwhelming for you, isn't it? If you need anything at all, please feel free to come find me."

Ari looked back over his shoulder in time to see Niklas moving closer to Evie. He signaled to Aulis, who moved in quickly; he stalked over to Evie, putting a proprietary arm around her waist. "I'll be there if she needs anything, don't worry. She is my responsibility."

Evie pushed away from him. "Responsibility? I'm not some unwanted package dropped on your doorstep. I'm perfectly capable of taking care of myself."

"Of course you are." Niklas said smoothly. "As soon as we arrive back at the castle, I'd be happy to be your personal tour guide."

Aulis growled at Niklas' audacity.

Evie smiled sweetly at Niklas. "Thank you. I'd like that very much."

She had pledged never to let another man control her, and she meant it with her entire being. Aulis wasn't going to be an exception to that rule – no matter how many butterflies he set off in her stomach.

Oberon approached the two men, who were now standing toe to toe in a silent standoff, and wrapped one arm around Evie's waist.

"Come, my child. I would like to show you my home." He said with a smile and kissed her on the forehead. He kept his arm wrapped around Evie, gesturing for Winnie and Colleen to follow as Ari and Taarmo led the way back to the portal. Aulis and Niklas were forced to bring up the rear, glaring menacingly at each other with every step.

Niklas was laughing inwardly; he hadn't had this much fun in years. Aulis had been knocked off his high horse by the human herself. He'd hardly been able to contain himself during that little scene. Now, he just had to figure out why the king was showing such a marked interest in the girl, and he knew just the person to ask.

Aulis was fuming. Did the girl have no sense of self-preservation at all? Couldn't she see through Niklas' glamour? He was going to have to enlist the help of Ari and Taarmo to keep a very close eye on Niklas and his men because it was only going to get worse when Niklas learned her true identity. Aulis was going to have to get her alone as soon as possible and explain things to her. He wasn't trying to control her; he was simply trying to keep her safe. He couldn't explain why, but she was very important to him.

Evie felt very safe with her uncle. He was extremely personable and reminded her of Winnie in a lot of ways. She turned to look at Winnie, who was laughing and joking with Taarmo, apparently thoroughly enjoying herself.

Evie also sneaked a peek at her mother. Ari was walking at her side, speaking very softly, and it appeared that Colleen was beginning to relax. Evie marveled at how different Ari was from his twin. They both had the same muscular build and jet-black hair, but there the similarities ended. Ari had a very soothing quality about him, an uncanny ability to soothe even the most frayed nerves. Her mother was a testament to that skill.

Aulis, on the other hand, positively exuded sensuality. Everything about him made her nerves sing; she couldn't look at him without getting weak in the knees and feeling her pulse race. His baritone voice held a promise all its own, leading to thoughts that made her blush just to think them.

When they reached the portal, Evie recognized where they were and blushed to the roots of her hair. Aulis looked at the circle of flowers, and a slow smile spread across his face as he looked at Evie through half-lidded eyes. She shivered to her very core.

Oberon watched the interaction and smiled contentedly. Yes, they would definitely make a good match. She would be safe in his care and, if the fire in her eyes was any indication, she would be good for him as well.

Winnie fanned her face, looking pointedly at Oberon. "We'd better get them to the castle quickly before we end up with the floorshow to end all floorshows." He chuckled as he grabbed Aulis by the arm. "Aulis, will you please take the ladies through the portal to their rooms?" He leaned over, whispering into Aulis' ear. "Colleen is to have Lyrr's room, Winnie can use my chambers, and I think Evie should remain under your protection." He tapped Aulis' chest with his index finger. "Take care, though, as I will not have her upset. Not only is she the Guardian, but she is my niece and…"

"My chosen mate," finished Aulis with a smile.

"I'm glad we understand each other." Oberon returned the smile.

Aulis gestured to the portal. "If you ladies will come with me, I will escort you to your rooms so you can relax and freshen up prior to the banquet." He held one arm out for Winnie, which she took willingly. He turned to Evie with a stunning smile and offered her his other arm. Evie looked at him breathlessly; since he was asking and not insisting, she decided she would take the arm he offered. She turned to see her mother taking Ari's arm in the same fashion. She studied the portal warily, grabbing Aulis' arm tightly before they stepped through. There was a blast of warm, sweetly scented air, and Evie felt dizzy. Then there was nothing at all.

10 WELCOME TO TUATHA

Evie woke in a colossal four-poster bed piled high with some of the most luxurious fabrics she had ever seen. Slowly sitting up, she cautiously pushed her hair back from her face and tugged the bust-line of her dress into place. She looked around the room, taking everything in.

The stone walls were adorned with elaborate tapestries. The floors were crafted of heavily scraped wood covered with thick woven rugs. On the far side of the room was a beautiful stone balcony. Where was she? She must be in her uncle's castle somewhere, but where?

Her attention was drawn back to the balcony by the sound of heavy footsteps approaching. Aulis slowly walked into the room and smiled at the sight of Evie in his bed with half-lidded eyes and disheveled hair. Evie blushed furiously, clutching a silken pillow to her chest with quivering hands.

"Wha... What are you doing here?" She stammered.

Aulis approached the bed, eyeing Evie with a predatory look. "What do you mean? This is my room."

Evie quickly scooted to the far edge of the bed, ready to flee. "Oh. I'm sorry. I don't know why I was brought here instead of being taken to my room."

Aulis crossed the room with inhuman speed and stood in front of Evie, preventing her from leaving. He pulled her off the bed into his arms.

"My love, this *is* your room. I told you before – you're mine. I know you understood the significance of finding my flower in your hair, not just once, but twice."

Evie trembled in his massive arms. "I don't understand. Why me? There isn't anything special about me. I have a very long line of failed first dates that can back that up." The pent-up resentment counteracted her fear, and her voice began to rise. "If any one of those men had seen anything worthwhile in me, I probably wouldn't be here right now."

Aulis sat on the edge of the bed, pulled Evie into his lap, and gently caressed her face. "I guess that proves something I've known for a long time – most human males are blind and stupid. From the very first moment I saw you, you stirred something in me I didn't even know existed."

Evie looked at him in disbelief as he took her face in his hands and kissed her tenderly with an expertise she had never known. Aulis couldn't think of anything but the tiny girl in his arms. Evie was amazed at the perfection of the moment and decided she must still be asleep; since she was dreaming, she might as well enjoy herself as she had in their previous dream encounters. She threw her arms around his neck and kissed him with abandon. Aulis paused, momentarily stunned at her sudden response. Evie thrust both hands into his hair, clutching the silky black strands in her fists. Aulis grabbed either side of her waist and roughly pulled her down to the silken sheets covering the bed. Evie gasped as they fell to the bed, and Aulis fanned her hair out around them.

Her heart pounded furiously when Aulis' eyes detonated into twin blue flames. She let one hand slide down his back as his lips expertly snaked down her neck. She could feel the slabs of muscle framing his spine. How could he possess such strength yet his touch be infinitely gentle? His mouth turned her pulse into lava, molten strands connecting the pulse point in her neck to her very core.

Aulis could feel her pulse racing faster with each touch of his lips, and his pants tightened until he thought he would burst through the seams. Evie reached between them and cupped him, hoping to ease his discomfort; Aulis threw his head back, revealing the cords in his neck as he moaned deeply. Caught up in what she thought was a dream, Evie began unbuttoning his pants, trying to remove the barrier between them. Aulis growled deep in his throat and pushed her dress down to her waist, devouring her nipples until they ached for more. She could hear her heart pounding in her ears.

Aulis abruptly jerked his head toward the door. Evie quickly realized this was no dream, and it was not her heart she heard pounding; rather, it was someone banging on the door. Every inch of her exposed skin blushed bright red as she pushed away from Aulis and desperately tried to cover herself. He slid off the edge of the bed and adjusted his painfully swollen phallus. All he knew was there had better be a good reason for the interruption or he might kill someone.

He flung the door open wide and snarled, "What *is* it?"

The young page winced at the sound of the door crashing into the wall, and the tone of Aulis' voice didn't make him feel any safer.

"I-I-I apologize, sir, but I have a message from King Oberon." The page stammered and swallowed nervously.

Aulis sighed in defeat. "What's the message?"

"He wanted you to know the banquet will begin within the hour. He would like you and Ms. Adair to meet him in his chamber and accompany him to the banquet hall. He requested that Ms. Adair wear her ceremonial robes for the banquet, but he would also like her to wear this."

He held a small box out to Aulis before turning on his heel and quickly disappearing down the hall.

Aulis shut the door with a thud. His eyes immediately sought out his bed, but Evie was gone. He heard a soft rustling and found her standing on the balcony with her face in her hands. Could she really be that shy? She was wonderfully responsive when she let herself go. Every time they were together the chemistry was explosive, but they always seemed to get interrupted. He vowed to himself he would get some uninterrupted time with her alone – and soon. He walked silently to the balcony so he wouldn't startle her. Evie jumped as his arms slowly wrapped around her waist and he pulled her back against his chest. She felt her heart hammer in her chest.

"Ionúin?" He whispered.

"Huh?" She replied quietly.

He pulled her head to his shoulder and brushed his lips against her forehead.

"It means beloved." He said softly. "You confound me. We have been together several times, yet you are still so nervous around me. I was just curious why."

She felt sick to her stomach. She really wasn't sure what she felt at this point and didn't feel prepared to have this conversation. He had introduced her to feelings and sensations so intense she hadn't known they existed. She turned slowly in his arms and forced herself to look into the fathomless blue pools of his eyes.

"Um... well... I'm not really sure where to start." She stammered. "Just yesterday, I was dealing with my asshole of a boss and all I could think of was spending a few days of peace and quiet with my favorite aunt in the country. Now, I'm in a place I thought was a myth, I'm about to have dinner with the king of the Fairies... and I'm in the arms of a fairy warrior whose legendary reputation with women goes back generations. I have zero experience with all of the above – so you're right, why in the world should I be nervous?" She managed a hint of her usual sarcasm and fingered her necklace anxiously.

Aulis couldn't believe his luck. It was exactly as Winnie had said; she was an innocent. He would be the first and the last man to ever lay hands on her. He broke from his daydream to look at her, and the smile quickly died off his face to be replaced with astonishment.

"Where did you get that necklace?" He asked, his voice just above a whisper.

Evie looked at her necklace. It wasn't anything special – to other people anyway. However, it held a lot of sentimental value for her as it had been a present from her grandmother on her mother's side. It was a black iridescent stone roughly cut in the shape of a flame, hanging from a simple black cord. She missed her grandmother terribly and, even after ten years, the pain was still raw.

She looked at Aulis, her eyes awash with unshed tears. "It was a gift from my grandmother on her deathbed. She told me to never remove it. It has brought me great comfort over the years; I can rub the stone and it's like she's still with me – I can almost hear her voice." She wiped her eyes with the back of her hand. "I know – it's stupid, right?"

Aulis lifted her chin with one finger. "Not stupid at all. You must realize things are not as cut and dried as you humans would like to believe; death is not always the end. This necklace is very special indeed. Your grandmother was right – you must never take it off unless instructed by the king himself." He smiled. "It would be impossible for another to remove it from your body while you live. It is yours to carry – until you pass it freely to another."

Evie rubbed her temples with her hands. "Stop, my brain can't process anything else right now. I need a shower, a nap, dinner, and a very strong drink… not necessarily in that order."

Aulis ran a powerful hand through her silken hair. "You shall have it all and more – starting with dinner." He handed her the box the page had brought in from Oberon. "Your uncle sent this for you to wear tonight."

Evie took the box in shaking hands and lifted the lid to find the most exquisite diamond ring, set with a crystal-clear blue and yellow topaz on either side. "It's the most beautiful thing I've ever seen," she gasped as she held it up to the light.

Aulis jerked in surprise. "This is a very unexpected move."

"What do you mean?" She asked.

"Evie, there is more at play here than you realize. I know you said you can't process anything else, but you need to know this for your own safety at the very least. They have never stopped the search for your father; however, in all these years there has never been even a whisper about the existence of his child. Your mother, Winnie, and Oberon have done an amazing job hiding your presence, and I promise that you are safe with me. However, I need you to follow my directions without question. I do not trust Niklas. He and his family have tried to remove

Oberon from the throne for centuries; most recently, they use his refusal to give up on the search for Lyrr as proof of his inability to be an effective leader. Niklas also has a strong rivalry with me and will do whatever he can do drive a wedge between us."

"Why are you telling me all this?" Evie asked desperately as she went back to rubbing her temples.

He sighed deeply. "The ring you hold has great significance. Oberon loved Winnie deeply, and he had this ring commissioned when he announced he was going to take her hand in marriage. However, after Lyrr's disappearance, they could no longer be together; it was too dangerous for her and your mother. But everyone within Tuatha De knows of the ring and its significance to the king. By giving the ring to you to wear, he is claiming you as part of his family – but you *must* not let anyone know you belong to Lyrr. It would put you in very real danger."

"Wait, I'm confused. If no one is supposed to know who I am, why is he giving me the ring to wear tonight?" She wailed.

He gently took her hands in his. "It's not just to wear tonight; it's yours to wear forever. He is showing his support for you to be joined with his successor in marriage. He is proclaiming you the next queen of the Tuatha De."

It was finally too much for her to bear; Evie's eyes rolled back into her head and the room went dark. She had no idea how much time passed, but she awoke on the floor, cradled in Aulis' arms.

"My love, are you all right? I'm sorry to put so much on your shoulders in such a short time." He grinned mischievously. "However, I thought all human girls dreamed of being a princess."

"Ha, ha, very funny." Evie shook her head. "So – now on top of everything else, I'm engaged to his successor? Great. So when do I meet him?"

Aulis stared at her in confusion. "You already have met him, Evie. You yourself participated in the ancient rituals when you presented the wine to Oberon and the flowers to his successor."

Evie's eyes went wide and her mouth formed an O. "You? You are his successor? I'm engaged to marry you?"

Aulis chuckled. "Yes; I'm sorry to disappoint you. However, I will have you and no other." He slid the ring into place on her finger. "The king will announce me as his successor at the banquet tonight, as well as celebrating the visit from the Adair women and the current Guardian. You will be the gorgeous confection to top the cake. The entire kingdom has been buzzing about the appearance of the Mark on my hand, and they are all dying to meet you – especially Kimbra, my brother's wife. Don't let her overwhelm you... She's been waiting for you for a very long time."

Evie giggled. "I doubt she will be the one to overwhelm me." She tentatively reached out and stroked the outline of the red and black tattoo on his hand. "It looks just like my necklace. Isn't that strange?"

There was a sudden knock on the door and Evie cried out in surprise.

"Ionúin, you must relax. No harm will come to you while I am here." He strode purposely to the door and swung it open wide. The page cowered in the hallway.

"Sir, the king is ready for you now."

"Give us one moment and we will be on our way." He said in an even voice.

The page visibly relaxed. "Yes, sir, I will let him know immediately."

Aulis slowly closed the door. "As much as I would like to stay in this room with you forever, I'm afraid it's time to meet your uncle for the banquet. Are you ready?"

Evie smoothed her hair back from her face and straightened her dress. "I guess I'm as ready as I'll ever be."

He pulled her into his arms and kissed her deeply, leaving her knees week and clinging to him for support. "My love, you continue to surprise me with your strength. I think I may have finally met my match – won't Ari be thrilled?" He asked sarcastically.

Evie laughed. "I think I like your brother already. I can't wait to meet his wife."

Aulis snorted. "You, Ari, and Kimbra will probably end up being the death of me, and then my little Lizbeth will be heartbroken."

Evie felt a sudden anger flare up at the mention of this unseen female. "So, who is Lizbeth?" she asked in a tone she hoped would pass for casual interest.

Aulis grinned at her widely. Nope, it had sounded just as jealous as she felt.

"Lizbeth is the baby daughter of Ari and Kimbra. She is my sweet little niece, and now she is yours as well. Be prepared, however; she is very shy around people she doesn't know well and can take quite some time to warm up."

He stroked her cheek. "You'll get to meet her later. She and Ari have a tendency to grace me with early morning visits." He said with a half-smile and held out his arm. "Are you ready? We can start meeting your list of demands, starting with dinner and a strong drink."

She took his arm and inhaled deeply. "Let's do this before I wake up or run home screaming."

They walked the halls as Aulis pointed out various points of interest in the castle; he was an excellent guide. Their tour was over all too quickly when they arrived at the king's private quarters. Aulis rapped on the massive doors, and they immediately swung wide. Two guards emerged from the room and stood outside the doorway as Aulis and Evie were ushered inside and the doors closed behind them.

Oberon rushed forward and grabbed Evie in a bear hug. "My child, I am so happy to have you here where you belong. You have Lyrr's eyes. Did you know that?" He beamed at her. "I wish I could tell the entire kingdom their princess has come home. However, I'm sure Aulis has explained why that isn't possible right now, correct?"

Aulis nodded his head.

"Evie," Oberon continued, "I'm depending on Aulis to fill you in on everything going on. I have complete faith in him, and I know he would never allow any harm to come to you. He is quite taken with you."

Evie blushed to the roots of her head and stared at the floor.

Oberon chuckled. "I see you aren't completely unaffected by him either. It's a good match, and I approve wholeheartedly. However, my child, I only want your happiness. I need to know you want this match."

Evie looked at her uncle in shock. Was he really letting her be in control of her own life? She looked at Aulis and could see the pain he tried to mask in his eyes. She tried to imagine walking away, never seeing him again, and found herself choking back tears.

"Oberon, at this point I can't imagine a life without him in it." She smiled shyly.

Oberon clapped Aulis on the back. "Well, my boy, you hit the jackpot. You have earned it all – you honestly deserve to be happy. I know the two of you will be fair rulers and will be loved by all within Tuatha De."

Evie gasped. "I'm really a princess?"

Aulis grinned at her. "For now. Ultimately, you will be queen."

Evie promptly fainted for the second time in her life. She awoke to two very anxious, very large men standing over her. Oberon was the first to speak.

"My child, are you all right?

"Yes, I'm fine… really. It's just been a lot to take in today. I promise I'll do my best to stay on my own two feet tonight." She said with a small smile.

Oberon beamed with pride. "I see Lyrr's eyes aren't the only thing you inherited; you possess his strength as well." He turned to Aulis. "She's truly fit for a king – strong and independent."

Evie couldn't believe her ears. These were the exact qualities that had run off her every suitor. Suddenly she felt more at ease in this strange world than she ever had in her own. She flashed a blinding smile at Aulis that took him completely off guard.

"I do believe you promised me dinner and a drink."

He grabbed her in a bear hug and swung her in a couple of circles, making her hair fly in an arc around them. Oberon glowed at the scene in front of him. He was thrilled to see Aulis so happy, and his heart threatened to burst with the joy of having Lyrr's child so close.

"What's all the noise about?"

"Aunt Winnie?" Aulis put Evie down so she could throw herself at her beloved aunt.

Winnie took Evie's face in her hands. "Sweet girl, you've never looked lovelier. You look truly happy."

"I am, and I'd ask you why you're in Oberon's room, but I already know the answer to that question." Evie held up her hand, and the light reflected off the magnificent ring. "Aunt Winnie, this is rightfully yours, and as soon as we can get everything sorted out, I'll return it to you."

Winnie looked at Oberon with raised eyebrows; he smiled and nodded his head in return.

Evie looked meaningfully from Winnie to Oberon. "Aunt Winnie, you deserve happiness more than anyone I know – you should be with Uncle Oberon."

He reached out and pulled Winnie into his arms for a tender kiss. When they separated, Winnie and Oberon's hair was a shade or two darker.

Evie stared openmouthed. "Aunt Winnie – your hair." She whispered.

Oberon smiled at her before putting his finger to his lips. "Shh."

Winnie beamed at her. "Come, child, let's go get some dinner."

"Wait, what about Mom? She's got to be freaking out... That is, if she's even conscious." Evie said sarcastically.

"Your mother is just fine. Last I saw her, she was curled up in a chair in Lyrr's room." Winnie smiled. "Ari offered to escort her to dinner and said they would meet us there." Winnie turned to Aulis. "That brother of yours is quite the charmer."

Evie rolled her eyes skyward. "Yeah, I can't imagine where he gets that." Aulis looked at her as the picture of innocence, and she burst out laughing.

Winnie tucked her arm into Oberon's. "Let's go get dinner; I'm famished."

The foursome walked to the banquet hall, utterly content in each other's company. As they came around a corner, Evie caught sight of her mother standing with Ari.

"Evie!" Her mother squealed in delight.

Ari turned to follow Colleen's gaze and stared slack-jawed at Aulis' overprotective stance near Evie. She was absolutely stunning. Could she truly be the human his brother had Marked? He knew she was the Guardian and she was definitely an Adair, and not to mention Lyrr's child. He met Aulis' gaze with questions in his eyes. Aulis nodded and smiled broadly, pulling Evie closer to his side.

Colleen noticed the possessive gesture and watched her daughter closely for her reaction. Evie smiled up at Aulis and leaned her head against his shoulder. Colleen breathed a heavy sigh of relief, overjoyed to see Evie finally get her chance at happiness.

"Colleen, you look lovely," Aulis said. "Ari, I would like you to officially meet Evie. It will be formally announced tonight, but Evie and I are to be wed. I wanted you to hear it from me."

Ari sprung forward, grabbing Evie and swinging her high in the air.

"It's about damn time if you ask me." Ari laughed, kissing her soundly on the cheek. "Kimbra is going to be beside herself."

Aulis plucked Evie from his brother's arm and held her close. She felt like a small child being passed between the two enormous doppelgangers. She was amazed at how much the two men looked alike – the jet black hair, crystal-blue eyes and heavily muscled physiques – but that is where the similarities ended. Ari had a very easygoing demeanor and made you instantly comfortable in his presence. Aulis was intense to the point of being intimidating.

The steward emerged from the banqueting hall.

"Sire, all is ready. Shall I make the announcements?"

"Yes. Start with me, Winnie, and Colleen Adair. Next will come Aulis and Evie, then Ari and his family."

"Understood, Your Majesty."

The small group began shuffling around to get into their respective plans in line. The steward banged his staff against the marble floor to command everyone's attention.

"May I have your attention please? Now arriving – His Royal Highness, King Oberon, and Ladies Winnie and Colleen Adair."

The room burst into applause as Oberon led the women to their seats at the main table on either side of his place. Everyone in the main hall turned expectantly toward the steward, anxiously awaiting the next announcement.

"Now arriving," the steward's voice boomed, "Lord Aulis and Lady Evie Adair."

The entire room erupted into thunderous applause with the exception of one person. Dahlia sat at Niklas' left, breathlessly awaiting the first glimpse of her rival.

11 A BANQUET

Aulis took Evie by the hand and led her to their places at the main table. When they arrived at their seats, Aulis turned to the crowd and lifted Evie's hand to his lips. Dahlia seethed with jealousy; the woman at Aulis' side was as stunning as everyone had said. Niklas looked at Dahlia with an amused glance. This was going to be even more fun than he'd originally thought.

"She's extremely beautiful, isn't she?" He asked silkily.

Dahlia glared at him. "Some might think so, but she isn't worthy of Aulis. What can a tiny little thing like that have to offer him?" She stared at Evie in pure hatred as Aulis gently pushed a lock of hair from Evie's face.

Niklas chuckled. "Well, it looks like she must be doing something right."

Dahlia shot him a look that would have withered a weaker man.

Oberon stood up and tapped his knife against his glass.

"Attention. Thank you all for being here tonight. We are celebrating the arrival of Winnie, Colleen, and Evie Adair. Evie is the Guardian for this generation." Oberon turned to Aulis. "In addition, I have a major announcement this evening. I would like to announce that I have chosen my successor – Aulis."

The room erupted into thunderous applause. Now it was Niklas' turn to glare in pure hatred, and Dahlia sat with her mouth hanging open in shock.

Oberon motioned for everyone to be silent. "I have one last announcement to make."

The room grew so quiet you could have heard a pin drop.

"On top of all the other exciting news this evening, our own Prince Aulis has finally chosen a bride! From this point forward, Evie Adair will be known as Princess Evie, future Queen of Tuatha De."

Aulis stood, pulled Evie to her feet, and kissed her gently. The cheers from the assembly grew deafening. Evie blushed furiously; she wasn't used to this kind of attention and was unsure how to react. She smiled and gave a small wave to the crowd, who returned the greeting with even louder cheers.

Dahlia glanced at Niklas' reaction and realized the announcement had been a complete shock to him; he had always assumed that, since Lyrr had no children, he would be the chosen successor.

Dahlia snickered and moved closer to whisper in his ear. "Guess you didn't see that one coming, did you? Now what are you going to do? Obviously taking the human from Aulis just got much more complicated."

The servers moved around the room with platters of food as the assembly took turns filing past the main table to congratulate the new couple and to pay their respects to the king and the Adair women.

Ari and Kimbra were first in line; she ran around the table and grabbed Evie in a tight hug. "I am so glad to finally meet you. I had just about given up on Aulis finding anyone who would truly make him happy."

A tiny blonde head popped over the edge of the table.

"Unca Owie, Unca Owie! I missed you."

Lizbeth jumped into Aulis' arms and buried her tiny face in his neck. Evie gasped at the pure beauty of the child. Lizbeth raised her head and looked deep into Evie's eyes.

"I'm Livbef." She said finally. "What's your name?"

Evie smiled; she absolutely adored children, and Lizbeth was no exception. "My name is Evie. It's nice to meet you. Your Uncle Aulis talks about you."

"I wuv my Unca Owie. Do you wuv him too?"

Evie blushed furiously. "Well, yes. I think I do."

Lizbeth studied her seriously. "You awe vewy pwetty." She reached out a hand to touch Evie's hair. "I like your hair."

Evie stroked the little girl's silky platinum hair. "I like your hair too; it's so very soft."

Lizbeth's next move shocked them all. She held her arms out to Evie, curled up in her lap and laid her head on Evie's shoulder.

Kimbra jumped forward to move the little girl. "I am so sorry. Let me take her before something happens to your beautiful dress." She fretted.

Evie waved her off. "It's OK. I'd like her to stay if you don't mind. She's a soothing presence." Evie said as she continued to stroke Lizbeth's hair.

Aulis looked at her lovingly. He was overjoyed that the two most important women in his life seemed to hold a natural affinity for each other. He smiled at Lizbeth, who had curled up trustingly in Evie's arms and fallen asleep.

Dahlia and Niklas were the next in line to greet the couple.

"Hello, Aulis." Dahlia purred and kissed him on the cheek. "I understand congratulations are in order. I have to say I'm surprised; you made no mention of this last night, you bad boy." She turned to Evie. "Congratulations my dear; I'd shake your hand but I can see your hands are full. You can always send her off to the nursery, you know." Her lips curled in distaste.

Evie seethed inside as the hair on the back of her neck stood on end. They'd just met, and already she couldn't stand this woman; it took some effort to keep her opinion out of her expression as she pointedly continued to stroke the baby's hair.

Niklas stepped forward and shook Aulis' hand. "Congrats, Aulis; very well done. I have to say, I haven't had a challenge this exciting in over 200 years. I look forward to it." He said for Aulis' ears only.

Aulis' fists clenched and his face reddened as he fought to maintain control of himself. Niklas laughed softly and decided to twist the knife a little deeper as he leaned over and kissed Evie lightly on the cheek.

"Hello again, Evie. Don't let Dahlia get to you; she has no maternal instinct at all. I guess congratulations are in order. I didn't realize you were so close to our Aulis, or was this a surprise for you as well?"

Evie blushed furiously.

"I see." Niklas said with a grin. "Well, I hope this doesn't change your decision to allow me to show you around the castle?"

Evie felt Oberon's eyes boring a hole through her; she didn't want to offend her uncle in his own home. "No, not at all. I'd be happy to let you show me around the castle."

"Perfect! I'll pick you up first thing in the morning. Where are you staying?"

Aulis spoke with his teeth clenched together. "She will be staying in my rooms while she is here."

Niklas smiled at Evie. "Fortunately, I know right where Aulis' rooms are. I'll see you after breakfast." He moved smoothly down the table to greet Oberon.

Evie flinched as she noticed Aulis' powerful hands fiercely gripping the edge of the table.

"Are you OK?" She whispered.

"We will discuss it later." He said through gritted teeth.

Evie found herself trembling at his cold, hard tone. "Oh. OK."

Kimbra watched the exchange with eyes that habitually missed very little and felt that cold protectiveness return; if Dahlia and Niklas thought they were going to ruin this for Aulis, they had no idea what they were about to run into. She looked at her daughter sleeping peacefully in Evie's lap and knew she'd extend the same protectiveness to Evie.

Ari saw the determined look in Kimbra's eyes and groaned. He had seen that look before, and it frequently led to a great deal of trouble for him. He reached over and pulled Kimbra's hand into his, giving her a meaningful look. She gave him an innocent smile in return.

Evie was a nervous wreck for the remainder of the banquet. She nibbled on cheese and a bit of roast pheasant that Aulis put on her plate. She was grateful for the soft weight of the sleeping child in her lap. Even that was over altogether too soon when Kimbra came to collect Lizbeth for bedtime.

"Don't worry; Ari and I will be back shortly, after we have tucked Lizbeth in with her nanny." Kimbra said softly in Evie's ear. Evie gave her a small smile in thanks; she had a feeling she was going to be good friends with Kimbra.

"Nectar, my lady?" A young squire appeared at her elbow, making her jump.

"Uh, sure… Thank you." She replied.

Winnie leaned across Oberon to caution Evie. "Careful, my dear; it's pretty potent stuff."

Evie grinned wickedly at her aunt. "You can still say that after drinking my attempts at bartending?" She considered the contents of the beautiful chalice. "It must be pretty harsh. Well, here goes nothing." She tossed back the entire portion.

Colleen gasped. "Evie, no!"

Evie licked her lips. "Wow. That's pretty good." She held her cup out for the nearest page to refill and hiccupped.

Winnie chuckled under her breath to Oberon. "We're in for it now."

Oberon watched her with an amused eye. "She's more and more like Lyrr every minute I spend with her. The nectar and Lyrr had quite a few adventures of their own, if I do remember."

Winnie shook her head ruefully. "You have no idea. She has a tendency to run barefoot through the woods after a drink or two."

Oberon laughed out loud before whispering, "In that case, she's just like Lyrr alright."

Colleen put her face in her hands, hoping Evie wouldn't get out of control tonight. There were too many wild cards, and she had no idea who to trust in this world, save Oberon, Aulis, and Ari.

Soon the servants cleared the tables and made room for the dancing that always followed a royal banquet. The musicians set up in the corner as the attendees milled around talking to one another. Aulis left Evie with her aunts while he met Ari and Kimbra at the door. Aulis clasped his brother's forearm with his hand before giving Kimbra a warm hug.

"So, what do you think?" Aulis asked while scratching a thumbnail on the marble pillar. He was desperate for them to like Evie; he just didn't want to *look* desperate.

"Anyone who Lizbeth connects with so quickly must be special." Kimbra said with a laugh. "Anyway, I really like her – you can see she's got spirit. I'm so unbelievably happy for you that I can hardly stop smiling."

Aulis heard the golden peals of Evie's laughter, so new in his ears but yet he would have recognized them anywhere. The smile quickly died off his face when he saw Niklas swinging Evie onto the dance floor. Aulis was enraged at Niklas' nerve; it was his own right to have the first dance with his betrothed. Niklas even had the gall to wink at him as they spun past! It was clear Niklas viewed the whole situation as a game and had made his first move. Evie was obviously flown with nectar; the color was high in her cheeks and her eyes were unfocused. Dahlia came by and took Aulis by the arm.

"Come, Aulis, it's been way too long since we danced." Dahlia purred. "Evie's in good hands."

Aulis' temper finally got the best of him; he grabbed Dahlia by the waist and swung her onto the dance floor. As they glided past Evie and Niklas, Evie narrowed her eyes menacingly. What was Aulis doing with that bitch? What exactly was their relationship? Evie had never experienced such a white-hot jealously before, and she hated every single second of it. As they whirled past, Evie grabbed another glass of nectar off a tray. The nectar launched a red bloom in her chest so bright she could practically see it, and her worries began to melt away. When the music stopped, she found herself standing in front of Aulis and Dahlia.

"Aulis, you always were an amazing dancer. All these years, you have always been my favorite partner... on *and* off the dance floor." Dahlia said breathlessly.

Niklas amusedly watched Evie clench her teeth together hard enough to make her jaw tic. He took a calculated risk and pulled her closer to his side, laughing. "Come on, my dear. I think they will want some time alone."

He took her arm and turned on his heel to lead her back to the dance floor. They made it perhaps two steps before Aulis caught her by the hand and dragged her back to his side.

"Niklas," he growled, "you overstep your bounds. I told you before: she is mine. I recommend not testing me where this is concerned."

Evie looked at him, wide-eyed. Could they really be fighting over her? Well, that was definitely a first! She knew there was some reason she shouldn't want to go with Niklas, but suddenly she couldn't remember what Aulis had told her. Further, when she caught the superior gleam in Dahlia's eyes, it angered her all over again.

"You know what I think, Aulis?" Evie said, the venom dripping from her voice. "I think you need to take a step back and decide what, and *who*, you really want. I refuse to speak to you, and certainly have no plans to return to your rooms, until *she* is gone from here altogether." She put a hand on one hip and made a concerted effort not to give in to any more hiccups. "And I recommend you not testing *me* on *this*." Her chest heaved up and down with anger.

Dahlia, Niklas, and Aulis stared at her in disbelief. No one ever talked to Aulis like that. He clenched his jaw in response; this tiny woman would be the death of him.

Evie pivoted on her heel. "Come along, Niklas; you promised me another dance." Niklas chuckled, threw his arm around her shoulders, and squeezed before leading her back to the dance floor.

Dahlia wrapped her arms around Aulis' neck, pressed her body against his, and breathed into his ear. "She's smarter than she looks. It appears we have some private time; shall we go to your rooms or mine? It will be just like old times."

"Get out of my sight. I will not be responsible for my actions if you stay here." Aulis ground out. It took every ounce of his self-control not to knock her to the ground. He strongly suspected she and Niklas had engineered all the trouble they were causing.

Dahlia smiled slyly as she backed out the door. "Anything that pleases you, Aulis; you know where to find me."

Aulis strode to the center of the dance floor where Evie had her head thrown back, laughing wildly while Niklas spun her about. He plucked her out of Niklas' arms and forced her to look into his eyes.

"Now, I've removed Dahlia from your sight; I assume you are going to keep your end of the bargain and speak with me?" Aulis asked her.

Evie's eyes shone a deep dizzying green like fresh clover in a meadow. "How did you get rid of her so quickly? Do you have magic powers? Hopefully there's a shallow grave out back somewhere." She twittered, the effects of the nectar making her head spin. She took an unsteady step forward and fell face first into Aulis' broad chest.

He smells so good, she thought. He smelled better than any cologne she had ever encountered. Clean yet spicy – and completely masculine.

Aulis shook his head. There was no way she could walk all the way back to his suite. He put an arm under her knees and picked her up. "I think you've had enough for one night. What say I get you to bed?"

Evie stared into his eyes and ran a fingertip up his arm suggestively. "Only if you are coming with me."

His eyes ignited with passion, and he carried her purposefully back down the labyrinth of corridors to his room, not caring what anyone thought. He kicked open the door to his room.

"Darling, I thought you'd never get here." Dahlia was artfully sprawled across his bed, clad only in filmy underthings that did nothing to hide the snow-pale skin underneath.

"What in the hell is *she* doing here?" Evie demanded, immediately struggling to dive at Dahlia.

"Aulis, you told me to get going, but you never said which room. I guess I should have realized you would want to meet in my rooms, since she would be here." She rose provocatively from the bed and caressed Aulis' cheek as she crossed the room to the door. "Put the little one to bed and I'll be in my rooms... waiting." The door slid shut behind her.

Evie thrashed wildly, trying to escape Aulis' iron grasp. "Put me down, damn you! You had me believing she was gone, and here she is half-naked in your bed – which apparently is normal!"

Aulis' emotions were still high. "No one *invited* her to come here!" He shouted back as he touched her feet to the floor. "I told her to get out of my sight. That was in *no* way an invitation to my bed. I'll say it again: there is you and only you!"

"I refuse to go through the pain of losing someone just as I begin to care for them. I'm not some little plaything you can use and throw away." She wiped a stray tear from the corner of her eye. "I'm also not going to be manipulated because of who my family is!" She pounded on his colossal chest.

He caught both of her tiny hands in one considerable fist.

"I wanted you *long* before I knew you were royal. I fell for you the first time I saw you dancing through the woods, all your beautiful hair flying out behind you." He pulled Evie close and lowered his face to hers. "In all my life, you are the only one I've ever wanted this way."

She so desperately wanted to believe him. Her knees buckled as his lips captured hers and his hands roamed over her silky skin. Her head fell back as if her hair was too heavy for her, and a soft moan escaped her throat as Aulis thrust his hands into her hair. She wrapped her arms around his neck and anchored herself to him. He plundered her mouth, savoring the sweetness left behind by the nectar. She felt their breath intermingle and tentatively stroked his tongue with hers, enjoying the responsive groan that emanated from the back of his throat. His mouth blazed a trail across her jaw and down her throat; if he continued on his current path, she felt her entire body was going to go up in flames. He was a blatantly male assault on her senses. She had never been so completely dominated by any man.

She looked over Aulis' shoulder, catching a glimpse of their reflection in the mirror, and gasped at the intimate scene reflecting back at her. He turned to follow her gaze.

"We make quite the scene, don't we?" He purred and turned her so they both faced the mirror. His hands ran down her arms, slid across her aching breasts, found the high slit in her dress, and made a path to her very core. She squirmed in his arms as her face burned with embarrassment, but he refused to let her turn away from the mirror.

"I want to see your face as I teach you the pleasure that will be yours every single night from this point forward. It will be you gracing my rooms, or no one." He whispered wickedly into her ear while his fingers traced her woman's jewel.

She watched as her eyes dilated and lips parted. She was no longer able to look away even if she wanted to. His sapphire eyes bored into her very soul. This man stirred feelings in her that she had never even known were possible. He continued to slowly rub her jewel between his fingers and watch her expression in the mirror as her pleasure grew.

Her knees threatened to give; she snaked her arms over her head and wrapped them around his neck, using him as an anchor. Her breasts heaved with her labored breathing. Her new position granted Aulis greater access, and he took full advantage by plucking at her hardened nipples with his free hand. Evie moaned in ecstasy and slowly sunk to the floor, no longer able to support her own weight. Aulis took the hem of her dress and gently lifted it over her head. Evie gazed at him through half-lidded eyes, clouded by passion; she had never cared for anyone enough to allow them to undress her before. He guided her body to the floor and raised her arms over her head, allowing her to grasp the foot of the bed. His tongue traced every inch of her body as she arched her back to meet him. She couldn't get close enough to him; she wanted him to fill her completely. The fire in Aulis' eyes combusted, and he tore her thong from her body. The feather-light caresses of his fingertips drove her to the edge of madness.

"Please, Aulis." She begged, no longer afraid of what they would share. She welcomed it – *needed* it.

In response he gently parted her knees. She closed her eyes and whimpered again in anticipation. She felt his silken hair brush against her thighs, then his warm breath on her mons. Jerking back, she scrambled to escape but only succeeded in hitting her head on the foot of the bed. He couldn't really mean to do that – it was so incredibly intimate. But the exquisite feel of his rough tongue sliding around her bud, followed by his lips suckling it, immediately stilled her. She didn't dare to make a sound lest she disturb the release she felt building inside her. Waves of pleasure crashed over her again and again until she screamed her release; it was even better than the time before. She peeked through her lashes at Aulis. His face remained so intense, and his lips glistened. He lowered his head and she tasted herself on his lips. It seemed so taboo that she felt her face heat under his scrutiny.

The throbbing subsided and she was eventually able to think clearly again. What was he planning? She knew he hadn't had an orgasm, so what was he waiting for? Was he just trying to satisfy her so he could finish with Dahlia – a woman who actually knew what she was doing? Not while there was breath left in her body. He rolled over to his side and studied her face. What was he looking for?

Evie decided to ensure that he had no need to seek satisfaction elsewhere. She pushed his pants over his hips and slid her hand inside, encircling him with her fingers. Aulis gasped and leaned back on his elbows, throwing his head back and lifting his hips to meet her hand. She took advantage of his movements and pulled on the waistband of his pants until they were inside out and on the floor. She wondered if she had the power to drive him over the edge as he had been able to do to her. She swept her glossy hair across the slabs of muscle on his stomach and continued down across his hips and over the velvet shaft jutting out of a nest of jet-black curls. His hips jerked at the sensation of her hair. Emboldened at his reaction, she took his full length into her hand, stroking from the base to the tip and back again. Sweat beaded over the surface of his body with his effort to maintain self-control.

Evie knew he was holding back. She wanted to see him wild and uninhibited with desire for her, and only her. Did she dare put her mouth on him? What would he do – would he be disgusted at her actions? She had so little experience and she didn't know if it was acceptable in this realm. She decided to take a chance. She continued to stroke him with one hand while using the other to caress him with her hair. Then she released her hair, slid down and wrapped her lips around him. He bucked and reared back, grabbing a handful of her hair while chanting her name – almost like a prayer.

Just when she suspected his climax was approaching, he pulled his hips back and dragged her up his chest so he could plunder her mouth. Determined to make him happy, she returned his passion kiss for kiss. She writhed wildly with excitement and ground against him, causing him to spill his seed across their stomachs where they were joined.

He smoothed her hair back from her face, his eyebrows drawn

together, and she panicked. He looked upset – had she done something wrong? She was afraid to ask, but more afraid of not knowing how he felt.

"Is something wrong?" Even to her own ears, her voice sounded strained.

He stood up and pulled her to her feet before striding to a large bathing pool near the stone balcony and filling it with warm water and eucalyptus oil. The soothing aroma soon permeated the entire room. He returned to Evie, swept her off her feet and carried her to the pool, where he lowered her gently to a bench below the scented water. She stared at him, mute, while he slowly sank to sit on another bench across from her. He took a deep breath before answering her.

"I'm so sorry, Evie. My behavior tonight was unforgivable. I promise it will not happen again."

Evie was devastated – he clearly wasn't impressed by her sensuality. What had she done wrong? It had started out so well. To her horror, she felt tears gather in her eyes. "I don't understand. Did I do something wrong?"

He stared at her blankly. "Are you serious?"

"I don't have much experience with men. If I offended you somehow…" She let her voice trail off.

He shook his head in disbelief.

"You think *you* have something to apologize for?" He moved across to the pool and sat next to her. "Ionúin, I completely lost control of myself. Tonight was supposed to be about you; I wanted you to understand how precious you are to me. Instead, I allowed myself to be selfish and behaved like an untried youth."

She ducked her head and stared at the small ripples in the water from their movements, trying not to stare at his naked form beneath the surface.

"I've never done anything like that before, and I was afraid I had done something wrong or, worse yet, that you didn't want me."

He lifted her chin with his finger so she was forced to meet his gaze.

"My love, how could you ever think I don't want you? You have no idea how difficult it is to restrain myself. I have to abide by the laws regarding relations between the Tuatha and humans. Winnie was quick to remind me of my place. As soon as we are married, I'm not letting you out of my sight, or my bedroom, for days."

Evie paused, considering all the implications what he'd said. "I didn't want you to go to Dahlia tonight… or any night. I want to be enough for you."

He stroked her hair. "Evie, you are *more* than enough for me. You are definitely worth waiting for."

"What would happen if we were to...? Is there some sort of consequence – I mean, how would anyone even know?"

"My love, you have no idea how tempted I am, but in the end I have too much respect for you to put you in that position. It's definitely going to put my self-control to the test – often." He planted a kiss on the side of her head.

"Maybe I can convince my uncle to have the ceremony sooner rather than later." She mused. "I can point out that it would be best since war is impending, and it's much safer for me here than back home with my asshole boss."

"You're pretty clever, and I think he'll give you anything you want. All you have to do is ask. He and I are quite close, so I'll also explain it will be increasingly difficult for us to share a room and remain unmarried. I *know* he'll understand that." He grinned at her.

She sighed. She wanted this to work out. The idea of being married to such a masculine presence with a tender heart was a dream any woman would kill for. Bouncing back from her failed relationships had been easy since she'd never been emotionally involved – but she knew there would be no recovery if she were to lose him now.

They allowed the hot water to soothe away stress and ease tense muscles until the water cooled. Aulis climbed out of the tub, and Evie watched his muscles ripple as he strode across the room. He was physically flawless. He grabbed two thick towels and caught her staring as he turned to make his way back to the tub. Her face reddened at being caught studying him. *Oh, who am I kidding – I'm leering at him like a cheetah stalking an antelope*, she laughed at herself.

He wrapped one towel around his waist and offered her a hand to help her emerge from the tub. When she stood, rivulets of water ran down her body, through the valley between her breasts and down her stomach. It was his turn to appreciate the perfection of her tiny figure. He licked his lips as he assessed every inch of her. She shivered under the scrutiny of his gaze. Surely he couldn't be ready for more?

He wrapped the towel around her and made his way to a curtained alcove in the corner of the room. He pulled back the curtain to reveal a closet that any woman would envy. There was a couch in the middle of the room, flanked on both sides by built-in shelves and separate areas for hanging. Aulis emerged moments later and handed her a length of impossibly soft material. Evie grabbed the material in both hands and quickly determined it was the Tuatha equivalent of a T-shirt.

"I didn't know what you might have packed, so I thought you might like to sleep in it tonight."

71

Evie knew she had T-shirts and shorts packed away in her duffel, but they were nowhere near as soft and didn't smell like him. She gratefully pulled the shirt over her head; it hung down to her knees.

He stared at her appreciatively. "It definitely looks better on you than it does on me."

"I seriously doubt that." She chuckled. "What are you going to wear?"

"I should probably wear full battle armor." It was his turn to chuckle as he strode back to the closet. When he came back, the towel was gone and in its place was a pair of thin cotton lounge pants.

He probably should've *gone with the battle armor.* He looked as good in the lounge pants as he had in the towel. *How are we ever going to get any sleep?*

Even his bed was intimidating; the four-poster was made of ornately carved, heavy wood and stood several feet from the large marble fireplace. She could only imagine how incredible the room must look in the wintertime with a fire crackling in the fireplace. She wondered if the weather there mimicked the weather back in Emory. If so, it would be at least November before she would get a chance to find out. She pulled the thick coverlet back and had to step on the edge of the bed frame to climb into the bed. It was by far the most comfortable bed she had ever known. She nestled into the massive mattress and pulled the covers back up to her shoulders.

Aulis flipped the coverlet back on the opposite side of the bed and slid in next to Evie. He immediately pulled her back against his chest and threw his arm over her waist. She shifted, trying to get comfortable, but it had a very different effect on Aulis. He growled low in his throat and kissed her neck where it met her shoulder.

"Sorry." She whispered. "I'm afraid it's going to be a long night."

His breath caressed her neck. "I'm not sorry at all. I'm going to enjoy every single moment."

She snuggled in closer and allowed her eyes to shut against the remaining light in the room. Moments later she was fast asleep.

12 A FORGOTTEN PROMISE

Evie awoke in the morning to a pounding sound. Was it her head? She didn't think she'd had *that* much to drink the night before. It took several moments for her to realize someone was pounding on the door. At some point during the night she had turned to face Aulis' chest and he had thrown his leg over her hip. She had no desire to move at all.

"Good morning, my love."

She looked up and found Aulis staring down at her. How long had he been awake?

"Someone is at the door." She whispered.

"I know. I was hoping they'd give up and go away." He grumbled.

The pounding continued.

"Obviously they aren't going to stop." His frustration was loud and clear in his voice. "It better be damn important or I may kill someone."

While Aulis answered the door, Evie slid out of bed and headed to the bathroom. Her bladder emptied and her teeth brushed, she stared at her reflection in the mirror. Her hair was disheveled, but she couldn't help but notice the glow in her cheeks. She looked as happy as she felt. She hoped Aulis was able to get rid of whoever was at the door, and then they could find some breakfast. She was starving.

She emerged from the bathroom to find Aulis and Niklas standing in a not-so-silent standoff at the bedroom door. They hadn't missed her entering the room, and Niklas called out.

"Good morning, Princess. You look lovely even first thing in the morning." He looked pointedly at her makeshift nightgown.

She crossed her arms over her chest, afraid of what the shirt might reveal. "Um, thanks. What has you up and about so early this morning?" She asked politely.

"I'm here to take you on your tour of the castle. Don't tell me you had forgotten?" He covered his heart with his hand.

She could see how upset Niklas' presence was making Aulis, and the sooner she could get him out of there, the better. She let a small trill of laughter escape.

"Honestly, you pounding on the door like the police woke me up. I haven't had time to think about anything yet this morning. However, you can clearly see I'm not dressed to go anywhere. Perhaps I can get a raincheck?"

"Absolutely not. I promised to show you around, and I always keep my promises."

Aulis snorted.

Niklas chose to ignore him and continued his coercion. "Go ahead and get dressed. I'll just wait for you outside. I won't take no for an answer."

He slipped past Aulis into the hallway and closed the door.

Aulis was clenching his teeth. "I don't like this at all. He cannot be trusted. I know he has something planned, but I haven't figured out what yet."

Evie crossed the room and wrapped her arms around his waist. "Don't worry. I seriously doubt he's going to give up, so let's just get it over with. I'm going to change clothes and let him take me on his tour. Maybe I'll be able to get an idea what he's up to."

Aulis wrapped his arms around her tightly.

"I really hate that idea, but I can't see where I have a choice. You are right; he's not going to give up. However, you can't let your guard down around him, not even for a second. He will have you giving up information you never intended to tell anyone. He's one of the most manipulative people I have ever known." He placed a finger under her chin and kissed her. "Promise me you will be careful. Don't allow him to corner you alone anywhere."

"I promise." She assured him. "Now, what to wear?"

"A large burlap sack?" He offered.

"Uh, no, remember I do have a reputation to uphold. I am the current Guardian and, thanks to you, I'm now a princess of the Tuatha De." She winked. "There is no way I'm going to embarrass you and my uncle by running around looking like a homeless person."

She grabbed her duffle bag and headed into the closet, where she dug through the bag until she found something other than running shorts and a T-shirt. She slipped Aulis' shirt over her head and set it down on the couch; she had every intention of wearing it again that night. She quickly dressed in matching colors from the skin out, as she tended to do. One more quick check in the mirror; she pulled her hair into a high ponytail and slapped on a little eyeliner and mascara. It was as good as it was going to get on such short notice.

She stepped out of the curtained area and twirled in a circle for Aulis' inspection. "So what do you think?"

"You look beautiful; I just wish it covered more." He sighed.

Evie looked down at her outfit. It was a simple, scoop-neck, jersey-knit dress in a brilliant blue that ended a couple inches above her knees. She had paired it with a pair of gladiator sandals, along with the ring her uncle had given her and the necklace she never removed.

"What are you talking about? It covers just about everything except my legs."

"I know. Can't we figure out a way to cover those up as well?" He grinned at her good-naturedly and then sobered. "Wearing the ring is a very smart move; it will serve as a constant reminder of your position. However, I want to give you something to go along with it."

He walked over to a box on top of the mantle and rummaged inside. "This was my mother's and her mother's before her. It goes back for generations, and now it is yours."

He slid something onto the ring finger of her left hand – a huge sparkling diamond surrounded by rubies and topaz, creating a flame effect.

Evie gasped. The ring was gorgeous – something she had never even dared to hope for. Was it possible this would work and she really would get to spend her life with him? She was afraid to get too confident since she usually had only one type of luck – bad.

"Thank you; it's absolutely gorgeous." She whispered fervently. "I promise I'll take good care of it."

He grinned. "It looks perfect on you. I must admit, though, I do have an ulterior motive. As long as you are wearing that ring, Niklas will have to respect my claim and keep his damned filthy hands off you. I swear if he dares to touch one strand on your head, it will take everything I've got to keep myself in check."

"Honestly, Aulis, I think you're being a little dramatic. I really don't think there is anything about me that is going to make him drop to his knees and declare his undying love." Evie snorted.

"Evie, you don't understand the severity of the situation. He is a troublemaker to the core, and his family has been trying to gain control of the throne for centuries." Aulis was somber. "Now you are here and, although no one knows, you are the rightful heir to the throne. Even if that weren't the case, you have been betrothed to Oberon's successor. He and I have always been at odds, and he goes out of his way to antagonize me. I can only assume he's just going to get worse now that I've been named to take the throne. I don't want to see you get used as a pawn in one of his childish games."

"Don't worry. I'm a big girl, and I've been dealing with immature assholes for years." Evie laughed. "I think I can handle myself."

He took her hands in his. "Promise me you won't get overconfident and let your guard down. He plays games, and he's very good at them. Many times people don't even recognize he's been toying with them until it's too late."

She grimaced. "If there's anything I know about, it's being manipulated and used. I've got a lot of experience in that arena."

He realized there was much he still didn't know about her background. She had obviously been through pain at the hands of others, but he would be damned if he'd let Niklas add to the list.

He followed her to the door and opened it wide, grimacing at the sight of Niklas leaning against a large pillar across the hallway. Niklas' face brightened and a smile spread across his face.

He reached out and kissed Evie's hand. "Wow, you look great. All eyes will be on us as we tour the castle and grounds today."

"You would do well to remember that." Aulis growled.

"Oh, Aulis, lighten up. Are you afraid of a little friendly competition?"

If they continued this banter, it was bound to escalate into an all-out physical fight. Evie pulled her hand away from Niklas and turned back to Aulis. She reached up and put her hands on either side of Aulis' face and pressed her lips against him. His arms went around her waist as he captured her lips.

He finally broke the kiss. "I'll see you in just a couple of hours."

"You betcha." She promised, hoping she'd made it clear to everyone where her loyalties lie.

Niklas took her hand and placed it in the crook of his elbow. "Come, my dear – let me show you our world."

She glanced over her shoulder to take one last look at Aulis. His mouth was set in a thin line, and he looked like he was fighting himself to keep from running after her. He stayed that way until she walked around the corner.

Was Niklas really that big of a threat, or was this more of a power struggle? He struck her as being an opportunist and even a little bit of a butt-kisser, but certainly not dangerous. However, she would have to trust Aulis.

Evie pulled her hand away and pretended to tighten her ponytail. "So, what's on the agenda for today?"

"Well, I thought we could start with the main audience chamber, then grab some breakfast in the gardens, and then off to the pool and wine cellar."

"Sounds ambitious." She had to admit to herself that she was really curious about what they would consider a pool; she seriously doubted it would be anything like what she was used to.

"Not at all. However, it might keep you away from Aulis longer than he would like." Niklas favored her with a conspiratorial smile. "In case you hadn't noticed, he's a bit of a control freak – it's going to be his way or not at all."

Yes, she had seen a bit of that from Aulis. However, she had chalked it up to him commanding troops for so many years; he had to be able to command respect and keep things under control. Why else would Oberon have named him as successor?

She straightened her shoulders. "Well, let's get started. There's no need to get him upset on purpose."

He chuckled. "Aulis is a big boy. I'm sure he'll be fine."

He motioned for her to follow him down the long hall. The soles of her sandals created slapping sounds on the marble floors. The halls seemed quite empty except for the occasional servant scurrying down the hall to tend to their duties. Evie now understood Aulis' hesitation about her going alone with Niklas. If the main hallways were this deserted, she could only imagine how secluded the wine cellar would be. She took a deep breath and assured herself that she could handle it. There had been plenty of other jerks who'd tried to overstep the boundaries she had drawn, and Niklas was no different… or was he? She never even thought to ask Aulis if Niklas possessed any special powers. She knew her uncle possessed powers, but was that just him, or did all the Tuatha have them? That piece of trivia seemed awfully critical now.

They arrived in the main hall, which was like the hallway – empty. Her senses had been assaulted the night before and she hadn't really had a chance to appreciate the beauty of Oberon's audience chamber. Large, carved marble columns stretched skyward to meet the soaring ceilings. The heavy wooden tables were still pushed against the walls from the dancing the night before. All of the furnishings were intricately carved and made of the same wood with a dark, glossy finish. The walls were adorned with beautiful tapestries depicting the Tuatha De celebrating the various seasons. What really drew her attention was the sunlight pouring in through a stained-glass window in the shape of the sun and a half-moon intertwined. The light created a reflection on the marble floors with the same sun/moon pattern. It reminded her of Winnie's instructions to only pick the yellow and blue flowers and of how the Tuatha had such a high level of respect for nature. She glanced down at the ring Oberon gave her; the same theme was in the stones.

"Of course, you saw this room last night, but it looks very different when it's empty." Niklas remarked.

"Yeah, and a lot bigger." Evie admitted. He bowed her through a set of French doors she hadn't noticed earlier, and Evie was faced with a scene she had only seen in movies. The gardens greeted them the moment they passed through the doors. Beyond the gardens and rolling into the distance was a terraced lawn that any high-end country club would have envied, with every third or fourth section adorned with a fountain. If it all lit up at night, it would create a magical effect. She would have to remember to ask Aulis.

Niklas studied her reaction. "Impressive, isn't it?"

Evie exhaled slowly. "That is the understatement of the year. This is incredible."

He chuckled softly. "If you think this is impressive, wait until you see where I have breakfast set up for us."

She raised her eyebrows. If the grounds got better than the gardens, she might not ever want to go home again. This sure beat driving through rush-hour traffic in the middle of the Texas summer to go to work for a jerk like Sean.

"Seriously? It gets better than this?"

He nodded. "Oh yeah, way better."

"I've got to see this for myself. Lead the way."

He continued down a wide path that began just to the right of the second terrace. The area was lined with trees that got larger and created a canopy over the path. She grew nervous as the area became increasingly secluded from the main building. She glanced backwards and realized they had just stepped out of what could only be described as a castle. A real-life fairy tale castle. She giggled at the irony since she was, in fact, surrounded by fairies. She wondered for the millionth time if it was all just a dream and she was bound to wake up in the hammock of Aunt Winnie's yard. If that was the case, she wanted to spend every moment she could with Aulis. Just as she was about to suggest they turn back, the canopy opened up to a grotto. At the center was a pool that resembled a lagoon, overlooked by a large cave with a waterfall cascading over the mouth of the cave.

"Oh. My. God." Evie breathed.

"I told you." He smirked.

"Is this Oberon's private oasis or something?" She simply couldn't believe her eyes.

"Nope. Anyone within Tuatha De is welcome to use it." He pointed off to one side. "See, that is our breakfast, just waiting for us."

She spied a long table that appeared to be made from a single slab of stone. On the table sat a buffet of platters containing fresh fruits and various pastries. In the center of the platters was a large pitcher of orange juice. Niklas strolled over to the table and poured her a large glass of the juice. She immediately drained it; she hadn't had anything in her stomach since the night before, and she hadn't eaten much then. It took a couple of seconds to realize it wasn't orange juice at all, but nectar.

"You could've warned me." She stared at him, the accusation clear in her eyes. Nectar had been at the core of Aulis' outburst last night. She was pretty sure he wouldn't like her sitting in this grotto dinking nectar with Niklas.

He had the nerve to laugh at her. "No one said to down the entire glass. I thought you knew what it was."

"Why would you assume that? I had never seen nectar before I arrived here."

He cleared his throat. "Well, you did get pretty well acquainted with it last night."

That was a very delicate way to put it, and she couldn't help but laugh. "OK, fair enough. I'll make sure to eat this time."

"Have a seat and help yourself. I highly recommend the chocolate croissants. The chefs make them fresh every morning."

Evie settled into one of the cushioned seats at the table, tucked her feet under her, helped herself to a warm chocolate croissant, and sank in her teeth. Melted chocolate oozed out of the buttery, flaky crust.

"Oh my God. That is amazing." She murmured and licked her fingers.

"We're lucky enough to have the best chefs anywhere… as well as the best view."

"I can't argue with either point – both are flawless."

He refilled her glass and she raised an eyebrow at him.

"Go ahead – now that you have some food in your stomach, it's safe." His face was the picture of innocence.

She punched him lightly in the shoulder. "Hah, hah… very funny." But she took another sip of the nectar and allowed her body and mind to relax. So far Niklas had been on his best behavior and hadn't tried to pull anything; she felt she could allow her guard to drop a little.

"So, are you up for some swimming after breakfast, before we tour the wine cellars?"

His question took her completely by surprise. "Sorry, I didn't think to pack a swimsuit." She smirked.

"Not to worry – just on the other side of the trees behind us is a cabana, and the staff stocks a selection of swimsuits for guests. They are all brand-new and you can keep whatever you wear."

She eyed the pool. The water called to her; she had always loved to swim. Being able to simply float on the surface of the water was more therapeutic than any counseling session. She would've given anything to have a couple of hours to herself in the lagoon. She glanced back at Niklas, who seemed a little too eager for her to agree to his suggestion. What would Aulis think if he were to come upon the two of them here in this lagoon? She grimaced. He would be furious. He had already proven to have a fairly strong possessive streak - or was it a jealous streak? She doubted he was following them around, but she still felt guilty at the thought.

Surely he would understand she desperately needed to unwind? She stared longingly at the water. She was quickly losing her internal struggle between wanting to relax in the water and worrying about being alone with Niklas in a swimsuit. She was torn out of her daydream by the sound of feet pounding against the stone of the pathway leading to the grotto.

"Ebbie!" Lizbeth threw herself into Evie's arms. "What'cha doin'? I'm gonna swim! You wanna swim wif me?"

Here was the answer to her prayers.

"Hi, Lizzie!" She hugged the little girl. "You know, I was just thinking about how pretty it is and how much I'd love to swim."

"Hi, Evie." Kimbra laughed. "I'm sorry you've been attacked during breakfast. She's developed quite an attachment to you." Her eyes swept the table and Niklas. "I hope we aren't interrupting anything."

Niklas opened his mouth, but Evie immediately spoke up.

"Not at all! Niklas came by the room this morning to pick me up for the tour he promised last night. We just finished breakfast, and he was trying to convince me to go swimming. The pool is absolutely breathtaking."

"He was?" Kimbra flashed a look at Niklas. "Well, I hope you don't mind if we join you? Lizbeth got up this morning and this was all she would talk about – I don't know what got into her."

"I'd love for you to join us. We can do some swimming and relax a little before Niklas shows me the wine cellars." Evie looked around her, hoping to spot the cabana.

"The wine cellars?" Kimbra's eyes narrowed.

Niklas' mask slipped into place. "No tour of the grounds would be complete without visiting our extensive wine cellars."

Kimbra clucked her tongue in response. "Come on, Evie, I'll show you where the extra swimsuits are."

Evie trotted behind Kimbra to the cabana, which was completely hidden behind the trees. Through the door was a small living area full of overstuffed couches with a door to a changing area off to one side and a galley-style kitchen on the other side. It was extremely warm and inviting. If she lived here, she could see spending a great deal of time here. Lizbeth ran ahead of them and jumped, giggling, onto the couch.

"Evie, you can go through the door there and you'll find an entire rack of suits. Pick whatever you like." She caught her bottom lip with her teeth. "I should probably warn you, the Tuatha De have a much different idea about modesty than most humans. We are in touch with nature and very comfortable in our own skins. No one would think twice about you wearing any of the suits in there."

"Ooo-K." Evie replied hesitantly. She walked into the changing room closing the door behind her. One look at the rack told her exactly why Kimbra has warned her. All the suits were two-piece and incredibly skimpy. She had never worn anything so revealing. If Kimbra hadn't said anything, she probably never would have emerged from the changing room. She flipped through the suits on the rack, finally settling for one in a vibrant blue with yellow accents; she decided to honor her family by going with the colors sacred to the Tuatha. She hadn't forgotten the fact that she was the Guardian and the future queen – she might as well start embracing their customs now.

She changed into the suit, adjusting it to cover as much as possible. She studied her reflection in the mirror. Whew. Well, if Kimbra was sure.... She hung her dress on an empty hanger and rejoined Kimbra.

"Oh, Evie, that suit looks like it was made for you. Aulis would be touched that you chose one in our colors."

Evie tugged at the top, making sure everything was adequately covered. "Are you sure it's not too revealing?"

Kimbra laughed and pulled her cover-up over her head. "Does this make you feel better?"

Kimbra's suit was every bit as revealing as Evie's.

"Yes. It makes me feel tons better. I've never worn anything like this before."

Lizbeth jumped off the couch and grabbed her by the hand.

"Let's go swimmin'. I wish Unca Owwie could come wif us."

Evie stroked her platinum curls. "Me too."

They stepped through the door back into the grotto, Lizbeth holding Evie's hand with an iron grip. Multiple voices caught her attention; who was Niklas talking to? She was already uncomfortable with the thought of being around him in her borrowed suit, much less having anyone else see it. Lizbeth rounded the corner first. Her eyes lit up; she dropped Evie's hand like it was burning her and took off running.

"Lizzie." Evie called after her. She and Kimbra emerged from the trees surrounding the cabana, and Evie froze in her tracks. Standing on either side of Niklas were Aulis and Ari. The twin colossi were identical in every way but their expressions. Ari waggled his eyebrows at Kimbra in obvious appreciation. Aulis wore such an intense expression that Evie squirmed and fidgeted with her swimsuit, rearranging it yet again. Niklas appeared less than happy.

"Hel-lo, ladies." Ari winked at them. "Mind if we join you this morning?"

Lizbeth threw herself into Ari's arms. "Daddy! Unca Owwie. Yeah! Come swimming wif us!"

Ari scooped the little girl into his arms. "You don't mind, do you, Niklas?"

Kimbra laughed. "Of course not; why would he mind? Lizbeth and I were already joining them. I was even thinking about tagging along when Niklas showed Evie the wine cellars. I thought I might grab us a couple bottles of the wine we had the other night."

Aulis turned to Niklas with flashing eyes. "The wine cellars? What would possess you to take her there?"

Niklas' smile didn't quite reach all the way to his eyes. "As I explained to Kimbra, what tour of our home would be complete without a visit to our extensive cellars? Anyway, it's fortunate you two came along when you did. I need to check on something but didn't want to leave Evie alone."

Evie raised an eyebrow. What was he talking about? He hadn't mentioned anything about needing to leave; in fact, his behavior had reflected quite the opposite.

"Niklas, I don't want to keep you from anything important. Thank you for showing me the grounds and for breakfast." Evie gestured toward the table.

The others turned to the table and then faced Niklas with the same surprised expression.

"Nectar with breakfast?" Ari asked casually.

Evie felt out of the loop. Aulis clenched his teeth until a vein throbbed in his temple. "You should hurry and tend to your business, Niklas."

The warning in his voice hadn't been lost on Evie... or Niklas, who said his goodbyes, kissed Evie's hand, and left quickly.

13 A LAGOON WITH A VIEW

"Did I miss something?" Evie asked quietly.

Ari wrapped an arm around her shoulders. "My little sister, it's very unusual to be drinking nectar this time of day, especially when we had so much of it last night. It stays in your system for hours, so it would only take one or two glasses before you were completely drunk."

Evie gasped. Well, so much for letting her guard down around Niklas! She'd thought he was on his best behavior, but the sneaky little bastard was trying to get her drunk. Now she wondered why everyone seemed so concerned about the cellars.

Aulis came to stand directly in front of her. "How many glasses?

"Huh?" Evie grunted.

He took her hands in his. "How many glasses did you drink?"

"Oh, only one before I figured out what it was, then I immediately had something to eat. He didn't tell me what it was when he handed to me. I just thought it was orange juice."

He moved Ari's arm and pulled Evie into his embrace. "I'm glad you're all right. I knew it was a mistake to trust him, so we sent Kimbra and Lizbeth to see if they could find you, and then we weren't far behind."

Evie grinned at Kimbra. "You were part of their little plan?"

"Guilty." She shrugged and chuckled.

Evie hugged Kimbra. "Thank you. I thought this setting was a little intimate, and I was beginning to get uneasy. By the way, what's the story with the wine cellars?"

Aulis growled low in his throat. "The cellars are vast and the racks of bottles act as a labyrinth for anyone not familiar with them. If he had cornered you there, no one would've heard you, and you would've gotten hopelessly lost if you had tried to run."

"Oh." Evie gasped. She had to start listening to her internal alarms. The last thing she wanted was to be trapped by Niklas. She had to admit that her day had taken a turn for the better with the arrival of Aulis and Ari.

"So, were you two planning to join us? I promised Lizbeth that we would go swimming." Evie grinned.

Lizbeth squealed and clapped in her father's arms. "The slide, Daddy... the slide!"

"Slide?" Evie parroted.

Aulis didn't respond; he was staring at her swimsuit intently, so Evie turned to Kimbra as she explained.

"Just to the side of the waterfall, the rocks create a natural slide. Also, if you look at the top of the waterfall, you will see a flat rock jutting out – that is what we use for diving."

"Awesome." Evie breathed. "It's even better than I thought." She turned to Aulis. "Are you guys joining us?"

A slow smile spread across his face. "I'd like to see someone try to stop me." He peeled his shirt over his head, revealing the slabs of muscle underneath.

She took a deep breath and a blush spread to the roots of her hair as her thoughts strayed to the night before.

Aulis leaned over and murmured into her ear. "I am very honored with your choice of colors. They suit you."

She shivered at the feel of his breath on her neck. "Th-Thank you." She stammered.

Ari shifted Lizbeth in his arms and clapped his twin on the back with his free hand. "I sure hate to embarrass you in front of Evie so soon. I mean, we know which twin is the better diver."

Kimbra rolled her eyes skyward. "Oh lord... here we go." She took her little daughter from Ari's arms. "Come on, Lizzie; Daddy and Uncle Aulis are going to start showing off. Let's head for the shallow end."

Lizbeth giggled and pointed at the two hulking men. "Daddy and Unca Owwie silly!"

Evie followed Kimbra and Lizbeth to the far end of the lagoon to a beach-entry. Lizbeth sat down and slapped at the water, splashing frantically. Suddenly she stopped splashing and pointed; Evie looked and found Aulis and Ari standing on the stone atop the waterfall.

"Spwash, Unca Owwiee!" Lizbeth cried.

Aulis pointed at her and grinned seconds before he leapt skyward and fell to the water in a perfectly executed cannonball. Water exploded into the air and rained down on the women and Lizbeth.

Aulis came up for air, shaking the water from his eyes. "Ha! Beat that one!" He challenged Ari.

"OK, hang on to Lizzie so she doesn't drown." Ari yelled back.

Kimbra rolled her eyes. "Oh, please. It gets worse every time they do this. Sometimes I wonder what gets into them; it's like they both have two separate personalities inside – one is a fierce warrior and the other is still a little boy."

"It's nice to see Aulis look so carefree. I've never seen this side of him." Evie mused.

"You will never see this side of him if other people are around. He only lets his guard down around family," Kimbra noted. "I know you feel like you haven't known him very long, but he genuinely cares for you. In all the years I've been with Ari, Aulis has never been this relaxed. You are good for him.

"Now, on the flip side, he's going to be extremely protective of you for several reasons." She continued in a low voice. "You understand the danger that comes with your position as the Guardian, and that is compounded by your parentage – which has to remain secret. But don't think those are the only reasons he may get a little overprotective. He has Marked you, and that means he will never consider another for his mate. There are many women who would kill for your position. Watch your back around Dahlia; she is dangerous. Aulis has snubbed her time and time again, but she refuses to take no for an answer."

Evie grimaced. "Yes, I'm all too aware of her. Upon our return to our room last night, she was there, half-naked and waiting on Aulis' bed."

Kimbra stared at her. "You're kidding me! I can't believe she would be so brazen. If he ignored her before, what made her think he would pay attention to her after he had *Marked* someone?"

"I don't know, but I wanted to drag that nasty bitch out of there by her hair." Evie muttered darkly.

The two woman made eye contact and broke into laughter. Evie suddenly felt hands on her calves and scrambled backward with a shriek.

Aulis' head emerged from underwater. "What did you ladies find so funny?"

Evie fought to regain her breath. She cupped her hands and threw a volley of water in his face. "You scared the crap out of me! Don't you think I'm stressed enough?" She laughed.

"Oh, I'm sorry, did I mess up your hair when I splashed you?" He teased.

"You call that a splash? You wouldn't know a real cannonball if it bit you in the butt."

Ari doubled over with laughter. "Finally, someone is on my side."

"Your side? Please. I'll show you both how it's done." Evie stood up, arched her back like a prideful cat and strolled to the steps leading to the diving stone.

"Oh, Evie... don't encourage them." Kimbra begged.

"What, you think she's going to outdo you?" Aulis taunted.

"Oh, the hell you say." Kimbra laughed and hurried to catch up with Evie.

The girls climbed to the top where Ari stood waiting.

"Are you ladies ready for me to show you how it's really done? I'll explain slowly so I'm sure you'll get it."

"Oh, that's it." Kimbra's hands shot out and hit Ari in the chest, knocking him off his perch and into the water below.

Aulis' rich laughter rolled throughout the grotto. "Nicely done, Kimbra."

Just as Ari surfaced, Kimbra sprung off her toes and flew into the air, tucking one leg into her chest before she hit the lagoon, sending water flying everywhere.

"Jacknife!" Ari cried.

Evie stood at the top of the waterfall and laughed down at the scene below. Kimbra was easy-going and fun to be around. She was someone Evie could see being a great friend.

Ari and Kimbra swam to the far end of the pool and plucked Lizbeth from Aulis' arms. They spread out and allowed the little girl to swim from one parent to another, leaving Aulis free to stroke his way to the center of the lagoon. He treaded water in the middle of the lagoon staring up at Evie.

No one had ever watched her with that kind of intensity. He made her vividly aware of her femininity and how different she looked from the rest of the Tuatha; it was the first time in her life she was glad to be tiny and curvy. The desire in his eyes was clear even from where she stood. She reveled in the realization she had her own powers. She arched her back, her generous assets threatening to burst free from the confines of her borrowed suit. She reached up, pulled the rubber band out of her hair, and shot it at Aulis, allowing her thick tresses to cascade down her back. He licked his lips in response.

"What's wrong, my love? Did you lose your nerve?" Aulis taunted.

Evie took two steps backward and then sprinted off the stone, tucking into a tight ball just before she hit the surface. Volleys of water arced through the air and crashed down. Evie finally came up for air and realized, to her horror, that the top of her suit had come undone at impact. She scrambled to pull it back into place before anyone else noticed.

"Oh, *yeah*! Nice one!" Ari crowed.

"Do it again! Do it again!" Lizbeth begged.

Kimbra was laughing too hard to respond, and Evie knew she had seen what happened but wasn't going to let on to the others.

Aulis was on her seconds after her head broke the plane of the water. His eyes devoured every inch of her while she clutched the errant material to her chest. His lips crashed down upon hers as his hands cupped her generous globes. She wrapped her arms and legs around him to shield anyone from seeing what he was doing. Her actions shielded her nakedness but also drove Aulis further over the edge. His erection rubbed her cleft, making her gasp.

Lizbeth's splashes pulled him from his passion-induced trance, reminding him they had an audience. Instead of releasing Evie, he dragged her through the waterfall into a hidden cave she hadn't known existed. A wide stone bench stretched from one end of the room to the other, and the waterfall shielded them from view. He glided to the bench and sat down, pulling Evie into his lap so she had one leg on either side of his. His assault on her lips was relentless, then his lips trailed across her jaw and down her throat, causing her to gasp and allow her head to fall backward.

"See what happens when you try to taunt me?" He murmured against her neck. "I've spent my entire life in total control of myself… until you came along." He moved his hips in a circular motion, grinding himself against her.

She moaned quietly. He was a force to be reckoned with. She knew they had to stop, but she couldn't pull herself away. "Aulis." She whispered.

He recaptured her mouth for several moments. "I love the taste of my name on your lips."

She blushed furiously before exhaling slowly. "Aulis and Kimbra are just on the other side of the water. What are they going to think? We should go back." She squirmed in his lap, trying to slide to one side.

His arms locked around her like a vise as he breathed his words into her ear. "They know exactly what I'm up to. Kimbra saw what happened when you hit the water, and they both watched me pull you here. I promise you, Ari and Kimbra have spent their fair share of time here."

Evie's hands flew to her heated cheeks. "Ohmigod. How embarrassing. What will they think of me? We're not supposed to be doing this."

"No, we're not supposed to consummate our relationship until we we're married. No one said anything about us doing *this*." He reached between them and slipped a hand under the edge of her bikini bottom. She inhaled sharply as his deft fingers quickly found her tender bud. Gently, persistently, he rolled it between his fingers, driving her to madness. The sensation built until she thought she would drown in the pleasure.

"Aulis." She panted, and he kissed her thoroughly just in time to catch her scream of release.

She lay limp in his arms as he re-tied her top and rearranged it. He sat her up and pushed her hair back over her shoulders.

"How can I face them again?"

Aulis chuckled and lifted her chin to face him. "My love, do you think they got Lizbeth by accident? When they were engaged and then newlyweds, they hardly ever came out of their rooms. Believe me, they are absolutely thrilled that I have found someone who can keep me on my toes. Of course, Ari loves the fact that you keep me in a constant state of arousal. I used to give him a bad time about trailing around after Kimbra – now he thinks it's funny that I have the same reaction to you." He slid off the ledge and pulled her onto his back. "Let's go rejoin them, and then we need to find Oberon as quickly as possible."

"What's the rush in seeing Oberon?"

"I won't make it another night. We have to be married this evening."

"Are-are you sure?" She stammered. "You've only known me a couple of days. Are you sure you want to be tied to me permanently?"

"I have never been more certain about anything in my life. We *will* be married tonight." He sealed his assertion with a deep kiss.

He was right. They emerged from beneath the falls, and all she got from Ari and Kimbra were smiles – knowing smiles, but fortunately no ribbing. She absolutely loved the people who would make up her new family. They would blend in very well with her mother and Winnie. Obviously the Adair women already had some favorites within the Tuatha De.

Evie grinned at Kimbra and shrugged her shoulders before wrapping her arms around Aulis' neck. She knew they would never give her a reason to feel ashamed of her love for Aulis – and then the meaning of her own thoughts hit her like a ton of bricks. It was love. She finally understood what people meant when they talked about a soul mate. She could no longer imagine a life without Aulis in it.

How could she love him after only a couple days together? How would they feel in two months, six months, six years, when the relationship was no longer new?

The way she looked at it, she had two choices: take a chance and hope things worked out, or hold herself away from Aulis and try to convince her uncle to delay things until they knew each other better. One look at Aulis answered the question for her. She wouldn't be able to be in the same plane of existence with him, much less the same room, without wanting to be with him.

"Unca Owwie, Unca Owwie…. Watch me!" Lizbeth pushed away

from her parents and paddled her way to her uncle in the middle of the pool. He plucked her out of the water and lifted her over his head while she giggled uncontrollably. Evie's heart melted at the sight. He obviously adored his little niece, and Evie could only imagine how he would feel about his own children. Lizbeth swam from one couple to the next until she wore herself out and was content to splash around in the shallow area. The men continued their earlier diving contest until they felt they had a definitive winner. Evie enjoyed the easy relationship she was developing with Kimbra; they never ran out of things to talk about. Evie hoped Kimbra would be willing to help her navigate the ways and customs of the strange, new land.

As Evie took a leisurely lap around the pool, a faint rustling in the trees caught her attention. When she turned toward the sound, the rustling stopped, but not before she caught sight of a retreating figure with long blonde hair. Had Dahlia followed them to spy? Maybe Kimbra was right – Evie would have to watch her back.

Evie glanced over her shoulder and made eye contact with Kimbra, who nodded in the direction of the rustling. She had heard it too. Evie ducked under the water and kicked her way to the beach where Ari and Kimbra were lounging.

"Hey." Evie greeted them.

"I take it you saw it too?" Kimbra acknowledged.

"Yes; was it Dahlia?" Evie glanced nervously over her shoulder.

"Who else?" Kimbra grimaced.

Ari was immediately on alert. "What are you two talking about? What about Dahlia?"

Kimbra smirked. "That bitch is sneaking around spying on Evie. You know she's always wanted Aulis, and I'm really worried about what she might do. She needs to be watched at all times."

Evie shook her hands in front of her face. "Wait, wait, wait. Please, I don't want to be any trouble, and I certainly don't want to freak Aulis out."

"Freak Aulis out about what?" Aulis' deep voice boomed behind her as he handed Lizbeth back to her mother.

"Oh, it's nothing. Don't worry about it." Evie assured him.

"Bullshit." Ari and Kimbra stated in unison, startling Evie.

"What is going on?" Aulis demanded.

"Kimbra and Evie spotted Dahlia spying through the trees." Ari put his hand on his twin's shoulder. "Kimbra thinks we need to have a member of the guard watching Dahlia – and I couldn't agree more."

Aulis swept Evie into his arms protectively. "Has she threatened you in any way?"

"You mean other than showing up half-naked in our bedroom last night?" Her eyebrows drew together.

Ari stifled a laugh and was rewarded with a dirty look from his twin.

"I told you she wasn't there by *my* invitation." Aulis insisted.

Evie patted his cheek. "I know, but it doesn't make me like it any better. As a matter of fact, can we change the locks or something? I can't be held liable for my actions if she shows up there again. I may be little, but I have a nasty temper."

Kimbra laughed. "I like her more every time she opens her mouth. I finally have an ally against you two bullies."

Aulis grunted.

"Oh, yeah. Be afraid, boys... Be very afraid." Kimbra gave Evie a high-five.

Evie's stomach growled and Lizbeth giggled.

"Unca Owwie, Ebbie is hungwy. Let's get cookies!" She squealed.

"How long have we been out here? Didn't I just have breakfast?" Evie mused.

Aulis growled. "Don't remind me of your breakfast partner. However," he looked skyward, "based on the sun, I'd say we've been out here for several hours."

Kimbra stepped out of the water and lifted Lizbeth out of the lagoon. "Come on, monkey; let's take Aunt Evie with us, and we'll get dressed so we can grab some lunch."

Aulis lifted Evie by her arms and set her feet on the flat stones surrounding the lagoon. Lizbeth immediately grabbed her by the hand and dragged her toward the cabana. "Huwwy, Ebbie, or the cookies will be all gone."

They dressed in record time. Kimbra handed her the bikini. "You might want to hang onto this. You probably haven't seen it yet, but Aulis has a private bathing pool off his balcony."

"Are you serious? How did I miss that?" Evie mused.

"I doubt you've seen very much of his suite save the main bedroom." Evie blushed furiously.

"Don't be embarrassed. I swear, I didn't see all of Ari's suite for almost a week. You're already ahead of me." Kimbra assured her with a wink.

"Let's go, Mama, I hungwy!"

14 LUNCH AND LEARN

They joined the men and, after Ari shifted Lizbeth onto his shoulders, the two men intertwined hands with Evie and Kimbra. The five headed off through the gardens and back into the main hall.

The tables had been moved back into place and lunch was being served. Sitting at the main table were Oberon, Winnie, and Colleen, with just enough empty seats for the newly arrived group. Just to their left sat Aulis' men, and on the other side sat Niklas with Dahlia with smiles plastered on their faces. Evie pulled closer to Aulis' side, and he wrapped his arm firmly around her as Kimbra and Ari closed ranks around her. Winnie started to rise from her seat but Oberon put a hand firmly on her arm.

"Evie, my dear. I hope these boys are taking good care of you. Did you get a chance to visit the grotto yet? It's always been one of my favorite places." He winked at Winnie.

Evie blushed furiously. He was obviously aware of the things that went on in the grotto. She couldn't deny they had been there since their wet hair was a dead giveaway, "Um, yeah. It's the most beautiful place I've ever seen."

Aulis led her around the far side of the table past his men to the empty seats, intentionally avoiding Niklas and Dahlia. He sat on one side of her and put Kimbra, Lizbeth, and Ari on her other side. There was no way for Niklas or Dahlia to get near her without getting through Aulis or Ari first.

Evie released a huge sigh of relief. She didn't want to have to engage in polite conversation with Niklas, and she wasn't sure she would be able to keep her temper in check around Dahlia after her actions the night before. No matter how highly Dahlia thought of herself, Aulis had chosen Evie. Just thinking about it made Evie smile. She would ignore the two vipers and enjoy lunch with her extended family.

Now that her nerves had calmed a bit, she found she was starving.

She eyed the platters full of meats, cheeses, fresh fruits, and a huge assortment of desserts. If they ate like this at every meal, she was going to have to start working out or she'd be clinically obese in no time.

A page came by and filled the crystal goblets sitting in front of each adult; Lizbeth was given a small glass of what looked like apple juice. Evie immediately recognized the contents of the goblets to be nectar. She raised the glass to her lips and allowed the nectar to fill her mouth. The taste was unparalleled, and its silkiness caressed her taste buds. Before she realized it, she had drained the glass.

Aulis chuckled and murmured into her ear. "Be careful, you may regret that. Remember what I said about it having a compounding effect? You had several glasses last night and one this morning. If you aren't careful, I'll have to carry you back to the room."

She giggled. "You say that like it's a bad thing. Maybe that's exactly what I'm looking for."

He leaned in close and nipped her earlobe. "You are going to be the death of me, I'm sure of it. I think I should talk with Oberon sooner rather than later."

She hiccupped in response, causing Kimbra and Ari to burst into laughter.

Aulis turned to his left, where Oberon sat. "Oberon, if you have a moment?"

Oberon clapped him on the shoulder. "Why so formal? Of course, I always have time for you. What's on your mind?"

Aulis cleared his throat, suddenly nervous. "Sire, Evie and I would like to be married tonight. We see no point in waiting any longer."

Oberon snickered. "You mean the two of you are having a hard time behaving yourselves?"

Aulis smiled and lowered his voice. "I won't deny it, but there's more to it than that. I suspect Niklas and Dahlia are up to something." He ran a hand through his long hair. "Dahlia showed up in my room half-naked last night, knowing that Evie and I were headed that direction. I'm sure you can imagine the grief *that* stunt caused. Then this morning, Niklas insisted on taking Evie on a guided tour of the grounds."

"That sounds harmless." Oberon noted.

"You would think so. And I've warned Evie to keep up her guard around them at all times. However, just as a precaution, I had Kimbra and Lizbeth 'bump into' them. Niklas had taken Evie to the grotto and had a breakfast all set up – including nectar, which he had tricked her into drinking – and was encouraging her to join him in the pool. When Ari and I arrived, we discovered he was planning to take her to the wine cellars."

Oberon narrowed his eyes. "Why would he take her there? It's dusty, dark, and damp, and there isn't anything to see unless you are a sommelier. I know the cellars like the back of my hand and I hardly *ever* go there."

Aulis nodded his agreement. "And finally, Evie and Kimbra saw Dahlia spying on the five of us while we were in the grotto today. What would be the point in that unless she was looking to cause trouble?" He shrugged. "After lunch I'm assigning Taarmo to keep a close eye on her – without Dahlia realizing she's being watched. I don't want Niklas to have the opportunity to compromise Evie in any way."

"He wouldn't dare!" The king's eyes practically shot fire.

Aulis returned his gaze steadily. "Oberon, I wouldn't put anything past him. Why else would he have planned to take her to the cellars? It's secluded, it's cavernous, and no one would hear her once they were inside."

Oberon leapt to his feet, clanging his knife on his goblet. "Attention, everyone." He commanded.

The room silenced and all eyes turned to him.

"I would like to invite you all to join us here tonight to witness the joining of the Guardian and my successor. Evie and Aulis are pleased take part in a traditional Tuatha wedding at sundown. While I will personally stand in for her father, Evie may choose three attendants, and Aulis may do the same."

"I will have Ari, Taarmo, and you, Oberon." Aulis grinned at him. "You'll just have to do double-duty tonight. You've been like a father to us since our parents died so many years ago; it only seems right."

Oberon smiled back at him, visibly moved. "I am happy to accept. Evie – who will you name?"

Evie fidgeted. She wasn't comfortable being the center of attention and would've been perfectly happy with a very small ceremony in Oberon's rooms with only family present. However, given Aulis' position, she knew that wouldn't be possible.

"I'd like to have Winnie, Mom, and Kimbra. Can we have Lizbeth act as a flower girl?" She glanced at Kimbra. "Wait, do you even have flower girls in your ceremonies here?"

"Absolutely. Ours is done a little differently, but the concept is the same." She assured Evie.

Evie turned back to Oberon. "Is that OK?"

He leaned over and took her hand. "Of course; it's your special day."

She leaned in to whisper into his ear. "Thank you for standing in for my dad. Maybe someday Aulis and I can renew our vows, and then it will be his turn."

He smiled at her. "I love the idea, and I promise you here and now that it *will* happen."

She leaned back in her chair, perfectly content with the way her day was shaping up. Then she made the mistake of scanning the room and inadvertently made eye contact with Dahlia. The fairy's grey eyes narrowed to tiny slits, and Evie knew she'd just been issued a threat. She stiffened in her seat and her pulse raced.

Aulis' gaze shifted from Evie to Dahlia and caught her expression. Dahlia's face brightened when she realized Aulis was looking at her, flashing him a brilliant smile.

Aulis pushed back from the table and paced to where Taarmo sat. Aulis whispered to his trusted guard and then strode from the room.

Evie stared at his retreating back, slack-jawed. What had just happened?

Dahlia waited a few moments and then followed. She knew the little human wouldn't be able to hold Aulis' attention for long; he had obviously wanted her to follow him. She sauntered through the archway into the hallway.

Aulis was leaning against a pillar down the hall. Her pulse raced at the sight of him. He was truly magnificent, deserving of so much more than some insignificant human. So what if she was the Guardian? He would have to marry her to keep her in line... for now. These things could always be dissolved later.

Dahlia put a hand on her hip to draw attention to the seductive way she walked.

Aulis glanced up just as she stopped inches from his face. She ran a long, perfectly manicured fingernail down his bicep.

"I missed you last night." She purred.

"Dahlia, what are you up to?" His eyebrows drew together.

"I'm sorry. I know I caused you problems with the little Adair last night. I should've known better. You are so private. I'll make sure to be more discreet in the future."

"Dahlia, there is *no future*." He stated with finality. "I am to be married tonight."

Taarmo sauntered out of the main hall and headed straight for Aulis. "What did you want to talk about, boss?"

Much to her horror, Dahlia realized Aulis was waiting for Taarmo, not her – but she would never let them see her composure slip. She smiled at Taarmo and turned on her heel to leave.

"We can finish our conversation later, Aulis." She said with a wink.

Both men shook their heads at her retreating form.

"Man. All the years she's been around you, and she just can't take a hint, can she?" Taarmo laughed.

"No, she can't." Aulis agreed. "That's exactly why I called you out here. I want you to keep an eye on her. I don't trust her, especially since she's suddenly started hanging out with Niklas." He grimaced. "I'm telling you, they are up to no good. When Evie and I went back to our suite last night, there was Dahlia half-naked on my bed. I thought Evie was going to kill her."

Taarmo grimaced in return. "I tried to warn you. Dahlia has tried to act like your wife anytime you aren't around – ordering your servants around and even trying the same tactics from time to time with your troops. The men ignore her pretty easily, but the servants are afraid of her; they don't know how much authority she really has. What can I do to help?"

Aulis' forehead creased. "I want you to keep an eye on her. Don't let her know you're watching her, but try to stay as close as possible." Aulis glanced around the hallway. "We need to know what she may be planning before she manages to do anything to harm Evie. If she so much as makes Evie cry, I won't be responsible for my actions."

They clasped each other's forearms in a show of solidarity.

"I'm her new shadow." Taarmo promised. "And I'm happy to do it because I really like your little human. She's got a lot of spirit – her personality fits right in with the Tuatha."

Aulis grinned. If only Taarmo knew how right he was – she was half Tuatha, and a royal at that. "I knew I could count on you. You understand I have every intention of turning control of the guard over to you once I have to take the throne? I can't imagine anyone who could do a better job. I wouldn't trust the safety of my family and our people to another."

Taarmo was floored. "I'm honored. Are you sure you wouldn't want Ari to take over?"

"I'm positive." Aulis gestured toward the banqueting hall. "He would rather spend his time with his family – which is the way it should be."

Taarmo stood at attention. "You have my word that I will do my very best."

"I know you will – that's why I chose you, both as my successor and to stand with me at my wedding. Now, let's go back and enjoy our lunch. I'm betting we'll find Dahlia already there." Aulis patted him on the back.

Evie breathed a sigh of relief when Aulis returned with Taarmo. She had watched Dahlia leave and knew Dahlia was trying to force some time alone with her betrothed; if Kimbra hadn't stopped her, Evie would've followed. However, Dahlia was already back in her seat and watching Aulis' every step.

Aulis strode straight to the main table. Once in his seat, he put a hand on either side of Evie's face and kissed her tenderly.

"Awww." A cry went up around the room. The couple broke apart and were forced to laugh.

Oberon leaned over. "See? You've already won them over. I suspect you two will be quite popular with our people for many years to come."

Evie cast a glance at Dahlia. She could think of at least one person she wasn't very popular with; she hoped Dahlia choked on her smirk at the wedding. Evie decided to issue a challenge of her own, stroking Aulis' silky black hair while never breaking eye contact with Dahlia. Kimbra attempted to stifle a laugh by taking a drink but only succeeded in choking herself. Ari looked at her strangely and thumped her on the back.

Dahlia's gaze spoke volumes. If looks could kill, she would've vaporized Evie on the spot. Feeling a little brave since she was surrounded by her family, Evie turned Aulis to face her and pressed her lips against his. He opened his mouth and she thrust her tongue inside. His arms shot out, pulling her out of her chair and into his lap. He buried one hand in her long hair while stroking her thigh with the other.

The sound of someone clearing his throat brought them out of a passion-induced haze.

"I think you two should start making preparations for tonight – separately – or you might not make it to your own ceremony." Oberon teased.

The entire room erupted into cheers and applause while Evie hid her face in Aulis' chest.

He lifted her chin so she faced him. "Do you know why they cheer? When the king and queen share such passion, it's considered a sign of great prosperity."

"But we aren't king and queen." She argued.

"Not yet, but we are next in line for the throne, so it's still considered a good omen."

Kimbra rose from her seat and took one of Evie's hands. "Come on. We have tons of things to do – especially since Oberon has stated this will be a *traditional* wedding." She leaned in close to Evie and Aulis. "Besides, if I don't separate the two of you, I'm afraid we're all going to get a floor show of epic proportions."

Evie took her hand. "OK, OK, you're probably right."

Aulis helped her to her feet, and she kissed his forehead in thanks. "I'm claiming your rooms for the girls. You guys can get ready in Ari's room. I'd like to feel a *little* comfortable while preparing to be put on display."

Aulis caressed her cheek. "You can have anything you want. Remember, though, that after tonight, they are *your* rooms as well."

Winnie and Colleen rose and joined the two women with little Lizbeth, and they all left the great hall together. Evie knelt down and allowed the little girl to climb on her back, and Evie carried her all the way to their rooms.

Evie allowed a feeling of great well-being to wash over her. Surrounded by these women, she was happier than she had been in a very long time. She had always dreamed of a large family, but it had been just her, her mom, and Winnie for as long as she could remember. Now she understood why. Her father had been ripped away from them.

Suddenly she couldn't stop the anger welling up within her. She vowed to get revenge on the creatures that had stolen her father and denied her the opportunity to form a relationship with him. She also felt anger on behalf of Winnie and Oberon. The same individuals were responsible for the couple not being able to marry when they should have. Oberon seemed to at least suspect who might've taken Lyrr, but she hadn't mustered the courage to ask him about it. Maybe Winnie or Aulis could give her some insight. She would have to do it when her mom wasn't around; there was no point in upsetting her unnecessarily.

Kimbra pushed the door of Aulis' suite open and allowed everyone to pass through. Once the door slid closed, she threw the bolt across the door. Evie raised an eyebrow at Kimbra as she let Lizbeth slide to the floor.

Kimbra shrugged a shapely shoulder. "We have a lot to do and very little time. I don't want us to be disturbed. I wouldn't put it past certain people to do everything they can to mess things up." She stared pointedly at Evie.

Evie knew she was referring to Dahlia. From what she had seen of the woman so far, she wouldn't put it past her to continue her quest to stand at Aulis' side – right up to the point where Aulis and Evie said "I do." He was definitely something to fight for, but Evie simply couldn't understand the drive behind Dahlia's obsession. What was she really after? Power? Money? Was she simply that fixated on Aulis?

"OK. Evie, time to start getting ready." Kimbra said, breaking Evie out of her daydream.

"Why do I get the feeling this is going to be more of a process than a day of pampering?" Evie grimaced.

Winnie snickered. "Honey, if we'd had more notice, you would be pampered from the moment you awoke until the moment you walked down the aisle. However, since you two are in such a hurry, we have to cram all the preparation into a couple of hours." She winked.

Evie blushed. "I don't want to cause some sort of scandal or cause anyone any unnecessary stress by hurrying things. We can certainly push things out a bit."

Winnie patted her hand. "Oh, no, there's no pulling back now. Oberon already announced it publicly. Everyone in Tuatha De will be there tonight to catch a glimpse of their new princess who captured Aulis' heart."

Evie dropped her head into her hands. "Ugh. I don't really want to be put on show. What if Dahlia or Niklas make some sort of scene?"

"They wouldn't *dare*." Kimbra growled.

"She's right." Winnie agreed. "First, it would reveal them for what they really are. Secondly, Oberon's judgment would be swift and harsh. He would take it as a personal insult."

Colleen pulled a brush through Evie's hair in long even strokes. "Evie, you're going to have to wash your hair if you want me to be able to do anything with it, since you went swimming this morning."

"OK. Why don't you guys pull everything you need together while I go wash my hair?" Evie suggested.

"Hurry, sweetie; we have a lot to do." Winnie insisted.

Evie bathed and washed her hair in record time. When she returned to the bedchamber with wet curls streaming down her back, the four-poster bed was covered in beautiful flowing fabrics of bright yellow, midnight blue, and snowy white.

Lizbeth's hair was fashioned in ringlets circled with a crown interwoven with tiny blue, yellow and white blossoms. She was skipping around the room with her curls bouncing on her shoulders.

"Lizzie, I love your hair. You look like a little princess."

"Fank you, Ebbie." She squealed and hopped up and down.

"Just wait until you see what we have in store for you," taunted Kimbra.

"Should I be afraid?" Evie asked cautiously.

"Be very afraid." Winnie chuckled.

Evie swallowed nervously and shifted from one foot to another, her eyes darting around the room.

"You two stop it. Can't you see she's nervous enough?" Colleen admonished.

Winnie and Kimbra each threw an arm over Evie's shoulders.

"We were just teasing you, sweetie. The gown and the accessories are exquisite. You'll see." Winnie comforted her.

Kimbra held up a fistful of diaphanous material for Evie to examine, grabbing it by the neckline so it morphed from a pile of fabric into a beautiful dress with panels in alternating sunshine yellow and midnight blue. Golden clasps at the shoulders were inlaid with the royal seal of intertwined sun and moon.

Evie gasped. "Is that for me?"

"Yup." Kimbra chuckled.

"It is breathtaking. I never dreamed to wear anything so beautiful. This would cost tens of thousands of dollars in my world."

"It's good to be a princess, right? Now step in and I'll zip you up." Kimbra knelt down and held the dress in place for Evie.

Evie stepped into the dress, marveling at the softness of the fabric; it felt like air against her skin. The dress rested on her shoulders, held in place with the clasps. The neckline was plunging and the colorful panels fell in graceful folds around her bare feet. Kimbra tapped Evie on the instep. Evie tentatively raised her foot and Kimbra slipped a golden anklet over her heel and twisted it into place. The anklet was covered in charms of suns and half-moons that tinkled when she moved.

Lizbeth danced around the two women. "Me too, Mommy! It's pwetty."

Laughter floated through the air.

"Well, you little monkey, you'll have to stand still for a minute so I can put it on for you." Kimbra grimaced.

Lizbeth went perfectly still and extended her pudgy little leg, pointing her toes to the floor. Kimbra slipped the anklet over her heel and Lizbeth immediately spun around the room like a whirlwind, making the charms sing.

Kimbra shook her head ruefully. "At least we'll know where she is tonight."

"No doubt about that." Evie laughed. "However, you could probably say the same thing about me." She twisted her ankle, making the charms jingle.

Colleen stepped forward, wrapping her arms around Evie. "You look so beautiful. Aulis is a very lucky man, and he is everything I'd always hoped for you and so much more. I only wish your father was here to see it." She wiped a tear from the corner of her eye.

Evie was stunned. Her mother had never voluntarily spoken about her father; being in Tuatha and staying in Lyrr's rooms must be making her very nostalgic. Seeing her mother's pain only strengthened Evie's resolve to find her father.

Winnie gathered both women in her arms. "He will have his chance, you'll see."

"Hug me too!" Lizbeth squealed and squirmed between the women.

Colleen surprised everyone by gathering Lizbeth into her arms. "Kimbra, go ahead and get ready; I'm happy to entertain Lizzie for a while."

Kimbra smiled brightly. "Actually that would be incredibly helpful."

She grabbed handfuls of blue material, handing one piece to Winnie and throwing another over her shoulder while leaving one on the bed.

"I'll leave your dress here on the bed, and as soon as I'm dressed, I'll relieve you of Lizzie duty and you can get dressed."

"Take your time. I'm in no hurry." Colleen stroked the little girl's curls. "Lizzie, would you like to hear a song I used to sing to Evie when she was little?"

Lizzie clapped her pudgy hands together. "Sing! Sing!"

Evie took advantage of having a few moments to herself. She glided over to the closet and its full-length mirror to study her appearance. The dress set off her complexion beautifully, and her hair was drying in ringlets around her face.

Kimbra approached her from behind. "Wait a minute, we're not quite done yet. Turn around for a second."

Evie dutifully turned around and found Kimbra standing before her with a handful of various cosmetics. She balanced the containers and used the brushes with the skill of a makeup artist. She finally took a step back and cocked her head to one side.

"Much better. Now I'm going to finish getting dressed." She smiled, turned on one heel and walked away.

Evie took a deep breath and turned back to the mirror, gasping at what she saw. Kimbra had given her the wildly popular smoky eye, and the effect was quite dramatic. The blue of the eye shadow complemented the dress perfectly and made her eyes really shine. She had also added a hint of blush – although Evie felt she would probably have plenty of natural blush that night. She knew she had never looked better, and couldn't wait to see what Aulis thought of her transformation.

The room was filled with the sounds of people bustling about, making their preparations. Evie walked out to the balcony, desperately looking for a little solitude before the wedding. Just a couple of steps out the door and she saw the private pool Kimbra had mentioned earlier. She couldn't help but blush at the memory of Aulis at the grotto and the thought what would take place within the privacy of the suite's walls that very evening.

"Evie – baby?" Winnie called.

Evie reluctantly rejoined the chaos in the main room. "Yes, ma'am?"

"It's time, love bug. Are you ready?"

Evie's heart pounded. She really hated to be the center of attention.

At least she was barefoot, which would help allay her fears of tripping and falling flat on her face. She still had to contend with all the unwanted attention and the fear that Dahlia was going to try to ruin the wedding. A wave of panic washed over her. She still had no idea what was expected of her. What was she doing? She had only known the man for a couple of days!

"No! I'm not ready. What am I supposed to do? We haven't talked about that yet."

Winnie massaged the back of Evie's neck. "Relax, kiddo. It's incredibly similar to a wedding in our world. Colleen, Kimbra, and I will walk through the arches made of hawthorn and rosemary and down the aisle, followed by Lizbeth. She will have her lemongrass basket full of lavender, but instead of walking down the aisle at a slow pace carefully dropping flowers, she will be dancing down the aisle tossing flowers. Tradition encourages her to give in to her fairy nature – which, thankfully, Lizbeth fully embraces."

The room filled with laughter.

"OK, I can definitely see that. However, what is *my* role in all this?" The tension was clear in Evie's voice.

"You and Oberon will follow behind Lizbeth. He will present you to Aulis, then stand before the two of you and begin the ceremony. The room will be decorated in pure white flowers intertwined with ribbons that compliment your dress. Nothing is supposed to outshine the bride. Your bouquet will consist of lavender and apple blossoms with lemongrass and baby's breath. The air will be filled with the sounds of thousands of tiny bells being rung by all those attending. These bells produce the smallest chime; it's actually very beautiful... and calming." Winnie stared pointedly at Evie.

"Does it show?" Evie wrung her hands. "I'm trying my best to stay calm, but I guess I'm not doing a very good job."

Colleen patted her hand reassuringly. "Sweetie, all brides are nervous at one point or another, and they've had months and months to plan. You've had a lot thrown your way in the last couple of days, and you've shown tremendous grace under pressure. It's a lot to take in, but you've done a wonderful job. You're very much like your father – he was the same way."

Evie hugged her mother. "Thank you so much. You have no idea how much that means to me."

Colleen wiped a tear from the corner of Evie's eye. "Now stop that or you're going to ruin Kimbra's masterpiece."

"All right, do you want to know about the rest of this ceremony? We're quickly running out of time." Winnie teased.

Evie's pulse raced. "Oh, geez. Yes, please tell me the rest."

"If you feel your emotions spiraling out of control, take deep breaths of your bouquet. The flowers were chosen for their aromatherapeutic effects as well as their symbolism. Remember, you couldn't ask for a better spouse. He clearly adores you and will treat you like a princess for the rest of your life. He will put your safety above all else."

Aulis' face came into focus in Evie's mind, and a warmth spread throughout her body. She knew there was no way she would have ever found someone like him in her world. For the shortest second, she wished she could see Sean's face when she didn't show up for work on Tuesday. Served him right, the jerk.

"Oberon will proceed through the ceremony. When it's time, he will have you repeat the words that will bind you together. Aulis will present you with your ring, handmade by the royal jeweler; Thuldin is a dwarf who has personally created all the jewelry worn by the royal family for centuries."

Winnie chuckled at Evie's stunned expression. "It's said that wedding rings made by a dwarf are very good luck. You will then slide the other ring onto his finger. Oberon will crown you both with a circlet of wildflowers. Then comes the best part – you get to seal it with a kiss. You will walk back down the aisle together and through the hawthorn arch. You will head out to the gardens for a few, precious moments alone before rejoining everyone for the reception."

"Why do we leave before coming back to the reception?"

"It gives the couple a few moments of privacy and, at the same time, gives the staff enough time to set tables up for the reception, dinner and dancing."

"Oh, well, that makes sense. Anything else I need to know?"

"Yeah – try to take it easy on the nectar tonight." Colleen grimaced.

Kimbra burst into laughter. "Don't worry about it, Colleen; she'll be Aulis' problem by then."

The women's laughter echoed through the room, but they were quickly sobered by a powerful knock on the door.

Kimbra crossed the room, slid the bolt back, and opened the door. "Hi there!" She cried.

Oberon strode over the threshold and headed directly for Evie. "You look beautiful, my child – a fitting bride for the future king of the Tuatha De." He kissed Evie on the forehead. "You look so much like your father; it's like looking directly into Lyrr's eyes." He turned to Colleen. "How have you managed it all these years?"

She shrugged her shoulders and blushed. "Every time I looked at her, I realized I had a piece of Lyrr with me. It was a comfort. It's not just the eyes, either; her personality is so much like his."

He took Evie's hand and settled it into the crook of his arm. "Well, shall we get on with things?" He leaned in close to whisper into her ear. "I just left Aulis and he's just as anxious as you – but I suspect for different reasons." He chuckled as the color spread across her face. He put his free hand over hers and led the women through the door. Evie was surprised to see members of the royal guard standing just outside the door to escort their party to the door of the great hall.

15 A CEREMONY FOR A PRINCESS

Evie felt the panic rise in her throat and desperately fought to remain calm. Kimbra handed her the bridal bouquet, and Evie immediately inhaled deeply. Her aunt had been right; the scent helped to soothe her raw nerves.

Lizbeth tugged on Evie's dress until she knelt down. "Ebbie, you look pwetty. Unca Owie will love you like I do." The little girl threw her arms around Evie's neck and kissed her on the cheek. Kimbra gathered her up and ushered her toward the arch for last-minute instructions. Before Evie knew it, her mother and Winnie had kissed her cheek and proceeded down the aisle, followed by Kimbra.

Lizbeth turned to Evie. "Ima good girl, I wait 'til you are ready – not before."

Evie looked down into the little face lit up with a beatific smile and felt her heart swell with love for the little pixie.

"OK, I'm ready when you are. You'll be the best flower girl ever."

Lizbeth grinned widely before darting through the hawthorn arch and then skipping and dancing down the aisle, tossing flowers as she went. It was so natural; no one could've choreographed anything more perfect.

Oberon patted her hand. "We're up. Are you ready?"

Evie watched the entire assembly rise to their feet and was struck by a wave of nausea. She took a deep breath and bit her bottom lip. She reminded herself of the prize to be gained, waiting for her at the end of the aisle, to be hers forever.

"OK, I can do this. I just want to make my father proud."

"You would – I promise."

Oberon patted her hand one more time as they passed under the arch and were greeted with the sound of thousands of tiny chimes, just as Winnie had promised. Nothing could've prepared her for the effect – it brought tears to her eyes and she couldn't stop smiling. When she finally turned her eyes to the front of the room, there stood Aulis and Ari. Ari's grin spread across his face, and he gave her a thumbs-up.

Aulis couldn't take his eyes off her; he placed his hand over his heart, his Mark visible for everyone to see. It was almost Evie's undoing. Finally they made it to the end of the aisle, and Oberon placed her hand in Aulis'. Aulis lifted her hand to his lips as Evie gazed at him with tears in her eyes.

Most of the ceremony passed in a blur. Evie simply couldn't believe she would spend the rest of her life with the colossal warrior at her side. She quickly snapped to attention when Aulis turned to face her with a ring in his palm. He took her hand and slid the ring into place as he recited his vows.

"The moon smiles on us today, our wedding day. Its light shines bright because our love is stronger than forever and our hearts beat as one. I promise to be faithful this day and all those to come. I will remain at your side in the joys and sorrows, sickness and health. I will always be there for you, to protect you, comfort you, honor, and cherish you, now and forevermore."

Evie felt a single tear slide down her cheek, which Aulis caught with his fingertip.

"Evie, repeat after me." Oberon instructed.

Oberon went through the vows line by line as Evie fervently repeated them. Then he placed an intricately carved golden band into her palm. She took Aulis' hand in her shaking hands and slid the ring into place.

Oberon turned the couple to face the assembly and placed matching crowns of flowers upon their heads. "Let no one, in this world or any other, sever the bond forged today. Let me present to you Aulis and Evie, your future King and Queen of Tuatha De."

The room erupted with a wild ovation. The sound of the chimes washed over Evie as Aulis bent his head and took her lips in a passionate kiss that stole her breath. When they finally parted, Ari raced forward and swung Evie into the air.

"Welcome to the family, little sister. We'll see you guys at the reception – make sure you don't sneak off to your suite before then."

Evie smacked him on the arm. "Stop it. I'm nervous enough already, so don't give him any ideas. I don't want to look bad in front of everyone."

Aulis pulled her to his side. "Come, my love, he can harass you later... and he will. Let's go enjoy a few moments to ourselves before we join everyone for the reception."

He tucked her hand into his arm and led her back down the aisle and out the doors leading to the garden as the sound of the chimes faded behind them. Once outside, he turned her to face him.

"I should probably warn you that once the reception starts, everyone is going to want to dance with the new princess. It's a big tradition, but

I'm not so sure I like it anymore." He chuckled.

"Do the bride and groom get to dance first? I know that's how it works in my world."

"Absolutely! I wouldn't have it any other way. However, that's part of why they give us this time together before the reception, as everyone wants a piece of us. It's considered good luck to dance with the bride and groom."

Evie peeked at him through her lashes. "Well, we better not waste what little time we have." She snaked her arms around his neck. She wanted to thoroughly enjoy her first few moments of married life.

His eyes flamed with passion. He lowered his head to hers and his assault on her lips was violent. She gasped and responded with every ounce of her being. He plundered her mouth, and she matched every stroke of his tongue. She anchored her hands in his hair as his hands roamed down her back. They staggered to a low stone wall around the balcony and Aulis dropped to the wall, pulling Evie between his legs so she was pressed fully against him and their faces were level. They were both breathless from the intensity of their kiss.

Suddenly they heard Ari clearing his throat knowingly. "Hey guys, they're ready for you. Oberon sent me out here to find you. I think he was afraid to send Colleen or Winnie since we had no idea what we'd find." He snickered.

"You jerk. Stop teasing me, or Kimbra and I will gang up on you." Evie stuck her tongue out at him.

Aulis burst into laughter. "Ari, I think she's got you. There's no *way* I'd want the two of them plotting against me."

Evie poked a finger in his chest. "You'd do best to remember that."

Aulis reached out and nipped the end of her finger, and her knees threatened to give out. If a simple kiss affected her this way, how was she ever going to survive the night? He was very experienced, and she knew nothing. She could only hope to find a way to keep him happy.

Aulis released her so he could stand up, then immediately reclaimed her hand. "Let's get this over with so I can have you to myself for several hours." He growled.

She blushed furiously, wondering if she'd always be red-faced around him. "Will we get the chance to eat something before we get passed around?"

Ari slung an arm around her shoulder. "Oh, hell, yes. In case you hadn't noticed yet, we don't miss any meals around here."

"Yes, I *had* noticed that. I'd just like to know how you all keep from being grossly overweight."

"Genetics, little sister. Aren't you lucky to be one of us?"

"Shh!" warned Aulis.

"Not to worry – I'd never put her in danger. I've waited centuries for you to find her." Ari squeezed Evie's shoulder before leaving to rejoin his family.

"Somehow I suspect I should be more worried about you and Ari than you and Kimbra." Aulis grimaced.

"You're probably right." She stood on tiptoe to kiss him. "Now let's get inside so everyone can stare. I'll be so glad when it's over and I don't feel like everyone is gawking at me all the time."

"My love, that will never end. How can you not understand how delectable you are? You are all curves, which is a rarity in my world. You have the size of the Adairs, but the eyes and spirit of your father; it's a potent combination." His eyebrows drew together. "You never have to worry about them acting on it, because I will *never* allow another to touch you. You are *mine.*"

She reached up to caress his cheek. "Aulis, how could anyone else hold any appeal for me after having you? No one could possibly ever measure up."

He chuckled, kissed her quickly and led her back to the reception. They were greeted by cheers and the ever-present chime of bells.

Oberon greeted them at the main table, hugged Evie, and clasped arms with Aulis. They were seated in almost the exact same places as at lunch, except Aulis and Evie were now seated at the center of the table. Oberon lifted his glass and tapped on it with a knife.

"If you will all give me your attention, I would like to raise up a toast to the next King and Queen of Tuatha De. May Aulis continue to fiercely protect our people as he has for centuries, and may Evie be as fair as she is beautiful. They will lead us into a new era of peace and prosperity."

Everyone raised their glasses of nectar and toasted the new couple. As soon as the smooth liquid coated Evie's tongue, she visibly relaxed. Aulis raised an eyebrow at her and she grinned in response. He would have to closely monitor her nectar consumption; it obviously affected her like it had her father. They dined on various meats, cheeses, olives, fresh vegetables, and desserts. Aulis made sure Evie ate her fill; he knew her nerves had gotten the better of her and she hadn't eaten anything since lunch. Then the servants quickly cleared the tables and pushed them to the outside walls to make room for dancing.

Oberon pulled the couple aside. "I have to make a personal request of you both." He had their full attention. "As much as you might want to, you cannot refuse to dance with Niklas or Dahlia. We received some new information about Lyrr and cannot risk those two finding a way to interfere. I don't want them to know they are being watched by the royal guard. I need you to act as though everything is fine. Can you please do that for me?"

Evie nodded quickly. "If it means we might be able to bring my father home, I'd be willing to do just about anything."

"I'll do it for you, Oberon, but I'm going to hate every single second of it." Aulis grunted.

"I know you will. However, I promise to do what I can to run interference. If it makes you feel better, I have Taarmo heading up a security detail for Evie tonight. No one but you will be allowed to take her from the hall." Oberon promised.

Aulis and Evie were both stunned, but Evie leaned in close to Oberon.

"Thank you, Uncle Oberon; I love you." She whispered.

He caught them both in a quick hug before pulling away with a tear in his eye. "I claim the first dance after Aulis."

"I wouldn't have it any other way." She assured him.

As the sound of music filled the room, Evie noticed a small group of musicians set up in a far corner of the room. She had never heard music so stirring. Aulis led her to the center of the dance floor as the other attendees formed a large circle around the room. He spun her around the room in perfect time to the music. Evie was stunned that a man as big as Aulis could be so graceful; he was the perfect dance partner. He placed his hands under her arms and lifted her high above his head. She allowed her head to fall backward as she giggled. He finally lowered her feet to the ground and pulled her tightly to him before fastening his lips to hers in a slow, gentle, heart-stopping kiss.

"May I cut in?" Oberon's voice brought her back to earth.

"Oh, of course." Evie stammered.

"Sorry to disturb you, Aulis – you definitely looked like you were enjoying yourself, but you still have to share her for a couple of hours." Oberon ribbed.

"I know, you keep reminding me." Aulis joked. "Take good care of her. I'm going to grab Winnie for a spin." He winked at Oberon and took off in the direction of Evie's beloved aunt.

"You look radiant, child." The king smiled down at her. "Your face glows with happiness. It's everything I ever could've wanted for you."

"Thank you." She smiled up at him. "You are a good match for Winnie. I can see why she fell in love with you, and vice versa. Is there any way you can ever be together? It all seems so unfair."

He glanced wistfully at Winnie, who was being twirled around the room in Aulis' powerful arms. "I swore not to marry until Lyrr was found. I wasn't going to let anything distract me from finding my brother and bringing him home."

"Then that is what we will do. Everyone deserves their happy ending. What can I do to help?"

"Child, you definitely have your father's spirit, but the path to find your father is riddled with danger. There is no way I would allow you to put yourself in harm's way, and neither would your husband. He knows of the dangers surrounding us and will be incredibly protective of you – *overly* protective at times. You are the Guardian, which means you protect the Relic as an ancient weapon against the dark forces that continue to plague us. I have long suspected there is a traitor in our midst; we only have to flush them out. I can't risk Lyrr's safety by accusing them outright. We must make them reveal themselves."

And that reminded her of something important. "Oberon, this may not be the place, but I feel like I need to come clean with you."

"What is it, Evie?"

"We have no idea where the Relic is. My mom and Winnie have been panic-stricken for days. They know of its existence, but my grandmother never told anyone what it looked like – only that we were the Guardians of the Relic."

Oberon surprised her by throwing back his head and laughing.

"Oh, dear child, do not worry. The form of the Relic is known only to the king and the Guardian – usually passed from one Adair to the next. Your poor grandmother passed away before telling you the full story, but not before giving you the Relic itself."

Evie shook her head. "I don't understand. You're saying I already have the Relic?"

"Yes, I am. You wear it around your neck as we speak."

Evie's hand flew to the necklace her grandmother had given her before she died, making Evie promise *never* to remove it. She had been wearing the Relic for years. "Is it dangerous wearing it out in the open like this? Aulis said he thought it was special the first time he saw it. Will other people know? How does it work?" Her hand covered the necklace protectively.

"Not in the least. Aulis is very quick to pick up on things, but only you and I know its significance. Of course, we will tell Colleen and Winnie to put them at ease, as well as making sure Aulis is aware as the future king and your mate. Don't worry about how to use it – we'll talk about that later."

Aulis and Winnie skidded to a stop next to them, making Evie squeak in surprise.

"Well, hello." Winnie winked at Oberon. "I can't remember the last time I danced with a real-live king."

Oberon plucked her from Aulis' arms. "We can fix that right now." And he spun her away.

Aulis pulled Evie back into his arms. "Could this night drag on any slower?" He waggled his eyebrows at her, making the blush rise in her cheeks again.

"Actually, I just had a very interesting conversation with Oberon, and we have a few things to talk about tonight. There's something you definitely need to know."

"Now you have me intrigued. Should we go ahead and leave the party now?" He pulled her even closer.

"Leave? Surely you're not thinking about leaving before we've all had a chance to dance with your beautiful bride?"

The couple turned to find Niklas standing at their side.

Evie felt an instant of panic. What had he heard?

Niklas held his hand out in invitation. "May I have this dance?"

She took one quick peek at Aulis out of the corner of her eyes. He was definitely struggling with the idea of this prospective dance partner.

"Of course." She took his hand and hoped Aulis would be able to hold it together.

She glanced at Aulis as Niklas whirled her across the floor and breathed a sigh of relief when she saw Kimbra claiming his hand for a dance. She hoped Kimbra could help keep him from making a scene. Evie knew he would never do anything to intentionally harm Oberon or her father, but she wasn't convinced he was in full control of his emotions at the moment.

"You are the most beautiful bride ever to grace these halls." Niklas purred.

"I seriously doubt that, but you are kind to say so." Evie reminded herself to be on her guard every second around Niklas. He was incredibly smooth, and she didn't want to be the one to cause problems for the family.

"Ah, but that is part of your charm. You have no idea how appealing you are to the Tuatha. Your brilliant hair, curves and tiny stature are foreign to us." His gaze caressed her face. "Even the color of your eyes is rare. The only Tuatha known to have eyes like yours was Lyrr." He looked over her shoulder. "Have you heard of him?"

Evie felt a brief surge of panic that Niklas might have figured out their secret, but she immediately pulled a wall around her thoughts and casually shrugged a bare shoulder. "I had never heard of him until we arrived here. I get the feeling from the stories that he and Oberon were very close."

"Yes, Oberon has sworn to find him at all costs. There are some who feel he neglects his people due to the search for his brother." Niklas was indifferent.

Evie surveyed the room. "Looks to me like you people have it all here. What could you possibly want for?"

"Oh, don't get me wrong – we live well, but the king's first responsibility should be to his people. His personal needs should come second."

She wryly reflected that it didn't take much to see he was not a big fan of Oberon's; could he be the traitor they were searching for? She was careful to speak casually. "The way I see it, his brother *is* one of his people. Wouldn't you do the same for your brother?"

"Ah, I forget. In the human world, family tends to come first. I imagine there are a lot of things here that seem strange to you." He gestured toward Aulis across the dance floor. "Take marriage for example – yes, the Tuatha mate for life, but there is nothing to stop them from taking other bed partners. We are comfortable with the complexities of our own sexuality, as you probably have noticed." He nodded toward Dahlia, who was striding toward Aulis in a dress so low-cut Evie wasn't sure how her bosom was staying confined. "Your new husband has enjoyed quite the reputation with the ladies for many years. Rest assured that if you ever tire of his wandering eye, there are many who would be honored to take his place and treat you like the princess you are."

Evie's eyes widened in surprise. Had he just propositioned her at her own wedding? Surely she misunderstood him! The music slowed to a smooth, flowing melody, and Niklas pulled her close against his body. Just as she put both hands against his chest to push him away, two strong hands clamped over her wrists.

"I believe this dance is mine. I haven't had the opportunity to dance with my new sister." Ari's face was a calm, smiling mask, but his voice carried a dark undertone. Evie knew he was sending Niklas a clear warning.

Niklas released Evie and kissed her hand before bowing low. "Remember what I said. I look forward to seeing you again very soon."

Evie shuddered in Ari's arms.

"Are you OK? Did he say something to you?" He scanned the room over the top of her head.

"No, it's fine. Everything has been a little overwhelming today, and the difference in customs makes my head swim."

"What difference in customs? Most of your human customs were taken from us. Your people seriously lack imagination." He grinned.

"OK, I'll tell you what he said, but you have to keep it completely to

111

yourself. I'm trusting you in this. I don't want Aulis getting fired up and doing something stupid."

"Oh, *ho*. You know my brother better than I thought. OK, lay it on me, little sister."

"Well, Niklas keeps referring to Aulis' *legendary* reputation with the ladies. You may or may not know – I have absolutely zero experience. I'm not ashamed of that fact, but I'm worried I won't measure up and Aulis will get bored. According to Niklas, the Tuatha do mate for life, but that doesn't necessarily mean they are *faithful* to those partners. I don't want Aulis to have to look elsewhere because I'm not enough." Her face was bright red and hot with embarrassment.

Ari hugged Evie quickly. "Oh, Evie, don't listen to him. Yes, the Tuatha mate for life and occasionally one will stray, but that is the *rare* exception – not the rule. A Tuatha with any self-respect would never feel less than the same respect for their spouse. I can assure you Aulis would never stray; can't you see how he feels about you? I've never seen him react this way to *anyone*."

"I'm just afraid that it's the anticipation that has him so wound up. He knew we couldn't be… well… intimate like that until we were wed. What if I'm terrible at it and I'm a huge letdown?"

Ari laughed and then immediately looked apologetic for his outburst. "No. I suppose that's a reasonable fear, considering the situation, but I simply can't imagine it." He said with deepest sincerity. "You will both have things to learn from each other. Kimbra and I were the same way, and anyone can see that she and I are still *very* much in love. You'll see."

Evie peeked around his shoulder. "Actually, the only thing I see right now is Dahlia rubbing herself all over your twin." She ground out through gritted teeth.

Ari spun her around so he could see what was going on and cursed under his breath at the sight. "She's a real piece of work. Evie, did you notice Aulis' response? Look how tense he is; he clearly doesn't want to be there, but he's trying not to cause a scene." He nodded at someone behind Aulis. "We're not the only ones who noticed how uncomfortable he was – Taarmo just cut in and took Dahlia. I expect your spouse will be here very shortly to claim you."

Just as Ari had predicted, Aulis appeared at his elbow and drew Evie into his arms.

"See?" Ari thumped her on the arm. "I told you." He grinned and walked away to find his own wife and child.

Aulis pulled her fully against his body and thrust his face into her hair, inhaling deeply. "You smell so good. I couldn't wait to get away from her. It took everything I had not to push her away and sprint over here, but all I could think about was what Oberon said."

Evie buried her face in his chest. "Could we take a minute to get a drink? I'm burning up."

"Absolutely." He gestured to a servant, who immediately brought them two glasses of nectar.

Evie tossed back the entire contents of the glass and melted against his chest. Aulis drained his goblet and looked down at his tiny spouse, who was staring at him with glassy and adoring eyes.

"What am I going to do with you?" He mused.

"I don't know – you tell me. You know I'm completely innocent. Well, at least I was until I met you." She giggled.

Aulis felt his shaft filling and fought to control it, but didn't know if it would be possible any longer. He surveyed the room until he found what he was looking for. He swept Evie into his arms and strode for the far corner of the room, putting her down just in front of Colleen, Winnie, and Oberon.

"We came to say goodnight. I hope everyone stays and enjoys themselves, but Evie and I are going to excuse ourselves for the night."

Evie kissed her mother, aunt, and uncle. "Good night. I guess we'll see you all in the morning."

Oberon leaned in close. "Don't forget to tell him, sweetheart. It's very important. We will see you at lunch."

Evie was surprised. "You aren't coming to breakfast?"

"I am, but I suspect we won't see the two of you until lunchtime."

"Oh." Evie whispered then giggled nervously.

Aulis swept her into his arms once more and headed for the hawthorn arch, which would lead them away from the party and to their suite. The assembly clapped and cheered as the happy couple departed from the reception with a full guard detail in tow.

Evie gave Taarmo a smile of thanks. She was so grateful for the men who were loyal to Aulis and watched over them. They parted company with the guards once they reached the suite doors.

"Not to worry, sir, we won't be too far away... just far enough." Taarmo assured them with a wink.

16 A ROYAL HONEYMOON

Aulis didn't put her down until he had kicked the door shut and thrown the bolt to lock the door. There was a large box on the bed tied with a large silver bow and a tag with Evie's name on it. Evie looked at Aulis with questions in her eyes.

"I'm just as curious as you are. Go ahead, open it."

Evie rushed to the box and tore it open. Inside was the most beautiful midnight blue lace nightgown. It had a plunging neckline and very short hem with a matching thong. She dropped the gown on the bed to pick up the card, which simply read:

Everyone should look beautiful on their wedding night. Love, your sister – K

When had Kimbra found time to slip in here and put the box on the bed? She was amazing. Lying next to the box was the swimsuit Evie had worn in the grotto.

"Kimbra always did have good taste. I'll have to thank her for this tomorrow." Aulis voice rumbled. "So, are you up for a dip in the pool?" He realized Evie was nervous, and he would need to take his time to woo her and make her comfortable.

"Sounds great. I didn't even notice the pool until this afternoon. It will be nice to have a swim without a full audience." She giggled.

He kissed her briefly. "OK, you go get changed and I'll meet you out by the pool."

Evie watched appreciatively as Aulis made his way outside. The muscles in his back rippled when he walked, reminding her of a powerful and possibly dangerous predator. She could see why he was so popular with women. Her teeth caught her bottom lip; she had unfortunately just reminded herself how little she had to offer him. She sprinted to the closet and got dressed in a flash. She admired her reflection in the mirror and adjusted her bikini top, trying to make sure everything was covered – and then remembered she was dressing for her new husband, so maybe less coverage was a good thing.

Finally satisfied with her efforts, she glided out the door and down the stairs to the private pool, where Aulis was waiting with a tray of cut fruit, a bowl of warm chocolate, a bottle of nectar, and a couple of glasses. This man never failed to amaze her – he thought of everything. He must've had this all set up before they even left the hall. He looked up from pouring the nectar to stare appreciatively.

"I definitely love the way that suit looks on you." He extended a glass of nectar to her.

She took the glass and chuckled. "I'm glad you like it. I'm still a little self-conscious in it."

"You could always take it off." He purred suggestively.

"You know, I think I'm getting more comfortable in it all the time." She savored the smooth, sweet taste of the nectar as she emptied the glass. "Someone is going to have to keep an eye on me to prevent me from becoming a total lush. That is the best tasting drink I've ever had, but it is potent."

"It definitely has a kick to it. Let's make a deal: you only drink it when you're with me or family – namely Ari, Kimbra, your mom, or Winnie. That way we don't have to worry about people trying to take advantage of you."

Evie thrust out her hand. "It's a deal."

Instead of shaking her offered hand, he pulled her close and plundered her mouth. She gasped and parted her lips. His tongue slid in and caressed the inside of her mouth. Evie was unable to refrain from moaning, and the sound only encouraged him. His hands roamed over her bare skin, leaving a trail of goosebumps in their wake. She was still shaking when they separated.

"So, um... Does everyone have their own pool?" The nectar was making her head a little fuzzy, and she desperately tried to change the subject.

He could see the effects of the nectar and handed her a large chocolate-covered strawberry. "No, it's a perk of the position I hold. These rooms will eventually pass on to Taarmo. Don't worry – I promise that Oberon's private pool puts this one to shame. His more closely resembles the grotto."

"Oooh." Evie cooed. "I think I could like that. If we had a pool like that, I might never leave our suite."

He took two steps toward her. "I like the sound of that."

Evie ran lightly around the edge of the pool and hopped down the stairs until the water reached her shoulders. The water was warm and soothing against her skin. Aulis strode to the edge of the pool and dived in.

Lit torches and starlight were the only sources of light, and it was impossible to see the bottom of the pool. Evie squealed when she felt a powerful set of hands on her calves, which slid up to her waist as Aulis' head broke the plane of water. The movement of his hands and the water against her skin were a sensual combination. She felt a warmth spread throughout her body followed by a new sensation – a craving that started in the pit of her stomach. She wound her arms around Aulis' neck as he reached beneath the water and lifted her legs so she could wrap them around his waist. She nipped lightly at his neck before licking and suckling the same spot. Aulis threw his head back and groaned as his erection thickened and grew to its full length against her buttocks.

"You are the perfect size to hold this way. It's like you were made for me." He murmured against her ear. He rotated his hips against her in a way that left her panting and clinging to him for strength. She was desperate for him to continue, filled with a longing she had never known before as she whispered his name into the darkness.

He placed his hands under her for support and then carried her up the stairs and out of the pool, heading straight for their bedroom. They left pools of water on the wooden floor with each step, but neither cared. When they reached the enormous bed, he laid her across the mattress, fanning her hair out before sliding in beside her. Evie's ample chest heaved with her labored breathing in a way he found irresistible. He stroked her cheekbones with this thumbs before leaning forward to kiss her.

He feathered kisses across her lips, then followed her jawline and down her neck. By the time his lips reached her collarbone she was arching up to meet him. He reached behind her and untied her bikini top before throwing it to the floor. He took her generous globes in his hands and worshipped them with his mouth. She had never experienced anything so erotic. Is this what she had been missing for so many years? No one had ever made her feel so deliciously feminine. He slid one hand down her stomach and peeled the rest of the wet swimsuit from her body. She lay before him completely exposed.

He knew he had aroused pure lust in his new bride, and he wanted to possess her body and soul. He pushed back from the bed to divest himself of his swim trunks, which were now painfully tight against his immense erection. He took his cock in one hand and lightly rubbed it against the satin skin of her thigh, causing her to whimper his name over and over.

She knew she was begging for something – but what? He had pulled the most delicious feelings from her time and again; would this time be the same?

He didn't know how much longer he could stand the tension. He slipped one hand into the cleft between her legs and rubbed her tender bud between his fingers before gently slipping one finger inside her. He was greeted with the moisture he was hoping to find and couldn't control himself any longer.

"Open for me, Evie."

"What?" She stared at him with unfocused eyes.

He nudged at her thighs with his knee. "Open for me, Ionúin."

Evie immediately obeyed and allowed her thighs to fall open. Aulis guided his crimson head to her honeyed opening. He settled the head on her bud, teasing her before sliding inside as she gasped. He held still, allowing her silken sheath to adjust to his fullness. He had never known such a tight fit; when he slowly slid his cock further in and then out, the edges of her sheath tugged outward with the friction.

"Oh. Oh!" Evie cried.

"Am I hurting you, my love?" Aulis asked through a jagged breath.

Evie raised her hips to meet his. "No, don't stop. Please don't stop." She begged.

The head of his cock caressed her bud with the rhythm of each stroke until Evie felt something tremendous and overpowering building within her. Her head thrashed wildly back and forth.

"Oh, yes – you feel incredible." Aulis moaned.

Evie felt her body splinter into a million points of light as Aulis roared his release. They lay side by side panting and completely spent. Evie could still feel the flutter remaining from her orgasm.

"I never knew it would be like that." Her voice was full of wonder.

He propped himself up on one elbow. "Well, I'm glad I didn't disappoint you." He tucked a piece of hair behind her ear.

"And I didn't want to disappoint *you*." Her voice trembled.

He took her face in his hands. "My love, it was the single best moment of my life. It's even better because I get to experience that with you every day for the rest of my life. People are going to talk about us." He winked.

"You promise? You would tell me if I did something wrong, wouldn't you?"

"Evie, how can I make you understand? I've never experienced anything like that before. I was hardly able to hold myself back as long as I did."

She rolled to her side and hugged him tightly. "So… Is it normal to want to eat now?"

The muscled cords stood out on his neck with sudden laughter.

"Actually, yes. Come on, we'll go back to the pool and have a snack." He reached out a hand to help her up. She immediately searched for something to cover herself. "Ionúin, don't worry. It's just the two of us; no one else will see you. How about this – we'll eat it in the pool?"

"That sounds great. Honestly, I keep waiting to wake up. This *has* to be a dream."

"I've been called a lot of things in my life, but never a dream." He smiled softly. "It's kind of nice."

They strolled hand in hand to the pool.

"Aulis, I feel pretty certain you have starred in more than one woman's dreams. Sad for them, though, because I'm not very good at sharing. It's going to be even harder after that religious experience I just had."

He chuckled as she sunk into the pool and he placed the tray of food at the water's edge. "Not to worry, I have eyes only for my mate. I just feel bad for you."

Evie's eyes widened. "For me? Why?"

"Because there is no *way* I'm letting anyone near you. My jealousy will know no bounds, and you may get tired of having me around all the time."

She splashed water at him. "I seriously doubt I could ever get tired of you. From the very first moment I dreamt about you, you set my very essence aflame."

He slid off the side and into the water. "I'll set you aflame all right. Oberon was right to tell you he would see you at lunch." He stalked toward her.

"Oh, wait!" Evie exclaimed. "I forgot that I was supposed to tell you what Oberon said."

Aulis immediately sobered and was once again every inch the powerful warrior. "What's going on?"

"Don't get all serious; it's just something that you, as the next king, need to know. I know the location and form of the Relic." It was hard to resist being just a tiny bit smug.

Not surprisingly, this fact did not lighten his mood; his face darkened even further. "Evie, you can't tell *anyone* what you know. There are people, I suspect in this very castle, who would try to use it for their own gain."

"I know, but Oberon said that I needed to let *you* know." She took her necklace in two fingers. "This is the Relic. I've been wearing it around my neck for years without knowing what it was."

Aulis stroked the surface of the necklace, marveling at its warmth. "I'm glad you told me, but you may regret it. You realize this means I won't want you out of my sight."

"Oh, no… You mean I'll have to spend more time with you? How will I ever survive it? Next you're going to tell me I'm going to have to continue having mind-blowing orgasms and glass after glass of nectar." She rolled her eyes skyward.

Aulis smirked. "I'm relieved you're taking this so seriously." He looked at her with one raised eyebrow. "Mind-blowing orgasm? It was really that good for you?"

"I don't really have any basis for comparison so I'll have to stick with my description. But don't go getting a big head about it."

He put her hand over his growing erection. "Too late. See what you do to me?"

"Already? You can do it more than once in a night?"

"Oh yes – many more times." He growled through a predatory grin.

Evie gulped as he reached under the water and once again wrapped her legs around his waist. Nothing could have prepared her for him reaching between them, parting her nether-lips and easing himself inside. Her inner fire threatened to consume her entire body as she felt the muscles of her sheath contract around his shaft.

"Oh, my God." She gasped.

Aulis captured her lips in a violent assault. His thrusts quickly matched its intensity, and Evie immediately knew what all her romance novels meant by "liquid tremors." Her body clamped down so fiercely that he couldn't withdraw even if he had wanted to. Two flutters of her sheath, and Aulis flooded her with his release. Her very bones felt like liquid and she clung to him with shaking arms. He let her feet sink to the floor of the pool, and her legs felt unsteady under her weight.

As he reached over the edge of the pool to the tray of food, Evie took the opportunity to study his naked form. He was an absolute work of art. The sheets of muscle along his arms and torso were perfectly chiseled. Her eyes trailed lower and she found the source of her pleasure nestled in a patch of black, silken curls; it was huge even at rest. His legs were heavily muscled and defined. If he were to walk down the street near her house, the sky would rain women's underwear. But she knew the best part about Aulis was that the inside was just as amazing as the outside – she had won the romantic lottery.

He turned back around with a roll stuffed with small pieces of chicken. Evie gratefully took the roll and inhaled it. The food in the palace was amazing; she could only hope that she had inherited her father's metabolism. Since she was part Tuatha, she no longer had to fear the old warnings about not eating in the fairy realm.

"Eat your fill, then I want to wash your hair – it fascinates me."

"You'll hear no complaints from me. One of the greatest pleasures in life is to have someone play with your hair." She popped the last of a second roll into her mouth. "I'm ready whenever you are."

"Then let's go."

They climbed out of the pool and wandered into the suite. Evie stepped into the bathing pool and sat on one of the stone benches lining the edges. Aulis sat behind her, taking her hair into his hands. He poured eucalyptus-scented soap into one hand and lathered it into her hair. He massaged her scalp until her relaxed neck no longer wanted to support her head; then he poured a basin of water to rinse out all the soap. Once finished, he climbed out of the pool and set a couple of towels on the edge before helping her up.

He wrapped one thirsty towel around her and led her to the pillows surrounding the fireplace. There he gently squeezed another towel around the length of her hair before taking a comb and carefully pulling it through her hair in long strokes.

Evie felt nothing but pure bliss and sat with her eyes closed as the comb removed all traces of snarls and tangles from her hair. She opened her eyes to thank him and wondered if he had ever grabbed a towel for himself since his bare knees were on either side of her. She leaned back experimentally and felt the head of his shaft buck against her hip. She smothered a gasp and was incredibly thankful he couldn't see how red her face must be. She had to wonder if this was normal for newlyweds, since that's what they were – or was it just another benefit of being with Aulis?

The comb was replaced by his hands slowly sliding through her hair. She had definitely woken a sleeping beast. His hands strayed to her shoulders, kneading the knotted muscles. She was amazed it was possible to be even slightly tense after the release she had found with him... twice. She gave into the pleasure of his hands on her skin and let her chin drop to her chest. The new position gave him better access to her shoulders and then to the edge of her towel, which he pushed down and cupped her generous bust; she gasped as her nipples rose and hardened under his stroking fingers. He jumped up off the floor and pulled her to her feet. Her towel fluttered to the floor. He picked her up and carried her to the bed. He set her down and lifted the covers so she could slide underneath.

"I don't know about you, but I'd really like to sleep in my *bed* tonight. One more episode with you and I will sleep like a baby." He grinned.

She scooted over in the bed and felt the unmistakable dip of him joining her. She turned to crawl into his open arms. She felt a slight ache between her legs but wasn't about to let that stop her from enjoying the sensations he was so quick to produce for her. He had already been spent twice, and he was happy to take his time to pluck and play her body like a delicate instrument. Over and over again, he took her just to the brink of madness, then pulled back and started again. He worshipped every inch of her body until she was feverish and shaking with need.

"Aulis, please – *take me*." She begged in a hoarse whisper.

Her words were his undoing. He covered her body with his and plunged hard, burying himself completely. He thrust in long hard strokes until they both screamed their release and collapsed against each other, exhausted.

Their ragged breathing echoed in the cavernous suite. Evie's body shuddered like the aftershocks from a major earthquake. She was completely sated and knew there was no way she'd be able to continue their loveplay without being miserable the next day. Aulis instinctively knew her body couldn't take anymore and pulled her back against his chest, dropping a kiss on the top of her head. He wrapped his arms protectively around her, and they fell asleep without so much as another word.

The sun rose high before Evie's eyes opened.

"Good morning, beloved. Did you sleep well?" Aulis' breath caressed her ear.

Her mind abruptly replayed everything they had shared the night before and how she had begged him in the end. Her cheeks flamed. "Y-y-yes. Thank you." She stammered.

He turned her in his arms so she was forced to face him. "Why are you suddenly shy? My love, the things that happen here in our rooms are perfectly natural – you should never be embarrassed around me. I always want to know what you are thinking."

"You may change your mind on that one; sometimes even *I* don't want to be privy to my thoughts." She giggled.

He pulled her into his embrace, and his erection pressed against her stomach. But she knew if she didn't eat soon, and go to the bathroom, there was no way she could survive another onslaught from him. As usual, somehow he knew what she was thinking.

"Don't worry. We're going to be social and go join everyone for lunch. You need to keep your strength up." He smirked.

She sat up in the bed and noticed the bloodstain on the comforter and sheets – the final evidence, and remainder, of her maidenhead.

Her hands flew to her cheeks. "Ohmigod. Aulis I am *so* sorry. I totally ruined them."

He took her hands in his and pinned her with his intense gaze, causing a shiver to run through her entire body. "You didn't ruin anything; I couldn't be happier. I am the first man to ever touch you – and I'll be the last." He kissed her tenderly before patting her backside. "Now go get dressed before I change my mind about joining everyone for lunch and decide to keep you here all day."

She hopped off the bed and felt a slight twinge between her legs, but it wasn't too bad. Then she remembered with chagrin that she had packed only a couple of outfits, and she had been in Tuatha long enough to run out of clothes.

Again he read her mind. "Sweetheart, I took the liberty of having a few things brought to my rooms for you. There are several outfits in the closet and more on their way. However, for today, why don't you put on your swimsuit and the matching cover-up, which is hanging in the closet? We can join Kimbra and Ari at the grotto after lunch. I want you to get to know them. Ari is the only family I have left, and he's very important to me... just don't tell him I said that." He winked.

"Actually, I really like Kimbra, and spending the afternoon hanging out with them sounds good. Only one problem." She grimaced.

Concern marred his forehead. "What's wrong?"

"I have *no* idea what you did with my swimsuit last night." She giggled.

He walked around the bed and then got on his hands and knees, pulling the bikini top from under the bed. "Here's part of it." He continued looking around and walked to the screen covering the fireplace, pulling the bottoms off the edge. "Here's the rest."

"I'm going to leave you to find where you tossed your trunks while I get dressed." She slung her suit over her shoulder, saucily turned a bare cheek to him, and walked into the bathroom. Once she had relieved herself and donned the swimsuit, she took a long look in the mirror. Her hair framed her face like a lion's mane. She had no choice but to put it in a ponytail until she could find something that resembled a straightening iron. She sauntered out of the bathroom and ran right into Aulis' broad chest. He had found his trunks and pulled on an impossibly soft T-shirt.

He kissed her long and deep. "Have I told you how much I like that swimsuit?"

"I think you may have mentioned it once or twice." She teased.

"Which is exactly why I had a cover-up made for it. If I like it that much, I can guarantee there are plenty of other men around here who feel the same way. Come with me." He pulled her into the massive closet and handed her a long sarong of the exact colors of her suit. "Here you go." He wrapped it around her, making sure to caress the tips of her breasts before tying it behind her neck.

She looked in the mirror and saw he had created a beautiful halter dress out of the sarong, which brushed the tops of her feet and swished around her ankles when she moved. "Oh, Aulis – I absolutely love it. I've never had such beautiful clothes."

"It's only the beginning, I assure you."

"What will I do for shoes?"

"You won't need them at all. I have no intention of wearing any today." He grinned. "Now, let's hurry to lunch. If we miss two meals, the teasing will be unbearable by dinner." He lifted her hand and kissed her ring before intertwining his fingers with hers.

17 THE DAY AFTER

They strolled into the banquet hall hand in hand, talking and teasing, to see that all evidence of the previous night's ceremony was gone.

Oberon rose from his place at the main table. "Well, well. I was beginning to think we would have to send your meals to your room today."

Evie blushed furiously while Aulis laughed out loud and pulled her closer to his side.

"I warned you." He murmured into her ear. "Imagine how bad it would've been if we had missed lunch."

Lizbeth jumped from the table and sprinted toward the couple. She surprised everyone by leaping into Evie's arms first. "Auntie Ebbie. I missed you at bweakfast but I saved you and Unca Owie a pwace for lunch."

Aulis plucked the little girl from Evie's arms and kissed her chubby cheek. "You did good, Lizzie. Any cookies left?"

She nodded, setting her platinum curls to bouncing on her shoulders. "Yep, I saved two choc'wate ones for you and Auntie Ebbie."

Evie waggled her eyebrows. "Now *that's* a girl after my own heart."

"So my bride has a soft spot for chocolate? That's a good piece of information to have."

"Stop teasing me, you giant. I thought you promised me some lunch. I'm *starving*."

He chuckled and led her around the table to their seats between Ari's family and Oberon, Winnie, and Colleen.

Colleen and Winnie grabbed Evie in a bear hug.

"Life with Aulis is definitely going to agree with you, my child. You are positively glowing." Winnie nodded.

Colleen searched her daughter's face. "Are you happy?"

Evie took her mother's hand. "Mom, before yesterday, I didn't even know this level of happiness existed."

Aulis immediately pulled her into her arms and kissed her tenderly. "I think that's the nicest thing anyone's ever said about me."

"You?" Evie snorted. "I meant the clothes and the food."

He picked her up in one arm and tickled her unmercifully. "Are you sure? Maybe it's not the clothes or food, but your amazing husband who would do anything for you?"

Evie giggled uncontrollably. "OK, OK. You win. Of course it's because of my amazing husband – anyone with eyes can see that." She wrapped her arms around his neck and kissed him before he lowered her back to the floor.

Oberon clasped arms with Aulis and then hugged Evie. "I can't remember the last time I saw such a happy couple. It will do wonders for the morale of our people – hope springs eternal."

Aulis pulled out a chair and sat Evie next to Kimbra as he took the seat next to Oberon.

Oberon leaned in close to Aulis. "I can't tell you how pleased it makes me to see my only niece in such high spirits. Her love for you is written all over her face. Remember, there are still those who would use that against you… and her. Keep a watchful eye at all times."

"I would defend her with my own life." Aulis shifted his glance to his bride before turning back toward the king. "I will kill anyone who attempts to harm her." He promised through a calm that was truly frightening.

Oberon patted him on the shoulder. "I have no doubt in your abilities, or your love for her. I haven't seen you look so much like Ari in a very long time."

"I look that bad?" Aulis protested before bursting into laughter.

"Hey!" Ari leaned around Kimbra and Evie. "I heard that. You could only dream of being as good-looking as me."

Kimbra and Evie rolled their eyes. The men were absolutely identical with the exception of their personalities.

Evie sensed a nagging presence and scanned the room. Yep, there was Dahlia, sitting next to Niklas and staring daggers at Evie and her outfit. *Why should she care what I'm wearing?* Evie thought. She unconsciously leaned closer to Aulis and he threw an arm around her shoulder and pulled her chair closer.

"Looks like you've completely lost Aulis. The little Adair must possess some fairly formidable skills we weren't aware of." Niklas ribbed Dahlia.

"Shut up. She's no match for him. He'll soon tire of her – you'll see. He won't want some little human midget long-term. He'll want a true Tuatha." Dahlia retorted.

Niklas raised an eyebrow as he considered. "Her size definitely doesn't look Tuatha – but that is part of her appeal. She's all creamy skin, brilliant hair and womanly curves. And every man dreams of possessing a woman who makes him feel needed – makes him feel like a man. Remember that."

"Oh, I can definitely make him remember he's a man. Never fear." She tossed her hair over one shoulder and drained the contents of her cup.

Evie shuddered.

"What's wrong, my love?" Aulis' face was mere inches from her ear.

"Dahlia keeps throwing dirty looks my direction and then whispering to Niklas. It makes me really uncomfortable. I get that she hates me – if someone took you from me, I'd be furious too."

"You didn't take me from her. I've *never* belonged to her." He stated flatly. "I never engaged in a long-term relationship, and now I know why – I was waiting for you." He turned her chair to face him. "Now, how about we give her something to stare at?" He lowered his head and took her lips, feathering kisses and then tracing the outline with his tongue until she was shivering.

Evie was incredibly thankful lunch was served at that moment to keep her from demanding he take her then and there. However, she didn't miss Dahlia's narrowed eyes – she knew a challenge had just been issued, with Aulis as the prize.

The remainder of lunch was blissfully peaceful as far as Evie was concerned. Her stomach was finally full and she felt reenergized.

Lizbeth rode on Aulis' shoulders as they made their way to the grotto for a swim. She was giggling as he tickled the bottoms of her feet. Evie watched and felt a longing. She had always loved kids, but since she couldn't make a relationship work for more than two days, she had never dreamed of having kids of her own. The thought of a son or daughter with their father's jet black hair and crystal blue gaze brought tears to her eyes. Was she being greedy? Should she dare to hope? She and Aulis hadn't ever had the chance to talk about things like children. She couldn't assume that just because he adored Lizzie he would want kids of his own.

They arrived at the grotto before Aulis caught her studying him. He handed Lizzie to Ari and followed Evie into the water.

"You are looking quite serious – are you having second thoughts about being tied to me already?"

She shook her head. "Actually it's kind of the opposite."

He tilted his head to one side. "What's on your mind? I was serious when I said I always want to know what you are thinking."

"I know, but you might not want to know this time. I'm not sure how you'll feel about what's going through my head right now."

He sat on the beach entry of the water and pulled her into his lap.

"Hey, guys? We'll be right back. Lizzie needs to use the bathroom and I'm going to see if I can find some of that good red wine we had the other night in the cabana." Ari called.

"Sounds good. We'll wait here." Aulis responded over his shoulder. "Now, my love – what's this horrible thing running through your mind?"

She laughed. "It's not really a *horrible* thing, I just don't know what your thoughts are since we've never talked about it."

He sighed. "Evie, just tell me."

"Well..." She looked down at the waves lapping the beach. "I was just watching you with Lizzie and wondered if you had ever wanted kids of your own."

He put a finger under her chin, forcing her to look at him. "Evie, are you saying that you would like to have children? My children?" He wore such a strange expression, she didn't know exactly how to respond.

"Well... Yes... that is – I mean, we've never really had a chance to talk about it." She gathered up her courage and took a deep breath. "Yes, Aulis – I guess that's exactly what I'm saying."

His face was unreadable.

"Come with me." He pulled her with him toward the hidden alcove behind the waterfall.

Evie braced herself for their first argument since he was moving out of earshot of his brother. She passed under the waterfall and wiped the water from her eyes.

Aulis stared at her. "You want to have children someday or are you telling me you want children now?"

"Aulis, I promise I'm not trying to force you into anything. I realize we haven't even been married a whole day yet. We can talk about this later – I don't want to argue with you." Evie attempted to smooth things over.

"Evie, answer my question - truthfully." He demanded.

She came to a decision. He said he wanted to know what she was thinking – so she would tell him.

"Aulis." She began slowly as she worked through exactly what she wanted to say. "I want your baby when you are ready to give it to me. If that is five years from now or this very second – I want it. I've always loved kids but never had a relationship get even close to the point where thinking about my own children was an option."

He stared at her silently.

"Aulis, please say something." She begged.

"It's all I *ever* wanted, and I want to plant my child in you right *now*." He grabbed her and held her in one hand while stripping their swim bottoms off with the other hand. His kiss held a frantic need she had never experienced before; it exploded into her core and spread throughout her entire body, setting it aflame. He alternated worshipping her breasts with his mouth and plucking at her nipples with his deft fingers.

"Oh, Aulis." She moaned.

He grabbed her hips with both hands and impaled her on his cock. His thrusting was frantic, quickly sending them rocketing to their release before starting all over again. It wasn't until they had both climaxed three separate times that he finally released her and gently pulled her bikini and his trunks back into place.

"I'm sorry to be rough with you." He murmured. "You just offered me the one thing I've dreamed of since Ari and I lost our parents so long ago, and I lost control. It's one of the reasons Lizbeth is so incredibly precious to us both. By the gods – I already want you again. I promise I'll wait until we are back in our rooms, if you promise to tell me if you are too sore. I know last night was the first time for you and you are so tiny – I don't want to hurt you."

She held a finger up to his lips. "Stop, I'm not a china doll. I'll let you know if it's too much but if I'm guaranteed orgasms like that, I doubt I'll ever say a word."

He kissed her deeply before pulling her onto his back and swimming back into the lagoon.

"Damn, Aulis, you've got to give her time to breathe." Ari teased.

"No way – not if we're going to start a family right away." Aulis grinned.

"Seriously?" Ari hugged his brother before pulling Evie off Aulis' back and crushing her in a bear hug. "I am so happy for you guys. Lizzie needs a little cousin to play with."

Kimbra extracted Evie from Ari's hug to give her an embrace of her own. "You have no idea how happy you've made him. Aulis has always wanted children – he just never found the woman he wanted to be the mother of those children. You've already seen how amazing he is with Lizbeth."

"She's easy to love... and so is he." Evie said quietly while watching the twin brothers throw each other around the pool, laughing. "While they're preoccupied, is there a bathroom in the cabana?"

"Yes, it's right next to the changing room. Go ahead, I'll let him know where you went."

Evie quietly climbed out of the pool and ran lightly around the corner to the cabana and the bathroom. Moments later, she was much relieved and anxious to rejoin her new family. She glided around the corner of the pathway to the cabana and froze at the sight in front of her.

Dahlia and Niklas had joined their little group at the grotto. Dahlia was in a charcoal grey bikini and had her arms around Aulis' neck, rubbing against him suggestively.

Evie promptly threw up in the bushes at her side. How could he do that after what they had just shared? She would be damned if she would let Dahlia know she had gotten under her skin.

Niklas spotted her as she straightened up and rushed to her side. "Evie, you look stunning. I swear you certainly do justice to the Tuatha style of swimsuits." He eyed her appreciatively.

"Yeah, if you like little girls." Dahlia sneered. "Most men prefer women, right, Aulis?"

Ari handed Lizbeth to Kimbra. "Take her back to our rooms right now. I'll be behind you in just a few minutes."

For once, Kimbra didn't argue at all. She gathered Lizzie in her arms and never looked back.

Evie's heart was pounding so hard, she was sure everyone must be able to hear it.

Niklas had placed an arm around Evie's waist and was stroking the skin just under the bottom of her bikini top.

Ari was torn: Should he help Aulis extract himself from Dahlia so he could deal with Niklas, or should Ari beat the crap out of him right then and there? The panic-stricken look on Evie's face made the decision for him.

He strode toward his sister-in-law. "Come on, Evie, I'll take you back to your rooms."

Evie wanted to reach for his hand but found she couldn't move. Her fear became palpable.

"Why would she want to go back to her rooms? We've got the makings of a great party right here." Niklas laughed.

"Niklas..." Ari's tone was one of pure warning. "Have you forgotten about the law preventing you from using your powers on a human? Especially one under Oberon's protection, not to mention Aulis' wife and *your* future queen?"

"You're right about one thing – she *should* be MY future queen." Niklas sneered.

Evie suddenly knew she'd had all she could stand and summoned every ounce of strength she had – which, she was surprised to find, was more than she'd felt like she had even a couple days before. She backhanded Niklas across the face, drawing blood from his nose. "ENOUGH! I will *not* be controlled by anyone. Do you *hear* me?"

Niklas stared at her in disbelief and calculation; there was no way she should've been able to break through his spell. There was clearly more to her than met the eye, and he was immediately determined to find out what it was.

A splash followed by a scream alerted them all to the fact that Aulis was also free of the spell Niklas and Dahlia had attempted to cast. Niklas had known it wouldn't hold Aulis long, but he'd hoped to be gone with Evie before Aulis broke free.

Ari pulled Evie behind him, and Niklas took the opportunity to disappear. Dahlia was still sputtering in the deep end of the pool. Evie patted Ari on the back and pivoted on one heel to leave.

"Ari, thank you for protecting me – you're the best brother-in-law anyone could ever want. Tell Kimbra I'll come by later. I'm going to my room; I suddenly feel very sick." She hadn't made it two steps before she blacked out.

She awoke in her own bed, nestled in fresh sheets and one of Aulis' T-shirts.

"Are you OK?" Kimbra's voice was full of concern.

"What happened?" Evie gingerly pushed herself to a sitting position.

"Do you want the long or the short story?" Kimbra's mouth turned up on one side.

Evie sighed. "Whichever one provides the most answers."

Kimbra nodded. "The long story it is. Well, I can only assume what was going on behind the waterfall while we had Lizzie in the cabana. Unfortunately, your heritage may have just bit you in the butt... twice."

"What do you mean?"

"Evie, I'm going to ask you a *very* pointed question, and you may not like it, but I need a straight answer." Kimbra looked more serious than Evie had ever seen her.

"Ooo-K." Evie plucked at the bedcovers.

"When you and Aulis were behind the waterfall, how many times did you make love?"

Evie gulped. Kimbra was right – she wasn't crazy about the question, but she wanted answers, and Kimbra was the only one offering to supply them.

"Three."

Kimbra burst out laughing. "Yep, that's what I thought. Stupid men, they never think about what they're doing." Then she sobered. "Evie, this is one of those situations where the Tuatha are very different from what you are accustomed to. When a Tuatha couple decides to have a child, it's *very* easy. All it takes is the consent of both partners and then making love three times in quick succession – usually over a single day. Ari and Aulis apparently are both overachievers in this arena, as that's exactly the same way we got Lizzie. To sum it up for you – you're pregnant."

"*What*?" Evie whispered in wonder. "I'd never been with *anyone* until last night."

Kimbra grimaced. "I wish Aulis had thought of this before. He is Tuatha, you are half – there was a chance that it would happen this quickly. I'm sorry it's such a shock." She patted Evie's hand. "But Tuatha women experience symptoms immediately. There's one more thing – it doesn't take us nearly as long to give birth. Your new little bundle will be here in about four months."

"Oh. Uh..." Evie's eyes threatened to roll back into her head.

Kimbra patted her hand more sharply. "Evie, stay with me – there's more and it's even more critical. Niklas and Dahlia broke multiple laws by trying to put you under a spell. Niklas was undoubtedly hoping to keep Aulis incapacitated just long enough to spirit you away somewhere. Imagine his surprise when you broke his spell quite easily! But now, Evie, he knows you aren't completely human. He still doesn't know your true heritage, but nothing will stop him from ferreting it out. Ari and Aulis are explaining things to Oberon right now."

Evie put her hands over her face. "Kimbra, every time I see that skank writhing all over Aulis, it makes me want to be violently ill. She is tall, thin, and beautiful, and I'm the exact opposite. Now you tell me I'm pregnant and will be huge within the next few weeks! How will I ever be able to hold onto him? I can't even begin to process it all." Tears streamed down Evie's cheeks.

Kimbra hugged Evie tightly. "No, baby, don't cry. I promise you, Aulis doesn't want anything to do with her. I suspect Niklas is stoking the fires to get her to continue pursuing Aulis in an attempt to distract him while Niklas pursues you. There is no way Aulis will think you are anything but stunning while you carry his child." She shook her head. "He has dreamed of a big family for centuries, and now he has a wife he adores who's willing to give him the child he so desperately wants. And I'll let you in on a little secret – Ari and I are expecting as well... as of yesterday. We were going to tell you guys at the grotto and then things got a little crazy. So, sister, we are in this together."

Evie hugged her back. "I'm so grateful that I have you! You're right; our men are stupid not to think of telling me something as important as this." She joked through her tears.

Both women jumped at the sound of the suite door slamming against the wall, revealing Aulis and Ari.

"Evie!" Aulis cried. He rushed across the room and sat on the edge of the bed, taking her hands in his. "Are you OK? I will kill him when I find him."

Kimbra stood up and took Ari by the hand. "Come on, they need some time together."

"What's going on? What do you know, woman?" He teased.

"I'll tell you in our rooms. Don't worry, I'm sure Evie will let Aulis come over and play later." She laughed as she mouthed a message at Evie before closing the bedroom door: "Tell him."

Evie looked at Aulis with tears streaming down her face. "Why didn't you tell me?"

"Tell you what? Evie, please tell me what's going on!"

"Aulis, I don't know how else to say this… You're going to be a father."

"But that's impossible. It only works that way with a… Tuatha." His expression changed from dismissive to disbelieving. "Do you really think it's possible?"

"Kimbra certainly thinks it is. Why didn't you tell me how things work here?"

He was stunned. "My love, I honestly never thought of it since you aren't full Tuatha. We've gone to such lengths to hide your lineage that I had forgotten it myself. What makes Kimbra think she's right?"

Evie groaned. "She said Tuatha show symptoms instantly. As embarrassing as it is to tell you all this, as soon as we emerged from the waterfall I immediately had to use the bathroom." She waved her hand in the air. "Then the moment I saw you with that bitch crawling all over you, I threw up. To complete the trifecta, I passed out as I tried to stalk off angrily. Not only that – she and Ari are expecting too, as of yesterday."

Aulis stared at her with a completely blank expression. "Beloved, there is only one way we can be completely sure. You're going to think I'm making this up, but I promise it's our way."

Evie groaned again. "Do I even want to ask?"

"What if it was something that promised you another mind-blowing orgasm?" He raised an eyebrow at her.

"Are you *serious*? If I find out later that you're full of crap, I'm going to get you."

"I'm quite serious. I would be able to instantly sense my own child."

Evie pulled the T-shirt over her head. "Let's do this – I have to know one way or another."

Aulis was instantly hard. He peeled off his wet swim trunks and flicked her nipples with his tongue. Evie was immediately wet; how did he manage to make her want him with a single flick of his tongue? He continued to suckle and then take as much of her breast as he could into his mouth. Evie arched toward him. She was almost frantic for him to enter her and desperately needed to feel him inside of her.

"Aulis." She whispered his name.

"Yes, my love." He reached between them and lazily rolled her bud between his fingers, setting her body on fire.

"Aulis, please."

"Trust me, my love." He whispered. "I'm going to enjoy every last second of this – child or not."

He proceeded to make good on his word, wiping away all the pain from Niklas and Dahlia's actions in the grotto. His lips trailed from her breasts across her stomach and down to her inner thigh, where he bit and licked. Her legs shook as he suckled on her bud and she begged him not to stop. He pulled back and inserted one finger, but Evie knew she was more ready for him than she'd ever been. He removed his finger and ran his rock-hard erection against her inner thigh before positioning it against her bud and sliding into her sheath. He suddenly went completely still and stared at her, wide-eyed.

"Kimbra was right."

From that point on his lovemaking was fast and furious. He no longer had control over himself and could think of nothing but burying himself further into his wife. After Evie experienced her third orgasm, Aulis allowed himself to roar his release. He stayed perfectly still, enjoying every last flutter and contraction of her inner muscles, before he gently laid his head on her stomach. "I love you."

As Evie fell into a deep sleep, she wasn't sure if he had been talking to her or their unborn child.

18 A NEW DAY

Evie opened her eyes as the sun blazed through the room. What time was it? It had to be late afternoon or early evening. Aulis' arms were still wrapped tightly around her stomach. It had certainly been one hell of a week. She went from working for an asshole boss and having no romantic prospects at all to being married to a warrior, finding out the identity of her father, and now discovering she was pregnant. How would she possibly explain this to her mother and aunt? Hell, according to Kimbra, it would be plainly obvious to everyone within just a few weeks. She quietly disentangled herself from Aulis' embrace and allowed her feet to slide to the floor.

Aulis' eyes snapped open. "What's wrong?"

Evie grimaced and blew a stray lock of hair out of her face. "Nothing, I just need to use the restroom. I could also use something to eat." She said apologetically. She didn't want to look like a pig.

He leapt out of his bed to his feet. "Anything you want. Go ahead and I'll pick something out for you to wear, and then we'll go find something to eat to tide you over. It's getting pretty close to dinner anyway."

"Sounds good." Clearly she had slept longer than she realized.

Evie quickly relieved herself and then stood naked in front of the full-length mirror. She ran her palms over her still-flat stomach, having a hard time believing she was carrying their child. Things were moving so quickly. She'd only been married for a day, and now she had to adjust to the idea of being a parent in just a few short months. She couldn't deny that she wanted the baby; she only hoped she would be a good parent.

Aulis rapped quietly on the door. "Evie, are you all right?"

Evie opened the door. "Yeah, I'm OK. It's just a lot to take in."

He gently caressed her stomach. "I know exactly what you mean. I got everything I ever dreamed of in the span of a couple of days. As you say, I keep waiting to wake up."

Aulis pulled a loose-fitting, emerald-green maxi dress over her head.

It was unbelievably comfortable; the only place it held her was where the straps rested on her shoulders.

"You think of everything, don't you? I don't know how you manage it." She mused.

"Actually, I have to give credit to Kimbra for this one. She had this sent over while you slept." He grinned.

Evie grabbed Aulis' hands in panic. "What are we going to tell everyone? If what Kimbra told me is true, we can't hide this for very long. In my world, it takes almost a year before a child is born – and here it's only four months. Can we even have everything ready in that time? We just got married, and haven't had time to really get to know each other, and soon we'll have another person to learn. What if I'm a bad parent — or spouse?"

Aulis gathered her into his arms. "Calm down, my love. I love you and that's all I need to know. I'm already completely in love with our child, who will have everything they could possibly need. We are accustomed to the short gestation time here, and I will have the craftsmen start work on a cradle immediately. You are a kind, beautiful person, inside and out; you will be a wonderful mother." He kissed the top of her head.

"As far as everyone else – we'll just have to tell them the truth. I'm afraid that your lineage may have been given away this afternoon anyway, first by breaking Niklas' and Dahlia's spell and now with the news of our little addition. I've already talked with Oberon, and he thinks it's best to simply come clean with everyone about your father. He would rather the people hear it directly from him than for Niklas and his men to start spreading rumors.

"Now, that being said – once the announcement is made, you will no longer be free to move around the grounds by yourself. You will need to have an escort of some sort at all times to ensure your safety until we can locate Niklas and get him under guard. The laws he broke today were major, and he *will* be punished for them. Unfortunately, Niklas slipped away while Ari and I were taking care of you and restraining Dahlia and he has gone into hiding. We'll find him; it's just going to take a little time." He lifted her chin. "Can you do this for me?"

"Yes, I can. I have a warning of my own, though – I cannot be held responsible for my own actions around Dahlia any longer."

"Fair enough – as long as your actions don't put you or the baby in harm's way." He chuckled. "Now let's go find you a snack and work out how we are going to break our news to everyone at dinner."

Evie happily munched on the cookies Aulis had procured for her as they strolled through the gardens and sat on the edge of a fountain.

"Hey, little sister, you look a lot better than the last time I saw you." Ari strode forward and hugged her tightly. He gestured to his wife. "Kimbra had a really interesting theory about why you weren't feeling well earlier." He stared at her. "Anything you two want to share with the class?"

Evie stared at him with wide-eyed innocence. "No, nothing I can think of. Do you have any news for him, Aulis?"

"Nope; he was in the meeting with Oberon and me earlier today, so he knows everything."

Ari's expression was crestfallen. "No news then?"

"Oh –" Evie pointed at him. "There is one *little* thing."

Aulis attempted to stifle a laugh.

"Something about a new cousin for Lizbeth." Evie said casually.

"I *knew* it! Kimbra is absolutely *never* wrong." He picked Evie up and swung her in a wide circle.

"Ari, put her down before you make her throw up." Kimbra rolled her eyes.

Ari was immediately contrite. "Oh, right. I'm so sorry, are you OK?"

"Yes, I'm fine; I didn't drop my cookies." Evie was determined not to grin at her own pun. "Feel free to swing Aulis around if you want."

"Woo-hoo!" Ari cried and proceeded to try to swing his twin around.

Evie embraced Kimbra and handed her a cookie. "Thank you – for everything. Clearly you were right. I appreciate the dress more than you can know. I apologize in advance, since I will probably lean on you pretty heavily over the next couple of months." She admitted sheepishly.

"Don't think another thing about it. These are my favorite dresses to wear when I'm expecting. I'll have several more sent up for you until we can go shopping."

Evie glanced around. "Where's Lizzie?"

Kimbra waved a hand. "Oh, she's playing with some of the other children in the nursery. Ari and I wanted to talk with the two of you freely without worrying about Lizzie shrieking about the new baby ...or babies, I should say." She patted her stomach lovingly.

"Dinner should be interesting tonight – that's for sure. You guys should probably announce your news first, since the news of who I *really* am will probably set the entire castle aflame."

Kimbra giggled. "You're probably right about that. Have you two told anyone yet?"

"No, we decided to surprise everyone at the same time. I can't even imagine how my mother is going to react to all of this. She's still so afraid of the men who took her and, ultimately, my father."

Ari slung an arm over her shoulder. "I bet she will be thrilled. How can she *not* be excited about her first grandbaby?"

"You've got a point there. My mother adores children." Evie gestured to Kimbra. "You saw how she was with Lizbeth the night of the wedding."

Kimbra nodded and smiled. "Yes, and Lizzie is still singing the song Colleen taught her."

Aulis came to stand at Evie's side and caressed her arm. "Evie, I don't feel right about Oberon, Colleen, and Winnie finding out about the baby with everyone else. I think we should go seek them out in Oberon's rooms and escort them to dinner. Kimbra, Ari, will you two join us?"

"We wouldn't miss it." They chimed in unison.

The four walked along the long marble hallways to the double-doors of Oberon's rooms. Aulis rapped on the door, and they were immediately admitted by Oberon's guard.

"Hello, Aulis, we were just about to head down to dinner." Oberon called from another room.

"We thought we would join you." Aulis replied.

"We?" Oberon poked his head around the corner and saw both couples. He rushed forward to hug Evie. "Are you all right? Ari and Aulis came to me this afternoon and told me of Niklas and Dahlia's treachery. I assure you that these deeds will not go unpunished." He searched her face and noted the anxiety he found there. "Aulis told you of my plan to reveal our kinship." It was a statement and not a question.

Evie nodded. "Are my mother and Winnie with you?" She scanned the room.

"Yes, they are. Colleen? Winnie?" He called out.

"Are we ready?" The two women emerged from the balcony to find the young couples waiting.

Colleen ran forward and embraced Evie for a long moment. "I knew there was something about Niklas that I didn't really trust. He reminds me of the man, Stanis, who abducted me in the woods so long ago. They have the same eyes."

Oberon's head snapped up. "Colleen, why didn't you say something before?"

She shrugged. "I didn't want to seem paranoid."

Oberon hugged her fiercely. "No, that's the best news I've had in months."

Ari grinned. "I bet our news is better."

All eyes turned to him.

"Well, my boy – out with it." Oberon grinned.

"Lizbeth is going to be a big sister."

Oberon clapped him on the back and hugged Kimbra as Colleen and

Winnie clapped their hands excitedly.

"I am very happy for both of you," the king said. "If this next one is even half as cute as Lizzie, we're all in trouble."

Aulis cleared his throat. "There's more."

Oberon's eyebrows drew together as he waited for the news.

Evie reached for Aulis' hand and blushed furiously.

Aulis reached out to caress Evie's stomach. "I'm going to be a father." The pride rang clear in his voice.

Colleen gasped.

Winnie whooped with laughter. "Well, you two didn't waste any time, did you?" She teased.

Evie's face grew redder until Oberon took her hands in his. "I promise you that we will have your father back in time to meet his first grandchild."

A single tear rolled down Evie's cheek. "Thank you, Uncle Oberon. It would mean the world to me." She tugged at the material of her dress. "Mom? Please say something."

Colleen's eyes brightened as her smile threatened to split her face. "Oh, Evie. It's a dream come true. I've always wanted a grandbaby to spoil rotten. I only worry about the danger of the impending war."

Aulis pulled Evie into his arms protectively. "No one will touch her, or our child." He promised.

Oberon rubbed his goatee. "I guess it's a good thing we already decided to make the announcement about Evie tonight. Considering her condition, no one would believe she was completely human anyway. Well, let's go have some dinner and turn the kingdom on its ear." He held out an arm for Colleen and Winnie and led the group to the dining hall.

Lizbeth's nanny was waiting at the door. "She was a complete doll – as always." She gave the little girl one more squeeze and headed to a table inside.

Ari scooped his daughter into his arms. "Hi, baby girl. Did you have fun today?"

"Yes, Daddy." She grabbed his face and blew a raspberry on his cheek. Evie saw the longing in Aulis' face and was thrilled she would be the one to give him the child he wanted.

Aulis was incredibly attentive at dinner, even going so far as to cut her meat for her. He waved off the page bearing nectar and instead drank water out of respect for Evie. She glanced at Ari and noticed he treated Kimbra with the same tenderness and consideration. It was the first time she had witnessed the twins acting alike.

"Aulis, you don't have to spoil me like this. You need to relax so you can enjoy your meal as well. You've hardly touched your dinner, and it's absolutely amazing."

"My love, you are giving me a most precious gift, and I can give you very little in return." He placed his hand over his heart. "I will do everything I can to make sure you are completely pampered for the next several months." He kissed her hand.

Evie sighed contentedly. How did she get so lucky?

Oberon rose and tapped his knife against his crystal goblet for everyone's attention. "Thank you for your attention. Last night we witnessed the marriage of Aulis and Evie."

The room burst into applause. He had to pause until it died down enough for him to be heard.

"Tonight I have some additional announcements." The applause gradually fell silent. "As you know, my brother, Lyrr, has been missing for some time. What you *don't* know is that Lyrr sired a child before he was taken captive. The child and her human mother went into hiding, apparently right under our very noses."

The room buzzed with excitement.

"Now Lyrr's child has come home to us."

The citizens of Tuatha scanned the room and craned their necks, wanting to have the first glimpse of their beloved Lyrr's child. Evie gulped and fought to remain calm. She noticed Taarmo had slowly made his way around the room and now stood at her back along with two other men she recognized from Winnie's yard.

Oberon finally continued. "Evie, wife to our Aulis, is Lyrr's only child and the rightful heir to the throne – which only further strengthens Aulis and Evie's position as our future king and queen."

After a split second of stunned silence, cheering erupted in all corners of the room.

Oberon held up his hands. "Wait a minute – that is not all." He turned to Aulis. "Do you want to share your news with your people?"

Aulis stood next to Oberon and took Evie's hand to help her to her feet. "I am thrilled to share with you that we will have a new little royal in just a few short months. Evie and I are expecting."

After another thunderstruck moment, the room erupted into another tumult of cheers. Evie looked at all the smiling faces and realized how much these people truly loved her father. She was so overwhelmed by the acceptance of an extended family she'd never known that tears flowed freely down her cheeks. Aulis wiped her tears and kissed her deeply while placing his hand protectively over her stomach. Evie wouldn't have thought it was possible, but the cheering grew even louder.

Aulis glanced over Evie's head at his twin. "So do you want to share your news while we're here?"

"Hell, yes." Ari grinned.

"Quiet, please." Aulis' voice boomed with the authority of a man who had commanded armies for years. "We're not done yet."

The room immediately silenced in anticipation.

Ari stood and pulled Kimbra to her feet before lifting Lizbeth to stand in the chair between them. "If one new Tuatha is reason to celebrate, then two should be even better, right?"

The cheers grew deafening. Evie could clearly see how the people of Tuatha loved the two brothers as well.

Lizbeth tugged on her father's sleeve. "Daddy, why is everyone yelling?"

"Lizzie, what would you say if Mommy and I told you that you were going to be a big sister?"

She jumped up and down frantically. "A baby! A baby! We get a new baby!" She turned and jumped into Evie's arms. "Ebbie, Ima be a big sister!"

"I know, and you are going to be the best big sister ever! Uncle Aulis and I are having a baby too, so you are going to have a new little cousin. You're going to have to show the babies how to do all the things you know how to do."

Lizzie let out a high-pitched shriek and jumped at Aulis. "Unca Owie, you're gonna be a daddy!! I so excited!"

It took a while for the room to calm down. Once Evie was seated, Taarmo leaned between the seats and clasped arms with Aulis. "Congratulations to you both! There isn't a single child within Tuatha De who will be loved more than yours – or one that is better protected. I pledge my life to the safety of your child here and now."

Aulis clapped his lieutenant on the shoulder. "You have no idea how much that means to me. You aren't just a member of my guard, but part of our family, and welcome in our home anytime."

Evie leaned over and kissed Taarmo on the cheek. "I hope that someday you get everything you've ever dreamed of." She told him quietly. "Thank you for taking such good care of me."

His face reddened and he straightened up. "You are going to be a highly popular and well-loved queen, you know that?"

Evie smiled up at him before suddenly squirming uncomfortably in her seat.

"What's wrong?" Aulis was incredibly in tune to her feelings.

"I really need to use the bathroom." She responded, red-faced.

"Come on, I'll take you."

Evie put a hand on his shoulder, holding him in his seat. "OK, Aulis, I have to draw the line at you escorting me to the bathroom. I'm not a toddler or an invalid."

"Evie, I already explained that you wouldn't be able to roam freely until we had Niklas in custody."

"Aulis!" She wailed. "I've got to have some independence or I will lose my sanity. Surely I'm not in any danger going to the bathroom here in the castle?"

Kimbra leaned over. "Aulis, I really need to go as well. We can escort each other – looks like we're going to be on the same bathroom cycle for a while." She grinned.

Aulis continued to grumble but finally relented after escorting them to the doorway of the dining hall. "Just call if you need anything; I'll be right here waiting."

"And so will I." Ari stood shoulder to shoulder with his twin. They formed a veritable wall of muscle and power.

"If one of us accidentally falls in, you guys will be the first to know." Kimbra wrinkled her nose at them.

The two women scurried down the hallway to the bathroom, Kimbra leading the way. Evie finished first and waited, leaning against a wall. She was suddenly overcome by a wave of nausea as a hot flash ran through her entire body. The bathroom was too stuffy; she needed some air before she passed out.

"Kimbra, I'm going to wait just outside the door. I'm not feeling so great. I'm burning up."

"One sec, Evie. I'm right behind you." Kimbra called, but Evie couldn't wait long enough to hear her.

Evie burst through the door, taking gulps of air, and almost ran headfirst into Niklas, who was standing with his arms crossed just a few steps from the door.

"Congratulations. Pregnancy agrees with you; you have a glow about you." Niklas' voice washed over her like a suffocating oil slick. "So, Lyrr has a child – who knew? No one ever breathed a word about it – which is probably a good thing since a war would have been waged for your hand in marriage alone. Now that you are carrying a royal heir, you are even more valuable."

Evie opened her mouth to scream but found she had no voice. She was hit with wave after wave of nausea until she was fighting not to be sick right where she stood.

Niklas continued relentlessly. "It's a shame Dahlia bungled things so badly, even with the spell I had cast on her; her will was stronger than I anticipated, just as yours was. Now that she knows I was manipulating her, she's no longer of any use to me. You, however, are a different matter altogether. I will treat you like the princess we know you are, and I will show you how a *real* man makes love to his woman."

Evie shook like a leaf, her hands pressed to her stomach.

Kimbra opened the door to the bathroom, saw Niklas, and summoned her husband with a blood-curdling scream.

"I should've known they wouldn't leave you completely alone." Niklas sighed in vexation. "I guess we'll have to finish our conversation another time. You *will* be mine, little princess; don't ever doubt that." He ran his hands in a caress over both women's stomachs as he melted into the darkness.

19 INTRUDER

Ari and Aulis raced toward the sound of Kimbra's voice, Taarmo and a full complement of the guard on their heels. Aulis was mere steps away when Niklas vanished into thin air, but not before Aulis caught his final threat.

"By the *GODS*! That son of a bitch was right here in the castle, not twelve inches from my pregnant wife! How in the *hell* did he get in here? I want the guard details doubled around Evie *and* Kimbra!" Aulis roared with such force that the chords in his neck stood out against his skin.

Evie took one look at Aulis and burst into tears. All she knew was that she'd needed him and he'd come. She couldn't help but feel that if she had waited for Kimbra, none of this would've happened. The guilt wasn't the only thing choking her; why was Kimbra able to scream when she, Evie, was unable to make any sound at all? She'd certainly been able to break the spell at the grotto.

The sight of Evie's tearstained face sent Aulis over the edge. He swept her into his arms and strode directly for their rooms. He kicked the door shut, sat in a large, overstuffed chair, and settled Evie into his lap. He pulled her against his chest and caressed her hair in an attempt to comfort her as she drenched the front of his shirt. "I am so sorry, my love. I should've known better than to let my guard down even for a second."

"No – no, it was all my fault." Evie shook her head. "I should've swallowed my pride and let you walk me down there, or at the very least, I could've waited until Kimbra was ready to leave. It was just so hot and stuffy in there all of the sudden; I felt like I had to get air."

"Evie, you should've been safe with Kimbra here in the castle. The nausea you described is not your fault – Niklas created that to draw you out." He explained gently. "I need to know exactly what he said to you."

Evie relayed what Niklas had said, word for word, and watched as Aulis' knuckles turned white and his voice turned to stone.

"If he thinks he will possess a single strand of your hair, he's even crazier than I originally thought. This is no longer some juvenile

143

competition between us; he now thinks he can use you to get the throne. Did he touch you?" He searched her eyes for the truth.

She shook her head again. "He barely grazed my stomach with his hand as he disappeared. I tried to scream for you, but I couldn't make any sound come out; it was like the nightmares I used to have as a child. If it weren't for Kimbra, I don't know what might've happened." She burst into tears again.

Aulis held tight to the tiny woman in his arms and silently planned a thousand painful deaths for Niklas.

The heavy door to their suite abruptly crashed into the stone wall, and Aulis tightened his arms around Evie to keep her from bolting from the room.

"How is she?" Oberon demanded as Winnie and Colleen raced in behind him.

"Damn it, don't *any* of you know how to come into a room like a normal person?" Evie screamed.

"Looks like she's in good hands." Winnie chuckled. Colleen stood just inside the door, wringing her hands.

Evie squirmed until Aulis allowed her to stand. She hurried over to her mother and wrapped her arms around the shaking woman.

"I thought they had taken you like your father." Colleen whispered.

"Mom, it's OK. No one even touched me, thanks to Kimbra's big mouth." She attempted to lighten her mother's mood. If her mother knew the truth – that Niklas had been close enough and *had* touched her – Evie worried her mother could come unhinged.

Oberon chuckled. "We are *all* thankful for Kimbra's big mouth right now. As a matter of fact, I expect her and Ari to arrive any second."

"Someone call my name?" Ari questioned as he led Kimbra into the room, Lizzie in her arms.

"As a matter of fact, we were all just saying how grateful we were for your wife's big mouth." Oberon winked.

"Glad I could be of service." Kimbra quipped.

"Actually, I'm glad you're all here." Oberon turned and called over his shoulder. "Taarmo, I need you to watch the door – no one gets within earshot."

"Yes, sir." Taarmo replied smartly and pulled the heavy door shut with a reassuring thud.

"Now, I've come to a very difficult decision." The king continued. "This last attempt within my own castle has made up my mind. Aulis, you are going to take Evie back to her world."

"The *hell* I am!" Aulis roared.

"Wait until I finish." Oberon ordered sternly. "You are going to take

Evie back to her world and stay at her little house. It would be a good opportunity for her to wrap up any loose ends before she joins us permanently. I'm sure there are things there that are important to her – family photos, mementos, etc. Colleen and Winnie will return to Winnie's house, and I'll have them contact you when you can return here. I am certain now that it was Niklas' family who took Lyrr, and we are finally going after them."

"Are you sure it was his family?" Aulis' tone was cautious. He wanted nothing more than to reunite Evie with her father, but he didn't want to get her hopes up unnecessarily.

"Yes; it was something Colleen said earlier. She recognized Niklas because he looks just like his *father,* Stanis – the man who abducted her years ago and who disappeared shortly after Lyrr. It all makes sense now. I'm leaving Ari in charge here with a guard detail, and I'm taking the rest with me to bring Lyrr home."

Colleen burst into tears and placed a shaking hand on Oberon's sleeve. "Do you really think you can find him?"

"Yes, and I will bring him home to you, your daughter, and his grandchild." He smiled at her reassuringly.

"Evie?" Winnie's voice held an edge of amusement. "You should definitely take Aulis when you go in to give your notice."

Evie's eyes narrowed against laughter; she loved her aunt's sense of humor. "Oh, most definitely. I can't *wait* to see Sean's face when he gets an eyeful of Aulis."

"Who is this Sean?" Aulis' tone carried an echo of jealousy.

"He's my boss and the reason I ended up at Winnie's in the first place." Her hands clenched into fists. "He's manipulated me and treated me like a slave the entire time I've worked for him: stealing my ideas, making me work weekends and holidays while he goes to the lake – you name it."

"Oh, yes, I look forward to meeting him." Aulis' smile was more of a baring of teeth.

"So it's settled." Oberon said. "Aulis, I want you to head out immediately. The only people who know of this plan are in this room and, of course, Taarmo. Aulis, watch Evie closely in her world. I have no idea how being back in her world may affect her health and the baby. Her symptoms may become more pronounced."

"Great." Evie grumbled. "More nausea is exactly what I was hoping for."

Kimbra handed Lizzie to her father and grabbed Evie by the hand. "Wait, I had some dresses sent up here earlier. You'll definitely want to take them with you. Like a true Tuatha, you will find your clothes become tighter by the day." She led Evie into the closet where she pulled out several lovely dresses in different colors, some with straps, some halters and some strapless.

Evie threw her arms around Kimbra. "What would I do without you? You've come to my rescue time after time."

Kimbra giggled. "Don't think anything of it. I'm so happy to have you around and to finally have a partner in crime against those two stubborn colossi."

Aulis and Ari walked up and the two women dissolved into laughter.

"Do you get the feeling they are laughing at us?" Ari asked with a furrowed brow.

"What else?" Aulis chuckled.

He took a large duffle bag from the closet, carefully folding Evie's dresses and placing them inside. Then he stared blankly at his clothes hanging in the closet. "I have no idea what is considered appropriate in your world."

Evie walked to the low-hanging bars and pulled shorts and cargo pants from the hangers. She pointed to the upper bars. "Any of those shirts are fine, but I'd need a ladder to get them down for you."

"No problem; I can handle that." Aulis reached over her head and plucked several shirts from the hangers. "Anything else we need we can buy in your world."

"Yeah, I guess I won't need my bank account anymore." Evie sighed. She had worked so hard to save what little money she had.

"No, I have plenty of money; there is no reason to use what you have earned. And shopping will help us kill time. Maybe we can find some things for the babies and Lizzie?"

Evie brightened. "Oh, I would love that. Maybe we can donate the things from my house that I don't need to charity? Fortunately the lease on my house is up next month. I'll just need to write a quick letter and mail one last check to my landlord."

"Anything you want. We'd better get going though. I want you to get some sleep tonight, and we still have quite a drive to your house, right?"

Evie grimaced. The thought of being stuck in the car for the ninety-minute drive home made her cringe; they would probably have to stop ten times for her to use the bathroom. She reached down to grab the handle of the bag, only to have Aulis bat her hand away.

"Are you kidding?" He snorted before slinging the bag over his shoulder.

Evie rushed to hug Ari and his family. She hated leaving them, but she assured herself that they would be back soon and promised Lizzie lots of presents when they returned.

"I'm going to create the portal right here in this room. I don't want to risk anyone seeing you all leaving." Oberon explained.

Evie automatically visualized the wall of shimmering air from the forest near Winnie's house, and it abruptly came into focus in the middle of the room.

Oberon jumped backwards. "Evie, did you do that?"

She stared at him blankly. *Had* she done it? She shrugged her shoulders.

Aulis caressed her hair like he always did to calm her nerves. "Evie, what were you thinking about just now?"

"I just thought about the portal we saw in the forest and how pretty it was."

"Well, my love, take a good look at *your* first portal."

Her mouth dropped open in disbelief. "I did this? How?"

Oberon stroked his goatee. "Apparently you are even more like your father than we thought. Aulis, you need to watch her like a hawk. It would seem our little Evie has some latent abilities, and she'll need to be taught how to use them."

"Abilities?" Evie gulped.

Aulis wrapped an arm around her waist. "I'll explain it all later. Shall we go?"

Evie nodded and they entered the portal, followed by Colleen and Winnie. They stepped out onto the soft grass of Winnie's yard, only steps from the back door; Aulis quickly ushered everyone inside.

"Colleen, I need to get Evie away from here as soon as possible. It is much safer for you to remain here with Winnie than to go to your home alone. Evie and I can grab anything you need. If Oberon is successful in his mission, you may not want to leave anyway." He winked.

Colleen blushed before putting a finger in the middle of Aulis' chest. "You'd better take good care of her. You have no idea what she means to me, and I promise you, there will be hell to pay if something happens to her."

He hugged the tiny woman. "Yes, ma'am. I feel the same way."

They quickly said their goodbyes and got everything stashed into Evie's car. Aulis took the keys before settling her into the front seat."You can drive?" She asked incredulously.

"It's not my first time in your world." He said quietly, but Evie caught the slight hesitation.

"Who was she?" Evie demanded.

He chuckled. "You."

"*Me*?!"

"Oh, yes. I've been watching you since the night you ran barefoot through Winnie's woods. You fascinated me, and I couldn't get enough. I didn't know how you knew Winnie, only that you were stunning, streaking through the woods with your hair streaming out behind you." His face reddened but the memory still made him smile.

"You could've said something sooner and saved us a lot of time." She grinned back.

He put the car into drive and they headed off. She looked at the display on her car and realized it was already Monday night. She grunted. She had to return to work the next day. Suddenly her outlook brightened; she had to go into the office only long enough to tell Sean where to shove it, and then never look back.

Her eyelids grew heavier with each mile. When she became aware that the car had stopped, she opened her eyes and realized they were parked in her driveway. "Oh, Aulis, I'm so sorry. It must've been such a boring drive."

"Not at all. I was relieved to see you get some sleep." He said as they got out of the car and he grabbed the duffle. "It's been a very hard day for you. Let's get your bag inside and then go to bed."

Evie yawned. "I think you're onto something there. I can hardly keep my eyes open."

He turned the key in the lock and pushed her front door open. Evie looked around at the house, grimaced at the amount of work she faced to pack it all up, and trudged into the bedroom. Aulis dropped the bag onto the floor with a thud and grinned at her modest queen-sized bed; it was a far cry from the enormous bed in his suite. "Good thing we're tired – this thing would never stand up to our lovemaking."

Evie giggled and headed into the bathroom. "You're probably right. I'm looking forward to getting back home to our room and our bed."

"Not nearly as much as I am." He called at her retreating back.

Evie emerged feeling completely refreshed and dug in her dresser for a long nightshirt. She quickly changed clothes and slid into bed, where Aulis pulled her into his open arms. Within seconds she fell into a deep, dreamless sleep.

She banged her fist on the snooze button when her alarm clock went off. Was it that time already? She had to get ready for work. She swung her legs over the bed and raced to the bathroom to empty her bladder, which was dangerously close to overflowing. Afterward she glanced at her reflection in the mirror.

"Holy shit!" She cried.

Immediately awake, Aulis bounded across the room and yanked the door open. "What's wrong?" He was completely alert – a skill he'd developed after years of training.

She slowly turned to face him and lifted the hem of her nightshirt, revealing a tiny mound protruding from her stomach. She looked like she was three or four months pregnant after just a couple days. Kimbra wasn't kidding about her clothes becoming tighter each day! Evie was thankful they had packed the dresses, since most of her clothes wouldn't fit her any longer.

Aulis stunned her by dropping to his knees and placing a kiss over her swollen stomach. "Do you feel OK? Can I get you anything?"

"No, I'm fine." She shook her head. "But I can see why Kimbra insisted I bring the dresses. I've got to get dressed for work – and hopefully no one throws a fit about what I'm wearing. Oberon had better be quick about finding my dad, or this baby is going to be born here and I have *no* idea how we'd explain that to the doctors."

"Sweetheart, you're only going in to quit and get your things. Who cares what they think about your dress?" He smiled while he addressed each of her concerns. "We'll just have to trust in Oberon to get things done quickly. Worst-case scenario, we'll sneak you back to Tuatha De to have our baby. Now, let's get this over with so we can go shopping for you and the baby."

Evie smiled back at him. "How can I turn that down? Can we fit breakfast into that equation somewhere? I'm starving!"

"Without question, we'll do that first – anything you want."

"I'm so glad you feel that way. I guess it doesn't really matter if I'm on time to work or not. There's a great place a few minutes away that does a skillet breakfast that sounds amazing right now."

"A *skillet breakfast*?"

Evie laughed at the face he was making. "Yeah, it has diced potatoes, onions, tomatoes, bacon, cheese, and it's all topped with eggs. Just wait, you'll love it."

He raised an eyebrow before cracking a grin. "I'll trust you on this. Now let's get dressed."

Deciding they were too hungry to take the time to shower, they took turns splashing water on their faces and brushing their teeth in the small bathroom. Aulis pulled a pair of cargo shorts and a black fitted T-shirt out of his bag. Evie selected a royal purple dress with a halter neckline. She pulled the dress over her head and quickly realized her stomach wasn't the only thing to have swollen; her bustline had increased as well – a fact that didn't go unappreciated by her husband.

Aulis reached around to cup her breasts and run his thumbs over her nipples. She gasped with pleasure heightened by the added sensitivity brought on by her pregnancy. Aulis was instantly rock hard, and his erection rubbed the cleft in her backside. With one hand he grabbed a fistful of material, pulling the hem of her dress up around her waist before sliding his hand under the waistband of her panties. He caressed her bud in long, languorous strokes until her legs shook. She had never wanted him so badly – was it a side effect of her pregnancy as well?

She whirled around and pulled his head down to hers, kissing him frantically while stroking the massive bulge in the front of his shorts. He'd never finished buttoning his shorts so she slipped her hand inside. He pulled the dress over her head with one hand before letting his shorts fall to the floor. He carefully laid her on the bed while devouring her with his eyes.

"Take me now. I need you." Her voice was hoarse with need.

He took his shaft in his hand, rubbing it across her bud until she thrashed against the pillows, then plunged inside her to the hilt. She met him stroke for stroke until they both screamed their release. The moment her tremors ended, she was stunned by the realization that she wanted him again. She threw a leg over either side of him, straddling him. She reached between them and rubbed his semi-hard cock on her opening. Before she could get him fully inside, her stomach rumbled loudly.

Grinning salaciously, Aulis jumped out of bed and set her feet on the floor. "As much as I would like to stay under you in this bed all day, we need to get you something to eat."

He handed her panties and dress to her and pulled his shorts over his hips, fastening them quickly. Within seconds he was fully dressed; the T-shirt showed off all the muscles in his chest and arms. They hopped into the car and Evie directed them to the restaurant. After they parked he rushed to her door to help her out, intertwining his fingers with hers and leading her inside. Evie stifled a chuckle when the hostess was unable to do anything for several moments but stare open-mouthed at Aulis.

"It's just the two of us." Evie finally stared pointedly at all the open tables.

"Oh, I'm so sorry. Yes, please follow me." The hostess stammered and tripped over her own feet in her haste.

If this was the reaction they would get everywhere they went in her world, Evie knew it would be a huge test of her self-control; she felt self-conscious and overemotional, and the first woman to touch him would probably pull back a bloody nub. She breathed a sigh of relief when their waiter came to the table.

"Hi, I'm Steve, and I'll be your server today. What can I get for you to drink?"

"Actually, I'd really like some orange juice – you can bring a big carafe."

"And you, sir?" He turned to Aulis.

"I'll just drink whatever she's having."

"No problem; I'll get it right out for you." He patted Evie on the hand and walked away.

Aulis pushed back from the table. Evie blinked and put her hand on his shoulder. "Where are you going?" She asked nervously.

"I want to know why he felt the need to touch you."

"Honey, you have to understand that's very common in this world – especially in the South and, for some weird reason, especially pregnant women. No one thinks anything about someone touching their hand or arm. Now, if he had taken me in his arms and embraced me, it would've freaked me out."

"If he had done that, I would've killed him." He said simply.

Steve came back to the table with the carafe and two glasses. "Do you know what you would like to order?" Something in Aulis' eyes made him take an involuntary step back.

Evie nodded. "Yes, can you please bring each of us the *Wanderer* skillet?"

"Very good; do you want them with everything?"

"Absolutely. Also, can you please bring out the toast as soon as it's ready?"

He looked at her strangely. "Um, OK. You don't want it with your meal?"

"Sorry, I'm starving." She shrugged.

Aulis leaned forward; his entire body was tense. "My wife is pregnant and hungry. Please bring her the toast she asked for."

Steve was immediately contrite. "I am so sorry. Oh, of course. I'll get it immediately." He hurried off and returned quickly with a plate piled high with toast and rack full of different flavors of jelly.

Evie smacked Aulis on the shoulder. "Be nice."

"I didn't like the way he looked at you; it was disrespectful." He groused.

Evie grabbed a piece of toast and spread a thick layer of grape jelly on it. "You know, it's going to be a very difficult visit here if we can't learn to control our jealousy." She bit into the toast and licked her lips.

Aulis stared at her thoughtfully. "You are jealous of other women? I don't understand. Why?"

Evie polished off the piece of toast. "Are you *kidding* me? Take a good, long look in the mirror. I think you'll notice that most men in my world don't look anything like you. When you walk down the street near where I work, I half-expect it to rain down women's undergarments."

Aulis roared with laughter. "I have to say that creates a very interesting mental picture. However, my love, I don't see anyone but you. It's that simple."

Evie snorted while putting jelly on a second piece of toast. "That's easy enough to say in here where we're surrounded by senior citizens. Wait until we get to my office where there are girls in their 20s running around in skinny jeans and low-cut tops. Then you're going to glance over at me with my newly rounded figure and realize you have better options."

He grabbed her face with both hands. "Listen to me – there is nothing they could give me that would be more important than you and our child. As far as I'm concerned, no one else exists but you." He released her face and caressed her hair. "I will admit that I'm a little concerned with how this world is affecting your pregnancy and the speed in which it's evolving. Even in my world, you wouldn't have developed quite this far yet. It's part of why I'm so anxious right now."

She caressed his cheek. "Don't worry, I feel fine. Of course, I'm still hungry and I have to run to the bathroom all the time, but other than that – it's all good."

"Two *Wanderers* – here you go." Steve placed the dishes in front of them.

"Thank you." Evie replied as Aulis' expression darkened.

"Can I get you anything else?" Steve looked like he couldn't wait to leave their table.

"No, I think I have everything I need right here."

The moment Steve left their table she turned to glare at Aulis. "What did I tell you about being nice?"

"He was staring at your top." He growled.

"Aulis!" She exclaimed, exasperated, "Can you really blame him? I was 'blessed' before the baby and now they are threatening to burst out of my dress. I'm going to tell you the same thing you told me: There is no one, and I *mean* no one, who could make me turn my eyes elsewhere. Sorry to tell you, but you're stuck with me. Now eat your breakfast." She grinned.

A few silent moments later, Evie sat back in her chair, rubbing her now-full stomach. Aulis licked his fingers.

"You were right." He said. "That was really good. We'll have to teach the cooks in Tuatha how to make it when we get back."

Evie hiccupped. "Yeah, I think it would be pretty popular. I know it's one of my favorites."

He laughed at her expression of complete bliss. "We should probably get to the office and get your things. Do we need a box or something?"

"Nah, I can always grab a box out of the copy room. I don't have many things there; just some photos and such."

He rose and helped her to her feet. It seemed to Evie that she actually waddled to the cashier; she was surprised when Aulis plunked down a credit card bearing his name on the counter.

"Where did you get that?" She demanded.

"We have things like this for emergencies. You never know when you'll find yourself in the human world." He grinned.

"What kind of credit line do you have on that?" She peeked at him through lowered lashes.

"And so it begins." He kept grinning. "I assure you it will cover anything you might want to buy."

Evie happily chatted with Aulis the entire way to her office, pointing out things along the way. "There's the airport. I wish we had time; there are so many places I'd like to see."

He shrugged. "I can take you anywhere you want to go directly from Tuatha. No plane required."

She blinked at him in amazement. "Be careful, or I'll have you traveling all the time. I absolutely love history and have never had the time or money to go anywhere."

Another grin lit up his features. "And how is this a problem?"

20 TAKE THIS JOB AND…

They pulled into the parking lot of her office, and Evie took a steadying breath as Aulis opened her door. "Well, here we go."

Aulis took her hands in his. "Why are you so anxious? You have complete control here – you no longer need this job. I will make sure you always have everything you need." He kissed her knuckles.

They took the elevator to Evie's cubicle on the fourth floor. She grabbed a copy paper box and had Aulis sit in the guest chair in her cube. Then she straightened her shoulders and prepared for battle as Sean caught sight of her and rushed over.

"Evie! Where have you *been*? Do you have any idea what time it is? I told you the new format of the newsletter had to go out today, and you just wander in two hours late? Maybe you don't want this job!" Sean bellowed for all to hear.

Aulis stood up slowly to stand toe to toe with Sean, who was a good foot shorter than him.

Sean quickly took a step back before recovering and plastering a fake smile across his face. "I'm sorry, I don't believe we've met. I'm Sean. Are you here to see Evie?"

"You could say that." Aulis' voice was low and menacing.

Sean finally took a good look at Evie, who was deftly tossing personal items into the box in her chair. "Evie, what is going on?"

"Sean, it's exactly what it looks like. As of right now, I quit. And I'm packing up my things because, for once, you're exactly right – I don't want this job." Her voice was matter of fact as she kept collecting and tossing.

"What!?" Sean's face was comical in its shock. "You can't leave – you have to put together the new format for the newsletter."

Evie paused, put one hand on her hip, tossed her hair out of her face, and looked straight into his eyes. "Watch me."

"Where do you think you're going to go? Anyone who checks your references will have to talk to me." He narrowed his eyes and waited for the threat to take effect.

"You know, Sean, that might've worked on me two weeks ago, but I don't *need* this – or any job – anymore." She let her voice register boredom, dropped the last item into the box, and closed the lid.

He glanced quickly at Aulis. "Oh, so he's going to provide everything for you now? What exactly do you have to do in return?"

Evie gasped at his audacity.

Aulis stepped in front of Evie. "No one speaks to my wife like that and remains upright." With the ease of training, he pulled one arm straight back and popped his fist into Sean's face, dropping him to the floor. Several people in the office began applauding.

"Oh my God, Aulis. Was that really necessary?" She chuckled.

He cocked an eyebrow at her. "Men like this will continue to treat people badly until they are taught a lesson. Furthermore, *no one* has the right to talk to my wife like that. Now, let's get your stuff to the car and get on with our lives."

On their way out, several men stopped Aulis and shook the hand that wasn't carrying the box.

"Thanks, man – I've wanted to do that for years."

"Yeah, no kidding."

"Evie, we all owe you one."

Evie grinned at the friends she would miss, hoping for their sakes that Aulis' "lesson" would resonate with Sean for quite some time. She put her hand in the crook of his arm as they walked out to the car. He got the box settled in the trunk and helped her in.

"OK, you tell me where you want to go. Do you want to go shopping for you first or the baby?" He grinned.

"Hmm." She rubbed her chin. "Let's go to the mall by my house. They have a couple maternity stores as well as several stores for kids."

"Sounds great – navigate away."

They walked through the mall hand in hand. Evie's shoulders relaxed as she took several deep cleansing breaths, relieved to be finally free of Sean. When Aulis absentmindedly caressed her stomach, her mind jumped to the issue of her serious lack of clothing; their first stop was a maternity shop where she was able to pick up a couple of dresses as well as some shorts and T-shirts. She even picked up a few things for Kimbra.

"Now let's head over to the children's store." She said as she walked with more purpose. "We can get things for Lizzie as well as the babies. I just wish I knew the sex of the baby; it would make shopping so much easier."

Aulis' blazing grin stopped her. "Do you want to know? I can tell you."

"What?" She gasped. "Are you serious? How?"

"I learned the sex of the baby the same way I confirmed its existence. I hadn't said anything because I didn't think you wanted to know." He shrugged and toyed with a stray lock of her hair.

She stared at him wide-eyed. "Oh, please tell me, Aulis." She breathed.

"Are you sure?" He caressed her hair.

"Absolutely. I want to know."

He smiled gently into her eyes. "Well, it looks like Lizzie will remain our only little princess for a while longer."

"A boy? We're having a boy?" She breathed.

"Yep, and so are Ari and Kimbra. He told me before we left. The two little cousins will grow up together just like Ari and I did." His excitement was written all over his face.

Evie grabbed him by the hand, hurried into the store, and headed straight for the toddler section. "We'll take care of Lizzie first, then the boys."

Aulis chuckled as he watched his wife go through rack after rack, pulling out things for Lizbeth that he knew she was going to love. Evie had a salesperson take everything to the register, then rushed to the boys' infant section, where everything was in blues, greens, and yellows. She chose two of most items – one for each boy.

Suddenly she turned to him. "Aulis, does it get cold back home? I know we have a big fireplace, but I wasn't sure."

"Yes, we have the same seasons as you."

"Good, because I really wanted to get this for him." She was softly stroking a blue and green blanket covered in monkeys.

"Well, he *should* arrive just about the same time as the cold weather. You might want to get him a couple of blankets and some lighter ones as well."

"Oh, OK." She abruptly stopped what she was doing. "I'm just going to get this one; I know of another place where I want to look. Are you up to making another stop for me?"

"I can keep up with you all day long. Are you sure *you're* up to it? I don't want you to get too tired."

"I'm actually feeling really energized right now. Let's take care of these things and then hit the other store."

Aulis carried her packages to the car and put them in with her box from work. He climbed into the car and stared at his wife. She was positively glowing. She looked beautiful.

They drove to the baby store and then a fabric store so Evie could get Colleen to make the baby a special blanket. After a couple more hours on her feet, Evie was beginning to look fatigued but was refusing to slow down.

"My love, I have a great idea. Let's stop somewhere for lunch. You haven't eaten in several hours. Surely there is somewhere around here where we can get something to eat. Is there anything you are craving?" Aulis suggested.

"Steak." Her response was immediate.

He couldn't hide his amusement. "Well, then, steak it is. Where should we go?"

"There's a place just on the other side of the highway; they also have the best strawberry lemonade."

"Then let's go." He ushered her out of the store and back to the car.

Evie had been much hungrier than she'd realized; Aulis stared in amazement as his tiny wife inhaled a steak, baked potato, and several pieces of bread. After the meal her eyelids were drooping and he knew she needed a rest.

"Evie, I'm going to have to insist that we go back to your house now. We can always come back out tomorrow. I think we have another day or two before Oberon calls us home."

She covered a yawn with her hand. "That actually sounds really good. I'm pretty tired now."

He got her home and unloaded all the packages. Evie was so tired that she was unsteady on her feet, and Aulis caught her just as she tripped on the edge of the rug in the den. He guided her to the bedroom and laid her down before pulling a blanket up around her neck. She was asleep before he could leave the room.

He picked up Evie's cell phone off the table next to the couch and searched until he found Winnie's number.

"Hello, baby." Winnie chirped.

"Hi, Winnie, it's Aulis."

"What's wrong? Is Evie OK?

"Oh, yes; I finally got her to lie down and take a nap. Winnie, how are things there? Any word from Ari or Oberon?"

"I heard from Ari today. He said reports from Oberon looked good, but they thought they were still at least a day from where Lyrr is being held. He explained to us that it would be extremely difficult to portal into Stanis' stronghold since they weren't familiar with the layout. I guess that makes sense; they probably don't want to portal into a wall." She paused. "Are you homesick already?"

"No, but I'm concerned about Evie."

"Why?" Winnie was more than a little alarmed at the heaviness in his voice.

"Oberon was right – this world is definitely affecting her pregnancy.

She got up this morning and she's already showing; that normally wouldn't happen for at least another week back home. I'm trying not to be overbearing and to keep her calm. I don't want to scare her, but Winnie, I don't want this child born outside of Tuatha – it's not safe. We can't go to a regular human hospital."

Winnie was thoughtful. "I understand. Keep doing what you're doing. If things get too advanced, bring her back here immediately. Even if it's not safe to return to Tuatha, we can handle things here."

"I knew you would understand." He breathed a sigh of relief.

"You might want to start packing up photos for her. I doubt she'll want to take much else with her – except for her books."

"Yes, ma'am, I'll get started while she's napping."

"By the way, Aulis – how did things go at her office today? Did you get a chance to meet her boss?" She asked coyly.

"You could say that." He mumbled.

"Let me just ask you one thing: when you left, was he vertical or horizontal?"

Aulis laughed. "Definitely horizontal."

"Good boy. That's exactly what I wanted to hear." She laughed freely.

"Winnie, is there anything we should gather from Colleen's house?"

"Just some clothes. She and Lyrr can clean out the rest. It'll be good for them to have some time together."

"OK, we'll do that first thing tomorrow."

"Sounds good. Take good care of our Evie, and we'll talk again tomorrow."

Aulis placed the phone on the arm of the couch and looked for a container to use for packing.

Evie's dreams were vivid and disturbing.

She was picking her way through a dark and forbidding forest. All around her, mangy wolves bared their teeth from their positions at the feet of what could only be trolls; the huge, misshapen creatures smelled as ancient and rotten as they looked, and, if the overpowering stench was any indication of their disposition, she was in serious danger. They and their wolves snarled and growled at her, but they didn't move to harm her; instead they seemed to be slowly, relentlessly, driving her toward a destination. She wound her way through the sunless gloom under the blackened and stunted trees, finally glimpsing a cavernous, crumbling castle. As she drew closer, she saw it bore more than a slight resemblance to the castle at Tuatha, although it was fatally marred by its serious state of disrepair. The castle stones were crumbling with age and decay, and every surface seemed to be covered in a thick layer of moss and mold. The trolls forced her to cross a splintering, swaying drawbridge to the castle gates, where she was terrified to see Niklas and an older Tuatha with the same pale, cold eyes.

"I told you she was beautiful, didn't I?" Niklas said with unwonted pride.

"Yes," the man purred, "she will be a fitting bride for the new King – my son."

Niklas turned to stare at her hungrily. "I'm coming for you, Evie. We'll be together again soon. I will always find you."

Evie woke up screaming. "NO!"

Aulis ran in and cradled her in his arms. "What happened? What's wrong?"

She buried her face in his chest. "I had a horrible dream."

"Tell me." Aulis nudged.

She told him of the dream and Niklas' dark promise to her.

Aulis swore colorfully and in Tuatha terms Evie didn't wholly understand. "He's trying to reach you through your dreams; it's something the Shadow Fairies excel at." He explained. "But I will never allow him to get near you – you are *mine*."

She breathed deeply of the natural scent of his skin through the thin T-shirt and rubbed herself against him; she needed to feel she belonged to him and that he still wanted her. She reached behind her neck, released the straps of her halter, and pushed the dress to her waist. Aulis stared at her bared breasts in shock before desire burned hot in his eyes. He peeled the dress from her body, and she lay before him in nothing but a thong. When she reached for him, he buried his face in her chest, loving each generous globe with his mouth as she thrust her hands in his thick ebony hair.

"I need you to put your brand on me. Leave nothing for anyone else." She begged.

Her words were his undoing. He tore her thong in his haste to remove it, and his clothes quickly followed it to the floor. They were both too feverish with need to draw out the loveplay; he positioned his cock over her bud and thrust home. Her sheath welcomed him with moisture and heat. She raised her hips, grinding him deeper, and he knew she was ready. He pulled in and out in long hard strokes until her entire body quivered. Their coming together was cataclysmic, and they collapsed on her bed.

"What did I do to deserve such a passionate, generous wife?"

"Just being yourself is enough." She said breathlessly. "You are my anchor, and I needed to reconnect with you after such a horrific dream."

He growled. "Don't remind me. I won't be able to let you nap alone anymore. If you sleep in my arms, you can pull me into your dreams if you need me."

She pushed up onto one elbow. "Really? You can protect me even in my dreams? This arrangement just keeps getting better and better."

He pulled her onto his chest. "No matter where you go, I'll always be able to protect you."

After a moment, she pushed off his chest and stood up. "For now, I just need to use the bathroom and get a drink – in that order." She hurried off to the bathroom.

When she emerged, Aulis was waiting for her with a large glass of ice water.

"Do you have any flaws at all?" She asked with a giggle.

"Oh, I assure you, I have plenty; however, you are my first priority. I called Winnie earlier to check in. She said that all we needed to grab from Colleen's house was clothes. She said we should leave everything else for your mom and Lyrr."

Evie wiped the beads of condensation from the outside of the glass. "Do you really think they'll finally be able to bring my dad home? I'm afraid to even hope."

"I have complete confidence that Oberon will succeed in his campaign. He is a fierce warrior, and he has been waiting for this for a long time."

"I hope so." She bit the edge of her lip. "I guess we can run by Mom's house tomorrow to grab some clothes, and then I need to get to packing things around here."

"I tried to get a start for you. I packed up your books and your photos; I wasn't sure what else you would want to take."

Her eyes filled with tears. "Thank you. Really, those are the only things I want; I don't need any of my clothes from here as I already have a closetful at our house – not that I'm dressed that often." She giggled. "Everything else can go to charity."

He pulled her into his arms. "You will have everything you could possibly need or want. Speaking of which – perhaps we should get dressed and find you some dinner?"

She looked down at her body and laughed. "I guess I'm getting more like my father's side of the family all the time. I didn't even realize I was still naked." She walked back to her bedroom, chose one the dresses Kimbra provided, and padded back to the den on bare feet. She plopped down on the couch and turned on the television. "How about if we just order some pizza and stay here tonight?"

Aulis walked in from the bedroom in a pair of shorts. "What is pizza?"

Evie laughed. "That settles it. I'm calling them right now." She picked up her cell phone and called the restaurant on her speed dial. They settled down on the couch and watched some of her favorite old movies while they waited for the pizza to arrive.

"This is the one thing I'm really going to miss." She reflected.

"What is that, Ionúin?"

"I'm going to miss my movies."

"Why will you miss them?" Aulis cocked an eyebrow at her.

"Because I can't take them with me."

"Who says so? You still haven't seen our entire suite." He shook his head at their omission. "We have a room with a TV and DVD player as well as a nursery all ready to be decorated."

"Seriously?" Her eyes lit up. "I can take my movies? Oh my gosh – we have to go out tomorrow and get some that I'm missing."

The doorbell rang. Evie jumped up to answer it, but Aulis sprang in front of her, pulled himself up to his full and imposing height, and swung the door open.

"H-h-hi. Your total is $22." The teenager at the door looked like he was going to wet himself.

Aulis took the box, handed him $25, and closed the door in his face. Then Aulis turned around to find Evie staring at him with her arms crossed over her chest.

"What?" He asked sheepishly. "I gave him a tip."

She burst into laughter. "What am I going to do with you?"

He grinned. "I can think of a few things."

They sat on the couch and watched the rest of the movie until Aulis polished off the last of the pizza. "OK, that's another winner. Can you explain to our cooks how to make this when we get back?"

"Yes, it's actually pretty easy to make." She replied before yawning.

He stared at her pointedly. "I think it's time to turn in for the night. Go get ready, and I'll clean up this mess and head in there."

Evie went into the bathroom and got dressed for bed. She had already pulled back the covers and was climbing into bed by the time Aulis entered. He didn't bother to remove his shorts and slid in beside her.

"Are you going to sleep in your shorts?" She asked.

"Yeah, I wanted to make sure you actually got some sleep. It seemed the best way." He grinned.

She snuggled in close and fell into a deep sleep free of nightmares.

21 ANOTHER SURPRISE

She awoke with Aulis hovering over her with a worried expression on his face. She rubbed the sleep out of her eyes, followed his gaze to where his hand rested over her stomach, and shrieked. "Oh my God! What is happening?" Her stomach was clearly more distended than the day before. She would not be able to hide her pregnancy any longer.

Aulis placed both hands over her stomach. "I don't know. Something about this world is speeding up the gestation process. At this rate, you could have the baby in a couple months."

Evie scrambled off the bed to the bathroom. She stood in front of the mirror after emptying her bladder and studied her new profile. She gently rested her hands over her stomach and felt a surge of love. She hoped her uncle would hurry so she and Aulis could return home; she felt so lost and hated seeing Aulis so nervous. If he was worried, she should probably be scared to death.

Aulis pushed the door open. "Evie?" He called cautiously.

"It's OK; you can come in." She had pulled up the hem of her nightshirt to examine the mound as she had done the day before.

Aulis stared at her in wonder. "I wish you could see yourself through my eyes. You are absolutely beautiful."

"I'm definitely a lot rounder." Evie joked.

He rested his hands over her stomach, and his face blanched when his touch was met with a kick from his unborn son.

Evie staggered backwards, startled. "You felt that too?" She whispered as she cradled the mound in her hands.

Aulis sprinted for the den and called Winnie.

"Hi there." She chirped.

"Winnie – have you heard from Ari this morning?"

"No… Why?" She asked cautiously.

"We've got a new development here, and I need to get Evie back to Tuatha as soon as possible."

"Aulis – take a deep breath and tell me what is going on."

"Evie woke up this morning and the baby has grown even more than yesterday. There's no way to hide the fact she is pregnant anymore. Not only that, I just felt my son kick."

"*What*?!" Winnie's voice rose an octave.

"What's wrong, Winnie? What's going on?" Aulis could hear Colleen's voice in the background, becoming more panicked by the moment.

"In a minute, Colleen." Winnie tried to calm her. "Aulis, here's what I want you to do. Put all of Evie's things in the car and then take her out to get any last-minute purchases she wants to make. Make sure she eats a good breakfast, then head over to Colleen's house to pick up her clothes. Once you've done all that, come straight here. Maybe being here at my house and closer to the portal to Tuatha will help her." Even though she couldn't see him, Aulis nodded in agreement while Winnie continued. "I'll find a way to get a message to Ari as soon as I can."

"Thank you, Winnie. We'll see you later today." He hung up the phone and stared at the floor.

Evie rested her hand lightly on his shoulder. "Are you OK?"

He could tell his abrupt departure had upset her. "I'm fine. I just needed to talk to Winnie to get her thoughts. Evie, you shouldn't be progressing this quickly. I'm worried about what will happen if we don't get you home soon. We're going to spend this morning finding your movies and grabbing anything else you want from this world. Once we're done, we will pick up the clothes from Colleen's and head directly to Winnie's. She has a theory that it might help you to simply be near the portal to Tuatha. She should've talked to Ari by the time we arrive."

"I'll start getting ready right now." She turned and hurried away before Aulis could see the tears. She was terrified. Why was this world, which had been her only home, affecting her this way? She wasn't willing to do anything to put the baby's development at risk. She rummaged through the shopping bags and found one of the sundresses they had purchased at the maternity shop the day before. She pulled it over her head and studied her reflection; she certainly filled the dress out a lot better than she had the day before. She was surprised that she felt cute in the short dress; she had been afraid that, once she was big enough to fit the dress, she would feel bloated and unattractive. She was still pivoting to see her reflection from all angles when Aulis walked in. He leaned against the doorframe and watched.

"Yes, you are unbearably cute." He agreed.

She turned and laughed that he had caught her admiring her new figure.

"I've already put your books, photos, and movies in the car. All we have left to load up is our clothes. Just throw everything into the bag and

I'll take care of it."

"Everything is pretty much packed up. I just need to grab the shopping bags from yesterday." Evie assured him.

"No, you need to go through the house one last time to make sure we didn't miss anything. You are not to lift *anything*. Do you understand?"

"OK, you win." She did one last pass through the main part of the house as he carried the last of the bags to the car. Her stomach growled audibly just as he came back inside.

"That's it. We're leaving now. You need to eat breakfast. We can replace anything that we may have left."

"Wait! What about all this stuff?" She wailed. "It was supposed to go to charity."

"I already took care of it." Aulis smiled down at her. "I told your landlord that you had to relocate unexpectedly. I gave him the last month's rent with a little extra, and he said he would arrange for the charity truck to pick everything up."

She went up on tiptoe and kissed him. "Thank you for taking such good care of me." She took one last look over her shoulder and waddled out to the car, surprised that she didn't feel more emotional about leaving; instead all she felt was hope for their future. Aulis hopped in and they sped off. Evie giggled when she realized they were going back to her favorite restaurant for breakfast.

He shrugged. "It was really good. Or would you prefer something else?"

"No, this is perfect."

They spent the better part of the morning hunting down Evie's favorite old movies and returning to the fabric store for more supplies. They pulled up to Colleen's house in the early afternoon. Evie turned her key in the lock, pushed the door open wide, and then stopped, her head cocked to one side.

"What is it?" Aulis was incredibly attuned to her emotions.

"I'm not sure." She shrugged. "It just doesn't feel right – it must be because Mom isn't here." She hurried to her mother's room and filled a suitcase full of clothes. Her unease grew with each passing moment, becoming unbearable when she was almost knocked to the ground with a flurry of vicious kicks from the baby. Aulis grabbed Evie's arm in one hand and the suitcase in the other and sprinted for the front door. He helped Evie into the car, tossed the suitcase into the backseat and gunned the engine, rocketing them out of the driveway.

Evie pressed both hands over her stomach. "It's OK, sweetheart. You're safe." She crooned to her unborn child. Aulis placed one hand over her stomach and the kicking quieted.

She leaned back into the seat, exhausted. "Aulis, what was that all about?"

"You were right when you walked in – something wasn't right." He said grimly. "Your instincts are quite good, and you need to listen to them. The baby felt it as well and tried to warn you in his own way. I suspect one of Niklas' men had been in the house; we may have even set off some sort of alarm. If so, they will probably know how your pregnancy has advanced. Now we have no choice but to return to Winnie's. You are in no condition to fight anyone off, and there are protection wards at Winnie's – no one is able to enter without her permission."

Tears streamed down her face. "I'm so sorry I didn't pay closer attention. I put you and the baby in danger." She felt her anger rise and her teeth clenched. "I'm so sick of people going out of their way to hurt my family. I swear I will get even one way or another."

Aulis stroked her hair. "Shh. It will be fine. We're going to be careful, though. I'll stop so we can grab something to eat and you can run to the bathroom, but we won't stop again unless it's an emergency."

"I understand."

Evie managed to hold out the remainder of the ride. The moment they pulled into Winnie's driveway, she felt, almost saw, a change in the air around her. It practically shimmered – like the magic that formed the portals. She wondered how she'd never noticed it before. Winnie and Colleen were waiting on the front porch.

Evie leapt awkwardly out of the front seat. "I'm sorry, I've got to use the bathroom." She squealed and rushed past them, leaving them staring after her.

Aulis climbed out of the car, stretching his arms over his head. He pulled Colleen's suitcase out of the car and strode toward the two women, following them inside the house.

"Sorry; we tried to make as few stops as possible, and she was a real trooper. Colleen, here is your bag, but you cannot return home until Lyrr has returned. It's not safe." He relayed the story of what had happened at Colleen's, as well as the nightmare Evie had experienced the day before.

Colleen nervously wrung her hands before hugging Aulis. "I can't thank you enough for everything you've done! I'm so happy you found each other."

He bowed in respect. "It is I who should be thanking you. You are the reason my soulmate even exists."

She blushed and twittered.

"Are you flirting with my *mom* now? Man, I leave you alone for five minutes to go to the bathroom, and this is what I get." Evie joked.

Winnie and Colleen turned to get their first good glimpse of Evie, and they both gasped.

"Looks like you've been eating well there, Evie girl." Winnie kidded.

"Har har, you're such a comedian." Evie grunted.

Colleen walked forward like a sleepwalker and placed her hands over the mound. "Oh, Evie. You look so beautiful. I can't wait to meet him, or her?"

"Him." Evie confirmed.

"I love him already." She breathed. Her hands were met with a light fluttering.

"Mom, I think he feels the same way." Evie smiled.

Colleen's eyes were bright with wonder. "How is it possible that you're so far along when I just saw you a couple of days ago?"

Evie shrugged. "We've been trying to figure out the same thing."

Aulis looked around the house. "Has Ari contacted you?"

"Funny you should mention that." Winnie scratched her head. "I'm surprised he's not here already. He and Kimbra have been popping in and out all day."

The back screen door slammed shut.

"Winnie? Are they here yet?" Ari's voice boomed through the house.

"Speak of the devil." Winnie murmured. "We're in here, Ari." She called.

Ari strode into the den and immediately caught his twin in a hug. "I came as soon as I heard from Winnie." He scanned the room until his eyes lit on Evie. "Oh, little sister – they weren't kidding." He strode toward her and dropped to his knees, putting his hands on her stomach; he received a light flutter in response. "Hey there, little guy. I can't wait to meet you." He hugged Evie gently. "How are you holding up?"

She crossed the room and sunk into an overstuffed chair. "It rates pretty high on my weird-shit meter, to be real honest."

Ari doubled over with laughter. "Well, I'm glad to see it hasn't affected your spirit." He turned back to Aulis. "So fill me in."

Aulis sighed and told Ari everything that had happened leading up to their arrival. In true twin form, Ari responded with the same colorful language Aulis had used earlier.

"Niklas had the nerve to send someone to Colleen's house!" Ari whistled and shook his head. "There hasn't been a trace of him in Tuatha since the night you left. Dahlia freely admitted everything once the spell Niklas cast on her wore off. We learned a great deal from her, and it's helped Oberon. They found Lyrr last night – they are just working on a plan to get him out. He's alive and in pretty good shape."

Colleen burst into tears and laughter simultaneously. "Lyrr's coming home!"

Aulis continued the conversation while Evie went to hug her mother. "Ari, I'm worried about Evie staying in this world any longer; you can see how far her pregnancy has developed in the few days we've been here. She looks like she's about one-third of the way through already. The baby needs to be born in Tuatha De so we can take care of both of them properly."

Ari nodded. "I understand completely, and I have good news. I've got your men doing a complete sweep of the castle, but they won't be done until tomorrow. As soon as they finish, I will personally escort you back to your rooms. Evie will have a full guard detail everywhere she goes. I have put the same guard on Kimbra, and it's been a sore trial. She's already chafing under the constant company. I only hope Oberon comes back sooner than later." He grimaced.

Evie's stomach rumbled and her cheeks reddened. "Sorry. I swear all I do is eat, sleep, and use the bathroom... You'd think I was a man."

Ari whooped with laughter. "Yep, that's our Evie all right."

Winnie and Colleen headed for the kitchen. "Let's see what we can feed our little peanut and then we can turn in early." Winnie said.

Evie yawned. "That sounds like a great idea."

The two older women fed Evie until she thought she would pop. She lowered herself to the couch and yawned again, her eyelids drooping. She felt herself being lifted into the air, and her eyes snapped open. Aulis had gathered her against his chest and was carrying her to the guest room they were using for the night. He eyed the full-sized bed and sighed. "The beds keep getting smaller and smaller. I will be so glad to be back in our own bed again."

Evie giggled. "Soon, there won't be room for both of us."

Aulis stared at her seriously. "I won't sleep without you, even if you have to sleep on top of me."

Evie's mouth went dry at the mental picture and she licked her lips.

"Oh no, not tonight." Aulis shook his head. "You've got to get some sleep."

Evie closed the bedroom door, pulled her dress over her head, and let it flutter to the floor. She pressed herself against him and waited for the kiss she knew was to come. "It's your loss." She shrugged one shoulder and climbed into the bed.

He stared at her helplessly. "Aren't you going to put on your nightshirt?"

"No, I don't think so. The sheets are so nice and cool against my bare skin." She squirmed in the bed.

Aulis' breathing was ragged.

"Come on – we can still cuddle, can't we?" She asked with large innocent eyes.

"Of course, you can sleep in my arms all night long if you want." He stripped off his T-shirt and shorts and climbed into the bed clad only in his underwear. Evie snuggled back against his chest, rubbing her backside against his groin. Aulis groaned quietly, knowing he was going to lose this battle and soon. Evie felt him lengthen and harden against her back. She reached behind her, took him fully into her hand, and was rewarded when she heard him suck in his breath. She turned over and pushed onto her hands and knees before straddling him.

"What are you doing?" He whispered.

"I just wanted a hug."

He held his arms open wide. Evie leaned forward and pulled on his waistband until his shaft sprang free.

"Evie." It was a clear warning.

"I just want to feel all of you."

He sighed. "Didn't we talk about this already?"

His arms wrapped around her and she reached between them, pulled her panties to one side and quickly seated herself on his shaft.

He grabbed her by the hips and growled. "That was sneaky."

She ground her hips against him in a circular motion. "Are you angry?" Her voice was pure seduction. She leaned forward and proceeded to ride his erect shaft until they quickly found their release. Evie fell asleep with him still fully inside her.

Aulis was propped up on one elbow and staring down at her when she awoke.

"What?" She blinked rapidly. "Is something wrong?" They had been presented with a surprise every morning so far, and she expected this morning would be no different.

"Nothing's wrong except for the fact I told you that I wanted you to sleep last night." He growled.

"I did sleep last night." She insisted.

"You know what I mean." He sighed.

"You didn't enjoy it?" Her face was crestfallen.

He rolled his eyes. "You can honestly ask me that? Of course I enjoyed myself, but it's selfish of me when you need your rest."

She stretched her arms over her head. "I can always take a nap later today."

"That's actually a good idea. I think I'll start making sure you take one every day. However, you can curl up next to me on the couch so you don't try any funny business."

She giggled. "Are you afraid to be alone with me?"

"Yes." He admitted with a brilliant smile. "It's not really your fault, though; it comes as part of the package during a Tuatha pregnancy. I promise it will get better after the baby is born." He winked.

"I wouldn't make promises you can't keep, especially since I felt this way about you *before* the baby." She waggled her eyebrows and leered at him until he laughed. "So what is on the agenda for today?"

"First we get dressed and get you something to eat – just like every morning." He quipped. "Then we hang around the house until we hear from Ari."

"Can we at least go for a walk or something?"

He put his hand under her shoulders and helped her into a sitting position. "I wish we could, but until we know where things stand with Oberon, I don't dare to have you out walking around in the open. Your condition is obvious to anyone who sees you. Remember, not only is Oberon fighting a battle to save your father, but we are still on the brink of war with the Shadow Fairies and Dark Trolls. The Shadow Fairies are true to their name. They are masters of stealth and the dark arts of control and manipulation."

"Like Niklas." Evie whispered.

Aulis' entire body stiffened. "What did you say?"

Evie cringed at his intense countenance. "I said they sound like Niklas. He seems to be able to come and go in the blink of an eye, and wasn't he using coercion spells against Dahlia and me?"

Aulis slapped his forehead with his palm. "How could we have been so blind? No wonder they always seemed to be one step ahead of us – we had one of them living in our midst. We suspected there was a traitor but never thought to look at someone with royal blood. Niklas' mother was Oberon's cousin and was never suspected of anything, right up until the day she died; but she never revealed the identity of his father. After your nightmare, I thought Niklas might be simply working with the Shadow Fairies, but it's so much more than that."

He paused, thinking, and then kept talking almost to himself. "I hope Ari gets here sooner rather than later this morning; this is critical information for Oberon. It's always been assumed that the Shadow Fairies were the ones behind Lyrr's disappearance. However, if the Shadow Fairies were the ones to abduct Lyrr, and Niklas is truly Stanis' only heir, we have a bigger problem than we originally thought."

"What about these Dark Trolls – that was them in my dream, right? What are they?" Evie swallowed against the lump in her throat. For the first time she was frightened by what faced them.

"They are every bit as nasty as the Shadow Fairies. However, where the Shadow Fairies use stealth and coercion, the trolls use brute strength. They are incredibly destructive, with no respect for life, and they will literally eat anything in their path. The Shadow Fairies use them like a brute squad. If you ever see one in waking life, call up a portal and get the hell out of there."

"Aulis!" She wailed. "I have no idea how I managed that the first time. How am I supposed to recreate it?"

He rubbed the stubble on his chin. "I know what we're going to do today. We are going to determine what your powers consist of and teach you how to control them."

"Do all Tuatha have powers?"

He nodded. "Yes, but the magic is stronger in some families than others and, Ionúin, you were born into one of the most powerful families the Tuatha have ever known."

"But I'm only half-Tuatha. What if I can't control the powers?" She could hear the blood roaring in her ears as her blood pressure spiked.

"Well, you may look like the women of the Adair clan, but everything else about you is pure Tuatha. I know you can do this. Perhaps we can find something that you can use to provide additional protection for you and the baby."

At that, her mothering instinct kicked in and he had her complete attention.

"OK, let's do this." Evie rummaged through the bag Aulis had put on a side chair until she found a pair of cotton shorts and a T-shirt. She turned sideways in the mirror and noticed a slight change from the day before, but she hoped it was minor enough that Aulis wouldn't notice. He had enough stress to deal with.

He stood behind her and studied her carefully. "What are you looking at, my love?"

"Just checking out the new outfit... You know – just being a girl." She hoped her voice sounded calm and even enough not to raise his suspicions.

He quickly threw on his own shorts and T-shirt and held the bedroom door open for her. The smell of freshly cooked bacon greeted them. Evie's stomach fluttered softly, causing her to place her hand on the small mound.

"Something tells me I'm not the only one who thinks the bacon smells good." She mused.

"Well, then, let's feed the boy some bacon." Aulis beamed.

22 TRAINING

After a long and mentally stressful day, Evie flopped backwards on the couch, exhausted. With Aulis' help, she had discovered that if she concentrated really hard, she could communicate with him telepathically. It hadn't worked when she tried it with her mother and Winnie; it seemed to be directly tied to her relationship with Aulis. They already knew she could call a portal, but Aulis felt it was too dangerous to try to actually call one up. He was afraid that Niklas and his men would be watching for any unusual portals. Aulis suspected she had other hidden talents as well but didn't want to tax her strength any further. Winnie handed him a blanket and looked pointedly at Evie, who wasn't even bothering to cover her yawns anymore. Aulis lifted her feet onto the couch and covered her with the blanket. Within moments she was fast asleep.

Aulis sat near her head and propped his feet on the table while he rubbed his temples.

"Knock, knock. Anyone home?" Ari's booming voice echoed through the little house.

"Shh! In here." Aulis replied in a low voice.

Ari strode into the room and spied Evie curled up on the couch.

"Ahh, sorry." He dropped into the oversized recliner at Aulis' elbow. "Looks like you guys had a rough day."

"You can say that again. It would appear that my wife has inherited abilities from her father."

"You're kidding." Ari raised his eyes in surprise. "How's she holding up?"

Aulis sighed and ran his hand through his hair. "Ari, she looks like a fragile, human Adair, but she's Tuatha through and through. She's a hell of a lot tougher than she looks. The baby's growth is slower than before, but I can still see a difference from yesterday, and she's been trying to hide it from me."

"Why?" Ari's eyebrows drew together.

"The only reason I can come up with is that she thinks she's protecting me." Aulis shrugged. "On one hand it's very heart-warming;

on the other hand, it's a very dangerous precedent to set. I don't want her hiding things from me and putting herself in further danger."

"I can see your point. So what do we do?"

The brothers sat for some time running through scenario after scenario, desperately trying to come up with a solution that would keep their families safe and not jeopardize anyone else within Tuatha De.

"Of course the best option would be to sit tight until Oberon returns with Lyrr." Aulis surmised.

"I agree, but that may not be an option." Ari was uncharacteristically grave.

"Ari, if we can't get her home soon.... At this rate the baby will be coming in a matter of weeks, not months." The anguish Aulis felt was written clearly all over his face.

"NO! HELP ME!" Evie screamed and kicked and clawed at the blanket. She sat up, blinking rapidly to clear her vision as she clutched at her stomach. Ari leapt to his feet and raced for the couch as Aulis snatched his wife to his chest.

"Evie? Evie?" Aulis shook her gently but his voice was frantic.

Ari took her hands into his and forced her to make eye contact with him. "Little sister, we are here. It was just a dream. Take deep breaths and try to be calm; your baby feels every emotion that you do. He is the cause of the cramping right now. Focus on deep breaths."

Evie's breathing gradually returned to normal, but tears streamed down her face.

"Tell us what you saw." Aulis begged.

Evie shuddered. "Very much like before. I was back at that old castle in the dark forest. The wolves and trolls were lined up on either side of the path as I walked toward the castle." She took a steadying breath.

"Niklas was waiting for me again. Aulis, he knows we're here and he said he's coming for me. I tried to reason with him; I reminded him that I'm already married *and* carrying your child. He told me none of that mattered and he could raise the baby as his own, but soon I would swell with *his* child." She grabbed Aulis' shirt with her fists as the panic rose again. "We have to leave here *now*. Where can we go that he cannot follow?" Abruptly she doubled over as the baby gave her a vicious kick that took her breath away.

Aulis nodded to his brother, and he and Ari placed their hands in the air just above the precious mound. Evie slumped against the back of the couch, reeling in pain. A soft glow began to emanate from the twins. Evie felt herself relax completely and the cramping lessened; she grasped the hem of her shirt and wiped the thin sheen of sweat from her forehead. The two men gasped at the sight of her bare stomach. The baby's movements were now clearly visible through her skin.

Ari jumped to his feet and paced furiously across the small room. "Aulis, I know you don't want to hear this, but we have to get her back to Tuatha *tonight*. I don't know how much of this –" he gestured toward her stomach "– is caused by being in this world and how much may be a product of something Niklas is doing through her dreams. I'll contact Taarmo right now and let him know what's going on, and have him prepare an elite guard detail to escort you home."

Aulis gathered his tiny wife into his arms. "I can't see any other way. Hopefully Oberon returns soon and she can enjoy the rest of her pregnancy surrounded by her entire family. Set everything up; I'll make sure she's ready. You might bring a couple extra guys to help carry back all the things she bought for the babies and Lizzie." He grinned.

Tears slowly slipped down Evie's cheeks. "I'm so sorry to cause everyone so much trouble."

He kissed the top of her head and wiped away her tears. "Stop apologizing. You aren't doing anything. Niklas and the damn Shadow Fairies are the ones causing all the trouble. You aren't responsible for any of this. Please try to relax and stay calm. I'm worried about how all this tension is affecting you and the baby."

"I'll try." She promised.

Ari returned to the den with a very worried Winnie and Colleen in tow. The women shooed the two men away and sat on either side of Evie.

"You boys go head and make your preparations. We won't leave her side in the meantime." Winnie promised.

"Mom?" Evie stared at Colleen's ashen face. "It's going to be OK. Dad will be home soon to meet his very first grandchild." She grinned, hoping to calm Colleen's shattered nerves.

Colleen laid her hands on Evie's stomach and sang quietly to her unborn grandson. Evie felt the tension melt away from the baby, and the cramping subsided even further. Evie exhaled a breath of relief.

"Mom, thank you – the cramping finally stopped. I think he likes that song as much as I did when you used to sing it to me." Evie smiled at her gratefully.

Ari had already sprinted out the back door and Aulis was dashing from room to room gathering all of their bags into the den. Evie watched Aulis and wondered if he was going to wear a rut in the carpet before Ari returned. His head whipped around at the sound of the screen door banging against the doorframe. Ari and Taarmo entered the den followed by four additional men, who immediately bowed in respect to Aulis.

Taarmo went down on one knee and kissed Evie's hand. "We're

honored to escort you back home, Princess."

Evie struggled to her feet. "Please stand. I should be bowing to all of you. You've gone out of your way to see to my safety and I'm so grateful. Thank you."

Ari and Aulis each grabbed a bag and flanked Evie on either side. Taarmo slung the last two bags over his shoulders and directed the remaining men to stand two in front and the other two should follow behind. Evie kissed her mother and Winnie goodbye.

"Will you come soon?" She asked anxiously.

"As soon as Ari calls for us. Don't worry, baby girl; your mother and I are perfectly safe here. The wards protect us completely and do not allow any magic creatures inside. They aren't as strong when we have Tuatha guests in the house."

Evie finally understood why she and Aulis were leaving but Winnie and her mom were staying. As long as she was there, the women weren't completely safe.

Colleen surprised them all by grasping Aulis' bicep in a death grip. "Protective wards or not, if there is any sign that she is going into labor early, you'd better send someone's ass here to get me immediately. Am I understood?"

Evie stared at her mother, openmouthed.

"Yes, ma'am. I will have Ari or Taarmo come collect you personally." Aulis assured her.

She hugged him tightly. "Take good care of her."

"With my own life, if needed." He kissed her hand, and the group walked out the back door and into the night.

They hurried through the trees to the circle of flowers containing the shimmering signature of a portal. Aulis and Ari took Evie by the arms and stepped through after the guards. They were met on the other side by Kimbra, Lizzie, and their guards.

Kimbra snatched Evie from the men and embraced her tightly. "I was so worried about you." She pulled back slightly and caressed Evie's swollen midsection. "Ari wasn't exaggerating when he said you were progressing quickly. Hopefully we can keep that little monkey right where he is for at least a couple more months."

Ari pried Evie out of his wife's arms. "Come on, you two, we can continue this reunion in Evie and Aulis' suite. The room has already been prepared for their arrival and all the wards are set, so you and Lizzie will be safe there. I thought you might enjoy a change of scenery."

"Oh, thank the gods!" Kimbra threw her hands toward the sky. "Let's go!" She scooped Lizbeth into her arms and they all hurried toward Aulis' suite.

Once inside their rooms, Ari and Aulis insisted on checking every inch of the suite before dismissing the guard to stand outside.

"Evie, where would you like me to put these?" Taarmo gestured toward the bags he was still holding.

"Oh my gosh. I'm so sorry. You can just put them over there." She pointed toward a sitting area within the suite.

He leaned the bags against a loveseat. "Just let me know if I can help with anything else." He bowed and left the room, closing the door behind him.

Evie waddled over to the sitting area and lowered herself carefully to the loveseat. "Lizzie, come see all the presents we got for you and your new little brother." Evie pulled the bags between her feet.

Lizzie skipped across the room and jumped onto the loveseat.

"Careful, Lizzie; don't mush Evie or the baby." Kimbra warned as she sat in the chair across from Evie.

"Ima good girl, Mommy." Lizbeth assured her. The little girl clapped and squealed as Evie pulled outfit after outfit out of the bag. Evie loved seeing the little girl so happy with her choices. Evie handed another bag to Kimbra.

"What's this?"

"I wanted to get a little something for the baby, and I picked up some seriously comfy maternity clothes while we were gone. I thought it was only fair since you had given me so many dresses." She gestured toward the bag. "I love that particular store and they have some great shorts and T-shirts. They are incredibly comfortable."

Tears formed in Kimbra's eyes. "Thank you so much. It was more than thoughtful, and I'm *always* happy to change up the maternity wardrobe." She giggled.

Evie had such a feeling of well-being. She hadn't been that relaxed since they left Tuatha. Even the baby seemed content for a change. Ari was right – the baby definitely seemed to feed off her emotions. She would have to be more aware of what she was doing. She leaned back and closed her eyes, simply enjoying being surrounded by her new family.

Her eyes snapped open at the feeling of two powerful hands kneading her shoulders.

"You look so peaceful. What is going on in that mind of yours?" Aulis purred.

She leaned a cheek against the back of his hand. "Did I fall asleep? I'm sorry to be so rude. I was just enjoying being at home. I haven't been this relaxed since the night we left. It just feels right here."

Aulis kissed her neck. "I'm so glad you are happy here. It means the world to me."

Lizzie yawned audibly.

"Well, I think that's our cue." Kimbra rose from the couch and Ari cradled his little girl in his arms. Kimbra hugged her sister-in-law. "We'll see you in the morning. Maybe we can take a dip in the pool with Lizzie here in the suite."

"Honestly, swimming sounds great. It would be nice to feel light on my feet for a little while." Evie giggled.

"Oh, please, you are still tiny. I doubt you've gained a single pound; that is all baby." Kimbra snorted.

"I told you so." Aulis wrapped his arms around Evie and pulled her back to his chest.

"See you guys in the morning. If you need anything, Taarmo will be just outside the door." Ari instructed and pulled the door shut behind him.

Evie hugged Aulis fiercely. "I love you."

"What was that for?" He brushed her hair back from her face.

"I just wanted to thank you for everything. I swear I feel better since we got here."

"It's entirely possible. The castle is not without its own magic."

She inclined her head towards the massive bed on the far side of the room. "I'm definitely thankful to be able to sleep in *our* bed tonight. I'm sure you'll be happy that your feet aren't hanging over the edge."

"You'd certainly be right about that. It will be nice to be able to stretch out." He glared at her sternly. "I want to make it very clear to you that you are doing nothing but sleeping tonight. We have no guarantee that being here will slow the baby's progression. I am completely aware of the change since yesterday despite your efforts to hide it from me."

Evie stared at the ground. She had been fairly caught. She should've known better than to try to keep something like that from him, especially with the connection he already shared with the baby. He confirmed the pregnancy and the sex of the baby when she couldn't.

"I'm sorry. You were already so stressed, I didn't want to upset you any further." She admitted.

"Never try to hide something like that from me again. We are in this together, and I can't help you if I don't know what is going on at all times." He chided her.

She wrapped her arms around his waist, burying her face in his chest. "I'm sorry. I'll never do it again. I promise to tell you everything as soon as it happens." She took a deep breath. She knew things hadn't slowed down, and she should tell him how active the baby had been the last several hours. She took his hand and placed it on top of her stomach where he could feel the rapid undulations.

"By the gods, that can't be comfortable. Are you sure you feel all right?"

"Absolutely. He's not hurting me like he was earlier. It's a totally different sensation." She lightly rested her hand on his.

He swept her into his arms and laid her on the bed, tucking her in before climbing in beside her. The stress from the day melted away as they drifted off to sleep.

Something, some strange noise, tugged the veil of sleep from Evie's eyes. Aulis jumped out of bed and bounded for the door. It took her several moments to realize it was Ari pounding on the door and shouting. "Aulis – wake up and open the damn door!"

Aulis threw the bolt back and swung the door open. Ari ushered Kimbra and Lizbeth inside before slamming it shut and locking it again.

"What the hell, Ari? Where's the fire?" Aulis grumbled, obviously still half asleep.

Ari pulled Kimbra forward. "Here's the fire. Our problem seems to be spreading."

Kimbra's hand rested on her distended stomach. She now looked every bit as far along as Evie.

Evie gasped and stumbled out of bed, grabbing her friend in a hug. "Oh, Kimbra. I hope this isn't my fault. I'm so sorry."

Kimbra surprised her by bursting into laughter. "I'm pretty sure you can't be held responsible for this little guy. The only one I can blame other than myself is Ari."

Ari snorted. "Very funny, Kimbra. I still don't think you're taking this seriously."

She waved him off with her free hand. "What good is it going to do me to get upset over it? The added tension and elevated blood pressure only stresses out the baby."

"No more cookies for Momma." Lizbeth said seriously.

Evie and Kimbra sputtered with laughter.

Aulis finally gathered his wits about him. "How the hell is this happening? Have there been reports from any of the other pregnant women within Tuatha?"

Ari rubbed his temples. "No, everyone else seems to be progressing normally. It only seems to be affecting *our* wives."

Aulis scratched at the stubble that was in danger of becoming a beard. "Let's think through this logically. What have Evie and Kimbra done or come in contact with that none of the other women have?"

Evie absently rubbed the side of her stomach where the baby was rolling. "We were both at the grotto that night with Dahlia, and then we were both in the hallway with Niklas the night he disappeared."

Aulis grabbed her by the shoulders. "Evie, we never really talked about this. I need to know *exactly* what happened before we got there that night. Did anything unusual happen?"

Evie bit her lip and concentrated on the events from that night, replaying them in her mind. Suddenly her eyes went wide. "There was *one* thing. Now that I think about it – it seems like such a strange thing to do."

"Evie, what thing?" Aulis was struggling to remain calm and not frighten his wife.

"After Kimbra yelled for you, and you started running down the hall…" She paused to make sure he was listening.

"Evie…" His patience was wearing very thin. He hated not having control.

"OK, OK. Once you two came into sight, Niklas reached out and barely touched both of our stomachs. Do you think it could have anything to do with all this?" She gestured toward her stomach and then to Kimbra.

"Son of a *bitch*! I will kill Niklas with my bare hands when I find him." Aulis howled.

Evie placed her hand lightly on his bicep. "Aulis, wait. I get the fact that he wants the throne, but doesn't the baby just strengthen your claim to rule? Oberon said I was the sole heir – that changed with this." She rubbed her stomach. "Why would he want to accelerate things? What would be the point in us delivering early?"

"I plan to ask the sorry pile of shit just as soon as we find him." He ground out through gritted teeth.

Ari flung the door open. "Taarmo!" He bellowed.

Taarmo's head popped into the room. "Yes?" He asked cautiously.

"I want Dahlia brought in here immediately. We need to determine if she can help us figure out where he is or what he might've been planning. She must've heard or seen *something*."

"I'll fetch her now." He disappeared down the hall.

Evie made an effort not to snarl. "You're really going to put me in the same room with that woman? In case you don't remember, the last time I saw her she was trying to dry hump you and stick her tongue down your throat. That's going to be *fantastic* for my blood pressure."

"Don't remind me or I'll feel the need to take a shower again." Aulis grimaced.

"Well, you *are* starting to look like a bit of a lumberjack." Evie gestured toward two days' worth of stubble on his chin.

Kimbra stifled a giggle as Ari narrowed his eyes. "You two are going to be the death of us. Here we are trying to work through a serious problem and you're cracking jokes."

Kimbra shot him a sideways glance. "Welcome to my world. You and Aulis have done this to me for *years*."

"It's not the same thing." He mumbled.

"Riiiight." She rolled her eyes.

Taarmo returned with Dahlia in tow. Evie couldn't help but notice the change in the woman's posture and mannerisms. Gone was the haughty stare, replaced with what looked like humility and sincerity.

She refused to meet Aulis' gaze and instead turned in Evie and Kimbra's direction. "Oh, *no!*" Her head whipped back to Taarmo. "Are they all right?"

"You tell us." Aulis' voice was clipped, but the underlying threat was obvious to everyone in the room.

"You don't think *I* had something to do with this?" She was as stunned as a bird flown into a sliding glass door.

"If the shoe fits...." Ari crossed his massive arms over his chest.

Evie almost giggled at the sound of such a modern, human phrase coming out of his mouth.

"I swear to you! I haven't seen either one since that night in the grotto – and the only reason I even remember that is because of what Taarmo told me." She picked at the ends of her blonde hair. Suddenly her head snapped up. "Wait, I think I remember something. Niklas mentioned something once about needing a major distraction that would keep you occupied enough that he could take something out from under your nose." She shrugged. "I just can't remember what it was that he wanted."

"Think carefully. Anything you remember could help us. Where were you when he was talking about the distraction?" Taarmo encouraged.

She stared off into the distance, desperately trying to recall anything, then sighed. "I just can't remember. The only thing I *do* remember is having the conversation while we were in his room."

Ari's hands came together in a thunderous bang. "What are we waiting for? Let's tear his rooms apart and hopefully we will come up with some answers."

Aulis shrugged. "I can't see that we have any other options. Taarmo, bring Dahlia along; maybe she'll remember more once she's in his rooms." He turned and took Evie in his arms. "You and Kimbra stay here where you are safe. Taarmo will escort Dahlia to Niklas' rooms and then will be just outside the door until Ari and I return."

She kissed him and took a step back. "I think you worry too much."

"I think you don't worry enough." He shot back.

"Aulis, I'm sure we'll be just fine right here. I don't know about Kimbra, but I could use some breakfast and some time to sit with my feet up. I'm still pretty tired."

He was immediately contrite. "Of course; how inconsiderate of me. I hadn't even thought about breakfast with everything else going on this morning."

"I'll have someone bring up a tray after I drop Lizzie off with her nanny. She'll be safest in the nursery, and I think the fewer people who know about what's going on, the better." Ari gathered his little daughter in his arms, and she blew kisses at Kimbra and Evie as the men walked toward the hallway.

Aulis turned over his shoulder before closing the door. "Remember what I said. Please stay here; don't wander off alone. I won't be able to focus on our search if I'm constantly worried about your safety outside these rooms."

The door softly clicked shut.

23 SEARCHING FOR ANSWERS

"Wow, for two men who are normally total opposites, they are singularly focused on the task at hand. Why do I get the feeling that we should all be very afraid?" Evie giggled.

"I know what you mean. It's like there's a shift in the universe." Kimbra laughed before plopping down in an overstuffed chair.

Evie eased onto the loveseat across from her. "I just hope they don't get too carried away. I'm not entirely sure why they are so panicked. Seems to me like the whole gestation process is already so fast – and I'm all for being able to see my feet again. I'll never hang on to my husband if I can't get my figure back." She winked.

"You know men – they hate change and anything they can't readily understand. I think with our boys it's the fear of the unknown. They don't know what's happening and they have no control over it. It's made worse by the fact that it looks like Niklas is the cause behind it." Kimbra absently rubbed her stomach. "I just can't figure out what he's up to. Why would he want the babies born early? Is it as simple as Niklas wanting the boys to stay distracted? What would be the point? What is he trying to hide? I honestly think that is what makes Ari and Aulis so nervous."

Evie shifted in the chair, trying to get comfortable. "I guess I can see where that would make sense." She pressed her hand to her side where the baby was pushing. "Did you hear about the dreams I was having when Aulis and I went back to my world?"

Kimbra shook her head. Evie took a deep breath and filled her in on the dreams that had begun as soon as they had arrived in her world. Kimbra slapped her forehead with her palm. "Oh, geez, no wonder Aulis is so freaked out. Does Ari know about this?"

Evie nodded. "Yes, Ari was there when I woke up at Aunt Winnie's."

"Well, that explains why Ari is so wound up as well. I can't say that I blame either one of them. Niklas and his family have been dabbling in some seriously dangerous magic." Kimbra's face was somber. "Aligning themselves with the Shadow Fairies and Dark Trolls is the equivalent of them declaring war on their own people. Niklas has always seen Aulis as competition and therefore a thorn in his side. As soon as Aulis Marked you, Niklas went out of his way to make contact with you. He saw it as a game – to see if he could steal you away from Aulis. For him to reach out to you through your dreams and threaten to raise Aulis' son as his own is the ultimate insult."

Evie ran her fingers through her hair and slumped back into the cushions. "No wonder Aulis bristled anytime Niklas was around. Now I feel really guilty for dancing with him and yelling at Aulis about Dahlia the first night I was here. It's a miracle I didn't cause a serious fight. I should've known Niklas was too anxious to spend time with me when he'd met me only a few hours before – and Aulis had *very* clearly noted our relationship. I think I owe Aulis an apology for giving him such a hard time."

Kimbra waved her hands in the air. "Please, girl – don't worry about it. That wasn't your fault. It was the combination of Niklas and the nectar."

Evie shook her head regretfully. "It's sweet of you to say, but I can't in good conscience blame it all on the nectar. I was already mad at Aulis when we got here. Every guy I've ever dated for any length of time has been completely controlling; unfortunately, Aulis was *very* much in control from the first time we met, and it rubbed me the wrong way. I was adamant that I was going to go things on my own terms and he could get over himself. Winnie'd made a big deal about his *legendary* reputation with the ladies, and it had set him up in my mind as a cocky jerk. When I saw Dahlia hanging all over him, it confirmed what I thought I knew, and jealousy got the best of me."

Kimbra smiled at her softly. "Evie, he hasn't had eyes for anyone else since the first time he saw you. I've known him longer than you've been alive, and I've never seen him so utterly infatuated. He truly loves you – you do realize that, don't you? He would throw down his own life to keep you safe."

Evie picked at her cuticles nervously. "It's a little disconcerting." She admitted. "I've never had such an intensely emotional relationship. He's everything a woman could ever dream about. Well, I certainly don't have to explain it to you – since you married his mirror image." She chuckled.

"Oh, I totally get where you're coming from." Kimbra grinned. "They are both definitely worth fighting for. There are times when I could throttle Ari, but I wouldn't change a single thing about him."

"I know exactly what you mean. I have some trouble when people try to control my actions, but deep down I understand that he's only trying to keep me safe. Sometimes the defiant part takes over, and that's when we fight."

Both women turned toward a knock at the door. Evie jumped up from the loveseat and crossed the room. "I believe that would be our breakfast. I don't know about you, but I am starving."

Kimbra's eyes widened in alarm. "Evie, no!"

It was too late; Evie had already flung the door wide open. She found herself face to face with Niklas, flanked by two heavily muscled men she didn't recognize. Niklas took a step forward and grabbed her by the shoulders.

"Hello, Evie. You are looking lovelier than ever." He dropped one had to caress her growing stomach and leered at her. "I have to say things are progressing quite nicely."

Kimbra rushed forward, only to be intercepted by the two men at Niklas' side. Niklas nodded to the two men, and Evie caught the now-familiar sensation of a portal opening. She couldn't believe what was happening. *This room is supposed to be the one place we're safe!* Frozen in fear, she did the only thing she could think of – she opened her mouth and released a primal scream to alert all of Tuatha as well as the human world. Within seconds, Ari and Aulis burst into the room, Taarmo and the rest of the guard hot on their heels.

Niklas was already at the mouth of the portal. He covered Evie's lips with his own, kissing her passionately before turning to smile at Aulis. "I should probably thank you for watching over her for me... both of them actually."

"How *dare* you?" Aulis roared and rushed toward the portal with his twin.

Niklas' men darted through the portal with Kimbra. Evie burst into tears at the look of anguish on Ari's face as he saw his wife fade away. Evie reached out to grab Aulis' hand as Niklas took one step backward, pulling her through the mouth of the portal. Her fingers brushed Aulis', and then he was gone.

"*Evie!*" Aulis bellowed and fell to his knees as the portal snapped shut.

Ari cursed vehemently, picked up the nearest side table, and flung it into the wall, splintering it into kindling. "Niklas has just made a blatant declaration of war." He snarled. "Let's regroup with Oberon and tear their stronghold down, stone by stone, until our wives are safely back in our arms. So help me, if our sons are born as captives to the Shadow Fairies, I will personally kill every last one of them with my bare hands!"

"You will have to get to them before I do. Niklas will die for this."

Aulis had gone cold and quiet, his voice shaking with the ferocity of his anger as he stared at the empty air where Evie had disappeared. "I no longer care what the repercussions are. I seriously doubt Oberon will deny me anything once he finds out what Niklas has done with his only niece." He stood up abruptly. "Taarmo, get the men ready – we leave immediately."

Ari put his hand on Aulis' shoulder. "One second, Aulis; we need to make a quick trip to the human world."

Aulis glared at his twin. "What is so important that we need to make a side trip, *now*?"

Ari uttered a single world: "Lizbeth."

Aulis' eyes gleamed at the brilliance of Ari's idea. "She'll be completely safe with Colleen and Winnie; the wards will prevent any magical being from setting foot on the grounds without their permission. Granted, Lizbeth could make the wards slightly weaker, but they have to be no less safe than the castle at this point. I know that Winnie and Colleen will protect her. Let's get her things and head there now. It's only right to tell them what has happened."

Sometime later, Ari and Aulis stepped through the portal in Winnie's woods with Lizbeth curled in her father's arms. She was excited about her first trip into the human realm to stay with her new "aunts."

Winnie opened the screen door at their knock and immediately knew something was wrong. "What has happened?" She ushered them inside.

Aulis took a deep breath and led Colleen toward the couch, where he proceeded to fill them in on everything that had happened since they had left Winnie's house the day before.

Colleen took one look at little Lizbeth and knew she had to hold things together. "Of course Lizzie can stay here. She will be a wonderful distraction and completely safe within the confines of the wards." She grasped Aulis' hands in hers. "You have to bring Evie back safely – she is all I have."

He enveloped the tiny woman in a bear hug. "I promise she will be back here safely, and as soon as possible."

Winnie smacked each giant on the back of his head. "You two better have both of those girls home before those babies decide to arrive. I have every intention of being there when they are born."

Ari kissed her cheek. "You got it."

Aulis nodded. "We wouldn't have it any other way."

The men hugged Lizbeth and said goodbye, leaving her in the very capable hands of Colleen and Winnie, who were introducing the child to a cartoon about a little yellow sponge when they left. Lizbeth giggled uncontrollably and waved happily at her father and uncle.

The twins strode purposefully toward the entrance to the portal.

"She's going to be fine. I can't imagine anyone who will dote on her more than Colleen and Winnie." Aulis assured his brother.

Ari chuckled. "Oh I don't doubt that." His face grew serious. "Right now, I'm more concerned about our other girls; the stress they are under must be astronomical. Kimbra fully understands a Tuatha pregnancy but, under the circumstances, I seriously doubt that even she can remain calm. And Evie...."

Aulis knew exactly what he meant. Evie was unfamiliar with so many things related to the Tuatha. Was she remembering to keep herself calm, or was she suffering from the same debilitating cramps she experienced at Winnie's? He felt so weak and impotent, tortured by the fact that they'd been taken out of his very room. *How the hell did Niklas manage to get back into the castle? Were we all so busy searching his rooms that we missed some sort of warning or clue?* He wracked his brain, going over every little detail in his memory. *Niklas must've had some sort of magical alarm set in his rooms; once we entered, it let him know that we were sufficiently distracted. I just can't figure out what's motivating Niklas. Is this another play for the throne, or something else entirely?*

Each lost in their own thoughts, the two brothers passed through the portal into the castle. They were met by the entire guard geared up and ready to leave, including King Oberon and his brother, Lyrr. Even after years of captivity, Lyrr looked every inch a royal. He bore a strong resemblance to Oberon except his eyes and hair were exactly the same shade as Evie's; to see him was to recognize her parentage.

"Oberon, I told Evie you would pull it off. How did you get him out?" Aulis queried.

Oberon's laugh boomed through the hallway. "I told her not to worry. It was much easier than we had expected; everyone in the castle was distracted, and now we know why. There was a single guard standing at the door of his cell, and he was easily glamoured with a little magic so he won't remember a thing. We portaled right into the detention area and, as soon as we had Lyrr from his cell, we portaled right back here. Honestly, it was quite anti-climactic after all this time of searching. If we hadn't been able to pry the location of the detention area out of the guard we captured, it would've been far more difficult."

The king's lips pulled back from his teeth in a vengeful snarl. "I was really looking forward to a fight. I owe them untold pain and bloodshed. Stanis thought to weaken our kingdom by keeping Lyrr captive, knowing I would be singularly focused on the safe return of my only brother. Little did he know it had the opposite effect; the entire kingdom rallied around the quest to bring Lyrr home. He *united* our kingdom instead of tearing it down. Now, it's *our* turn to bring Stanis and his fortress down stone by stone."

"I think we can accommodate that urge to fight. I don't plan to leave a single person standing who tries to stop me from bringing my wife back home where she belongs. They *will* pay." Aulis' words came out like grit through clenched teeth.

Lyrr came forward and stood toe-to-toe with Aulis, assessing every inch of him. Aulis couldn't help but marvel at the resemblance he shared with Evie, astounded that no one had noticed it earlier. Since there had never even been a hint of Evie's existence, and Lyrr had been gone so long, perhaps no one had put two and two together.

"You are the one who is married to my daughter?" He stared pointedly at the Mark on Aulis' hand.

"Yes, sir." Aulis answered without hesitation.

"My brother has told me a great many things about how you have cared for Evie. He holds you in very high regard. Oberon spent far more time with you and Ari than I have over the years, but I always respected your work ethic and loyalty to our realm." Lyrr stared into his eyes. "You understand that I was unaware of her very existence until Oberon brought me home. I was robbed of my opportunity to watch my daughter grow up, and now I find she is already married as well."

Aulis held his arm out to Lyrr. "I would happily marry her again so that you may give her away, sir. And I swear you will not miss the opportunity to watch your grandson grow up."

Lyrr's face brightened as he clasped arms with Aulis. "Grandson? You must really love my Evie to go through that whole ceremony again." He smiled slightly.

Aulis was not to be deterred. "Yes. And we will make those responsible for your absence pay... with their lives."

Lyrr clapped Aulis on the back. "Oberon, I see why you like this boy. Given time, I think I may also approve."

Oberon chuckled. "I told you. Now, let's get going before those babies are born somewhere other than Tuatha De."

Evie emerged from the portal, took one look around, dropped to her knees, and promptly threw up.

"Is that the way you greet your new home?" Niklas chided.

Kimbra shook loose of the large men and rushed to Evie's side. "Niklas, you idiot, do you have a shred of compassion?" She demanded scathingly. "You know how a Tuatha pregnancy works – the more stress you put her through, the worse things are going to get. And not that you care, but it's certainly not going to endear you to her at all. The least you could do is to get us inside and out of this cold drizzle."

Evie looked up through the fog and mist at the slavering wolves and Dark Trolls lining the path to the crumbling castle. It was exactly as she had seen in her last dream, and it was even more frightening in person. A single thought spread a small beam of hope: Her father was here – and Oberon and his guard were here somewhere looking for him. Aulis and Ari would join forces with them, and she and Kimbra would be saved. *We just have to hang on for a little while.*

She took a deep breath, forcing herself to remain calm, and staggered to her feet. "I need to lie down." She said simply.

"Of course; the castle is a short walk, and then we will get you settled into your new rooms." Niklas wrapped a proprietary arm around her. Evie turned her head slightly so only Kimbra could read the look on her face – she was going along with things for now until they could come up with a plan. Kimbra nodded almost imperceptibly.

Niklas was so pleased that Evie wasn't fighting him that his mood improved with every step toward the castle. "Don't let the exterior fool you; we have all the comforts of home." Evie was chilled by how friendly and ordinary his voice sounded, as if nothing was unusual or amiss. "I'll take you to your room, start a fire in the fireplace, and then have something brought up for both of you to eat. My apologies; I only had one room prepared, so you will have to share with Kimbra until we can have a room plenished for her as well. It might take a day to get it all done." He even sounded apologetic, right on cue – the perfectly charming host embarrassed at being caught out.

Evie rested her fingertips lightly on his forearm and tried not to think about it. "I'm happy to have Kimbra with me." She cooed. "It will make me a lot more comfortable and help me adjust to my new surroundings." She desperately hoped she wasn't laying it on too thick.

Niklas beamed at her. "Of course! She can stay with you as long as you want – at least until our wedding tomorrow night."

Evie fought back the bile rising in her throat. "Thank you."

What is he thinking? She was already married to Aulis, carrying his son and heir; she wasn't free to marry anyone else. Out of the corner of her eye, she caught a look of pure disbelief flash across Kimbra's face. Evie couldn't bear the thought of facing Aulis again if Niklas touched her, but she instinctively knew Aulis would kill Niklas for this. The remainder of the walk to the castle, she focused on keeping her breathing steady and calm for the sake of her son.

Kimbra gasped when the large wooden doors to the castle creaked open. The inside was every bit as plush and impressive as Niklas had promised. Evie couldn't help but notice how similar it was to the royal palace in Tuatha De. The floors were made of glossy stone with designs inlaid in the stones. The walls were covered with the same type of rich tapestries. The halls wove in a familiar pattern through the castle to reach the various bedchambers. They finally came to a stop in front of a set of ornately carved doors. Niklas pushed them open, revealing a room absolutely identical to Aulis' suite in every respect. Evie stared in disbelief. Obviously Niklas' need to compete with Aulis was much greater and darker than they'd originally thought.

"What the..." Kimbra stepped into the room and turned in a slow circle.

"How clever! I love the design." Evie chirped. Her voice sounded unnaturally high even to her own ears. They were obviously dealing with a very sick man, and she resolved to do everything within reason to keep him content.

Her comment hit the mark and Niklas smiled broadly. "I'm so glad you like it. I want you to be happy here. I'll go see about getting some lunch for you ladies; it's probably a little late for breakfast now. I'll be back in just a few minutes." He shooed the men out of the room and closed the door behind him.

Kimbra spun on Evie and whispered fiercely. "We are in serious trouble here."

Evie nodded and whispered back. "I know. He's incredibly unbalanced and obviously has a sick fascination with Aulis. Up until now, I just thought he was a jerk – I mean, no one could expect *this*."

"If Ari or Aulis sees this..." Kimbra gestured around the room, "they are never going to let him leave here alive."

Evie dropped onto a loveseat and was struck with a sickening sense of déja vu; it was the same spot she'd been sitting in when Niklas had knocked on the door. "Who are we kidding? This suite isn't going to be what pushes them over the edge. The simple fact he took us signed his death warrant." She noted grimly. "His plans to marry me, and this sick little shrine he's built, are only drying the ink. I've had only a very small glimpse of Aulis' temper, and what little I saw, quite frankly, scared me."

Kimbra eased herself into the chair across from Evie. "Honey, you haven't seen anything." She chuckled and massaged her temples. "Both of those boys have a fairly long fuse – Ari's is longer than Aulis', but at the end of that fuse is a truly frightening display of temper. I can assure you it's not going to be a quick death. Niklas and his group have a lot to atone for, starting with the abduction of your father."

Evie leaned forward. "Do you think my dad is still here? I know

Oberon and a portion of the guard went out to bring him back home. Surely Ari and Aulis will be here to join them?" She kept whispering, afraid the walls might have ears.

Kimbra leaned back into the cushions. "It's only a matter of time before our twin mountains of muscle come crashing through the front door. I just hope that Oberon has already freed Lyrr so the full guard can help our boys. I'm afraid of what Ari and Aulis might do if left on their own. I seriously doubt they're thinking very clearly – and that makes them even more dangerous than normal."

Evie sighed. "We need a backup plan just in case they aren't here before tomorrow night. I can't marry Niklas – just the thought of it makes me sick to my stomach. If he laid a hand on me, I'd never be able to look Aulis in the eyes again. I'd feel too ashamed."

"Oh hell no." Kimbra spat. "There is *no* way I'm going to allow things to go that far. If they don't make it here before the ceremony, fine – we can deal with that. It's not a real wedding as far as our laws are concerned anyway. But there is no way I'd let you go back to Niklas' rooms with him afterwards. I don't care if we have to find a cubbyhole somewhere to hide in – intimacy with him is not an option."

"OK, so what do we do?"

The two women bent their heads together and plotted until Niklas returned with a servant in tow, bearing two huge trays of food.

"I wasn't sure what you would want, so I brought several things – along with an entire tray of cookies." His face was so hopeful Evie couldn't help but compare it to a small child looking for a parent's approval.

Evie and Kimbra assessed the trays. They were filled with fresh fruits and vegetables, freshly baked rolls, and various thinly sliced meats.

"Everything looks delicious. Thank you for taking such good care of us, Niklas." Evie smiled.

"You even found the good double-chocolate cookies." Kimbra grinned. "Thanks, Niklas, I'm impressed."

Niklas' cheeks reddened. "Thank you. I'm glad you like it. I'm going to leave you to your lunch while I see to the preparations for tomorrow with Father." He bowed to each of them and left the room.

Evie raised an eyebrow at Kimbra. "Nicely done. Has anyone ever told you that you would've made a good actress?"

"Please! You learn those skills as soon as you get married and your darling husband tries to cook for you." Kimbra smiled softly at the memory. "I would never hurt Ari's feelings when he went to so much trouble."

Evie giggled. "I hate to be selfish, but I'm so glad that they took you too. I would've been a wreck if I was here alone."

"Yeah, but if you needed a little getaway before the baby came, I could've come up with several better places than this." Kimbra smirked. "Seriously, though, I'm glad you aren't alone. I think I'd be more stressed and upset at the thought of you trying to navigate all this craziness by yourself. I know Ari will have Lizzie in good hands, but I miss her little chunky cheeks."

"You are the strongest woman I've ever met." Evie said in awe.

"No, I'm just a mom. You have the same strength – you'll see." She reached for the tray of food. "Let's get something to eat while we can. I'm not going to assume that anything around here is going to remain stable and predictable."

"Good point." Evie agreed and reached for the tray.

24 GIRL POWER

The women were left to themselves for the better part of the day, which they used to work through one plan after another. Niklas would occasionally pop his head in to ask Evie a question regarding what she wanted at their ceremony. Each time she forced a smile to her face and told him she was sure she'd be happy with anything he chose. He seemed happy to handle all the details himself, and Evie was relieved he couldn't see through her smile to the disgust just beneath the surface. She was afraid of what he might be capable of if he knew the truth, and she was in no condition to defend herself.

"I hope you ladies have enjoyed your day." Niklas commented as he breezed in with their dinner delivery. "I wanted you to have a chance to relax before your weddings tomorrow."

"Weddings?" Kimbra queried.

"Oh, I'm sorry." He said ruefully. "I guess in all the excitement I forgot to tell you. My father has always admired you from afar and, since you are here with us, he is planning to take you as his bride."

Evie looked at Kimbra with wide eyes.

Kimbra merely smiled. "He does me too much honor."

"Not at all. You are a very worthy bride." He motioned for the servant behind him to set down the trays. "I will leave you ladies to enjoy your dinner and get some rest. Tomorrow is going to be a big day." He kissed their hands and left the room, turning a key in the lock as he left.

"Great. I guess that ends any thoughts of wandering around tonight." Evie grimaced.

"Is he crazy?" Kimbra whispered in disbelief.

"I thought we already established that."

"Ari will definitely kill someone over this. What is Niklas' father thinking? I've never even met Stanis – how does he know who I am?"

"Looks like something other than looks run in their family." Evie joked.

"Ugh." Kimbra grunted. She lifted the lids covering the trays and whistled in appreciation. "If I didn't know better, I would think they are trying to fatten us up. This is impressive."

Evie glanced at the tray full of roasted chicken and beef as well as potatoes, rolls, and another tray of desserts. The reminder of the wedding coupled with the fact they hadn't seen any evidence of Aulis or Ari had made her appetite fade away, but she knew she would need her strength and forced herself to eat. They talked for a couple more hours before they decided they would turn in. Evie faced the bed, which was an exact duplicate of the one she shared with Aulis, and felt the nausea rise again. How would she ever get through the night?

She climbed into the bed and scooted to the spot Aulis normally occupied. She turned on her side and focused all her thoughts on her husband, willing him to come to her in her dreams.

"Aulis – can you hear me?" She stepped through the door to their suite.

He was waiting for her near the pool outside their balcony. She ran into his arms and buried her face in his chest. "Is this real? Are you truly here?"

He placed his hands on either side of her face and tilted her head to face him. "Are you all right? Is Kimbra safe?" His voice was as anxious as his expression.

"Yes, we're fine. They've treated us like royalty since we arrived. But, Aulis, I'm scared and I need you here. Niklas spent the entire day making preparations for a double wedding tomorrow. He plans to marry me while his father takes Kimbra as his bride. You have to hurry. I can't stand the thought of having to stand next to him and go through that sham of a wedding."

"He's doing what!? Has he completely lost his mind?" Aulis didn't hide his shock and anger.

"I think that's exactly what has happened. Aulis, it's so much worse than we ever imagined. He is completely obsessed with you."

"What do you mean?" His eyes narrowed dangerously.

"I mean, Kimbra and I were put into a suite that is an exact duplicate of our rooms in Tuatha... down to the smallest detail. You have to hurry. Please!"

"Do not worry, my love. Ari and I are coming for you. I told you before – you are mine, and I will never allow another to possess you." He touched his forehead to hers. "Just keep yourself safe and play along for now, and I promise you – they will die for the crimes they have committed against our family. Take care of yourselves and the babies. I love you."

The sound of a key turning in the door pulled Evie from her dream and into an upright position in the bed, startling Kimbra.

"What the hell?" Kimbra grumbled.

"Someone is coming." Evie whispered.

Niklas knocked lightly on the door as he entered. "Good morning, ladies. I've brought you some breakfast. Your dresses will be ready shortly. They required a little altering to accommodate, ahem, your new figures. I will be back as soon as they are ready. In the meantime, here are a couple of dresses for you to wear around the suite." He laid a length of pink and purple material across the foot of the bed and left the room, locking it as he went.

Kimbra eyed the dresses warily. "I'll wear the pink one."

"Deal." Evie replied. She threw back the covers and sucked in her breath. "Oh my God." She placed her shaking hands on her distended stomach. She looked like she was ready to give birth any second. "Kimbra!" She whispered helplessly.

"I'm not going to be much help here, I'm afraid. It's taking all I have to remain calm." Kimbra's voice was shaky.

Evie turned to face her sister-in-law and saw Kimbra was in exactly the same predicament. If he hadn't already told them he was having the dresses altered, Evie would've suspected Niklas was trying to speed up the birth so she wouldn't be hugely pregnant for his wedding.

"What do we do? I'm afraid to do anything strenuous or stressful for fear that I will go into labor. I simply cannot have this baby here." Evie insisted with a firmness just short of panic. "I need Aulis and my family near me. And I've never had a chance to ask anyone – is the birthing process the same as it is in the human world? I don't know what to expect."

Kimbra laid a hand on her shoulder. "Take a deep breath. We will get through this. If you remain calm, everything should be fine. If you *should* happen to go into labor, I'm here." She assured. "I've already done this once and I can walk you through it. You will come out like a champ. Just focus on the fact that Ari and Aulis *will* come, and they will have us home in plenty of time for the babies to be born."

Evie sighed heavily. "OK, I can do this. I'll start with breakfast and we'll work our way from there." She eased out of bed, shuffled to the tray, and uncovered the aroma of freshly cooked omelets and bacon. She popped a piece of bacon into her mouth. "You are right about one thing – the boys *are* coming. I have that assurance directly from Aulis."

Kimbra slid out of bed and toddled to the tray. "What do you mean, directly from Aulis?"

"I had a dream last night where I was able to talk with him."

Kimbra stared at her in awe for a second. "The Anum Amhrán." She breathed.

"The *what*?"

"The Soul Song. It's the only explanation of you being able to talk to Aulis through your dreams. I've heard about it all my life, but I never actually thought I'd witness it." She grabbed Evie's hands in hers. "Evie, this is incredibly rare. You must not let *anyone* know about this. I think it'd certainly put Niklas over the proverbial edge."

"I don't understand. What is the big deal?" Evie shook one hand free and picked up some more bacon.

Kimbra sighed. "I wish I had more time to properly explain things. Let me sum it up the best I can. The legend says the one who possesses the Soul Song will also come into vast magical powers – enough to rule the entire realm. If he finds out, Niklas and his people will think to use you for their own personal gain."

"Wait, why would you think the legend is talking about me? How do we know that it's not talking about Aulis? I don't have any special powers."

"Did you reach out to him last night, or did he call to you?"

"Um, I reached out to him." Evie said quietly.

"There you go – that's how I know. I have the ability to speak telepathically, and even *I* can't get in touch with Ari."

Evie waved her hands in the air. "No more surprises today. I can't take any more."

"What did Aulis say to you?" Kimbra probed.

"He said that he and Ari were coming and that they would never let us marry anyone else. He said to just play along and trust in them to take care of everything. He also said Niklas and whoever else is here will die for their crimes against our family."

"Told you." Kimbra snickered.

"I also told him about all this." Evie gestured around the room.

"Well, that should've hit home and given him an idea of how crazy Niklas has become."

"Now what?" Evie asked.

Kimbra took a plate and piled it high with food.

"Now we sit and have breakfast and wait for our men to come through." She smiled confidently.

Aulis woke the moment Evie dropped the connection, springing off his pallet and onto his feet. He glanced around the camp; everyone was still sleeping, except Ari. His twin always had an unnatural connection to

195

his emotions and was wide awake, watching his every move.

"What is it?" Ari scrambled to his feet.

"Evie reached out to me through my dreams."

"The Anum Amhrán?" Ari whistled low. "She's an impressive little thing."

"They are in far more danger than we could've imagined." Aulis ran his hand through his hair and filled Ari in on everything he had learned, desperately trying to remain as calm as possible.

Ari shook his head in disbelief. "Are you serious? He's actually created a replica of your rooms back home? Man, that's incredibly disturbing."

"How do you think I feel?" Aulis grimaced. "Now I'm going to have to completely redo my entire suite when I get Evie home. I won't have her reliving his disaster every time she enters our rooms. What is going through Niklas' head to do something like this?"

"I can't even imagine." Ari shook his head. "So how does this change our plans?"

"It doesn't – except the men aren't going to get as much sleep as they'd like."

"Shall we?" Ari grinned.

"Absolutely." Aulis turned slightly and bellowed across the clearing. "Everyone on your feet! We move out in fifteen minutes."

Men scrambled from under their blankets and jumped to their feet, making preparations before they were even fully awake; they had been under Aulis' command for so many years that they didn't even hesitate when he gave them an order.

Oberon and Lyrr lifted the flap to their tent and zeroed in on the twins. "Aulis, my boy, any reason why you've got us all up at the crack of dawn?" Oberon raised an eyebrow.

Aulis and Ari strode over and relayed the message Aulis had received from Evie.

Lyrr burst from the tent, rubbing his bloodshot eyes. "You heard the man; there's no time to waste! Let's move out." He roared.

Oberon stroked his goatee thoughtfully. "Niklas and Stanis are even more unbalanced than I had realized. We can't just go crashing through the front door."

Lyrr, Ari, and Aulis turned to stare at Oberon in a mixture of confusion and disbelief.

"Why not?" Lyrr demanded.

"My brother, we have some very precious cargo currently under their control. Niklas and Stanis can't be dealt with like normal, rational men. We have to be very careful and not do anything to put Kimbra or Evie in harm's way."

"Oberon, I respect what you say and agree with you on the need to plan carefully. However, neither man will come out unscathed for putting my wife, Kimbra, and Lyrr through all this. I want to tear them apart with my bare hands. The moment the women are safe, I can no longer be held responsible for my actions." Aulis said through gritted teeth.

"As long as you can control the rage until the women are safe, then whatever happens next will stay there." Oberon patted the younger man on the back.

Aulis and Ari paced restlessly while the troops finished packing and doused the campfire. Oberon sought to distract them.

"What is your plan for bringing our girls home?"

"We're going to slip in during all the excitement of the weddings." Aulis' lip turned up in a cold sneer. "Everyone should be focused on the ceremony, so we can probably blend right in with the crowd. Ari and I will come in from two different directions to confuse anyone who might recognize us." His sneer turned into a grin. "Ari and Oberon will take a small group through the back of the castle, while Lyrr and I waltz right in the front door, in disguise of course. I believe even they would notice if their prize prisoner openly walked in the front door. I'd like to keep them under the impression they still have him for just a bit longer – Oberon's glamour on the guard should help that out tremendously. I want the remainder of the battalion to circle around the castle; leave them no room to escape. As soon as we find Evie and Kimbra, I want Oberon and Lyrr to open a portal to Tuatha immediately. If either one should go into labor early, I want it to happen at home. If I'm not there, make sure you have someone get Colleen and Winnie the moment they go into labor."

"Colleen!" Lyrr whispered, suddenly wistful. In all the excitement I hadn't even thought of being reunited with my beautiful Colleen."

"Lyrr, it only seems appropriate that you be the one who tells Colleen when Evie has gone into labor." Aulis grinned.

"I wouldn't allow anyone else to tell her." He said emphatically.

"Then... Let's move out and bring our wives home!" Ari crowed.

Evie forced herself to eat, even though the very smell of the food nauseated her; she knew she had to put the welfare of her child first. She found that if she took very small bites and took her time, she was able to keep everything down. Kimbra ate with gusto and appeared completely calm and collected.

Evie couldn't figure out how she managed it. "Kimbra, how can you stay so calm? I'm fighting to keep the food down; I'm incredibly worried that I'm going to sneeze and throw myself into labor."

Kimbra shrugged and swallowed before smiling brightly. "I have complete faith in Ari. I don't have to worry – I know he'll come. I've been with him for so long that there's no room for doubt. Evie, take a deep breath and focus on Aulis and your baby. Do you really think he would abandon you now?"

Evie shook her head. Of course Aulis would come to her rescue; she just hoped he would make it in time. She took a deep breath and forced some of the tension leave her shoulders – until a knock on the door made her jump and her stomach cramp.

"Hello, ladies; I hope you enjoyed your breakfast. Your dresses are ready, and I wanted to deliver them myself." Niklas laid the dresses on the edge of the bed before joining Evie at her side. He took one look at her drastically swollen figure and inhaled sharply. "Are you feeling all right? What can I do to make you comfortable?"

Evie caressed her stomach. "I'm fine, Niklas. Don't worry about me. Things are moving much faster than I expected, but I think I still have some time. "

Niklas wrung his hands together and bit the edge of his lip. "It isn't supposed to happen this fast. Father said...." He trailed off.

"What?" Evie turned on the loveseat to face him.

"Oh – nothing. I will be back to escort you to the ceremony shortly. I have to go." He turned and abruptly left the room.

Evie couldn't help but notice he'd been completely flustered, seeming almost as surprised by her rapidly advancing condition as she was. Was he being manipulated by someone else? His father? Evie knew absolutely nothing about his father, save the fact he might be the one responsible for her own father's disappearance so long ago.

"What the hell?" Kimbra mused. "What do you think that was all about? He looked rattled."

"I don't know. I think he's surprised at how far along we are. What does that mean for us? Does he have someone else pulling his strings? Who came up with the spell, enchantment, or whatever is causing the pregnancy to accelerate?" Evie caressed her stomach as she was caught by another cramp. She had to calm down; clearly her anxiety was being passed along to the baby. Aulis, Ari, and Kimbra had already warned her about trying to stay calm.

"Those are all really good questions, Evie, and I intend to get answers to each and every one." Kimbra's mouth set in a thin line.

The two women scooted to the edge of their seats and rose to their feet. Without talking about it, they both knew they wanted to be dressed and ready to go when Niklas came back; they were both unpleasantly unsure about what might happen if he was pushed too far in any direction. Evie pulled the dress up over her hips and found that she really had to work it over her stomach; it was extremely close to being too tight. Kimbra was in the same predicament. Evie smoothed her hands over her stomach and fought against the sensation of a band tightening around her. A knock at the door alerted them to Niklas' return.

"Are you ladies ready to go?" Niklas' expression didn't belie any of the anxiety he'd shown earlier. He glided over and took Evie's hand, lifting it to his lips. "You look absolutely ethereal. No one has ever seen a more beautiful bride."

Evie struggled to keep from throwing up and replied carefully. "Thank you, Niklas. That is a very nice thing to say."

He held out an arm for each woman. "Shall we go, then?" He beamed with pride at the prospect of his new bride.

Having no other options, Evie and Kimbra took his offered arm and left of the suite. Niklas was animated on the way to the ceremony, telling them of the history behind the castle and his family's plans for the future. Suddenly he stopped in the middle of the hall and turned to face Evie. "What are we going to name our baby?"

"Uh... ah... I think we probably still have some time to work on that." Evie stammered.

His eyes sparkled at the possibilities. "Father already has a name chosen for his new son. He plans to name him Dmitry. I think it's a good strong name, don't you, Kimbra?"

Kimbra was clearly stunned; she had not expected the conversation to turn in this direction. "Well, yes, Niklas. I think it is a very strong name." She replied in a soft voice.

They finally came to a cavernous room with a stone archway. It was not in the same condition as the rest of the castle and seemed to reflect a different style of architecture. Niklas noticed Evie studying the room as he led them in. "This is the oldest area of the castle. It's considered a sacred place to us and a fitting location for the start of our new life together."

There was stone as far as she could see. The entire space looked like it had been carved out of the mountains behind the castle. The walls were rough hewn out of jagged stone, while ancient, wickedly pointed stalactites dripped from the ceiling. Evie thought it looked more like the location for a human sacrifice than a joyous double wedding; her panic grew and she felt the familiar tightening around her midsection. She took a deep breath and steeled her nerves, determined to remain calm at all costs. Kimbra glanced at Evie with wide eyes, and it didn't take a seer to know she was nervous as well. They finally crossed the space and came to a stop in front of a man who looked like an older incarnation of

Niklas.

"Ladies, this is my father, Stanis. Father, I would like for you to meet my bride – Evie."

One good look at Stanis threw Evie's panic into overdrive. He had the same eyes as Niklas, but Stanis' had a very dark ring around them, giving them a deeply sinister appearance. Evie knew to tread very carefully. If she thought Niklas was unstable, this man was probably a thousand times more dangerous.

Stanis took her hand. His grip felt like stone. "Yes, Evie. I would've recognized you anywhere. I would've known your parentage even if Niklas hadn't told me."

"You know my father?" Evie asked cautiously. She was almost afraid to hope.

"Of course." He blustered. "He has been here with us these many years."

"He's here now?" Evie glanced around the room. "May I please see him?"

He patted her hand. "Of course. It will be my wedding gift to you." He motioned for a nearby guard. "Please have Lyrr brought down to watch his only daughter marry."

The guard nodded and took off toward the back of the cave.

"Thank you." Evie graced him with a blinding smile. Perhaps if her father was still here, he would be able to help them.

Stanis turned to Kimbra and kissed her hands. "I need no introduction to know who you are."

"You have me at a disadvantage." Kimbra fought to match his composure. "You know me, but I have never met you."

"My dear, I've been watching events unfold in Tuatha for a very long time. I noticed your beauty years ago; you have a grace and strength about you that is very appealing. Not to worry about your little girl. I will have her brought here to live with us. I wouldn't make you leave her behind."

"Thank you, Stanis. I would be heartbroken without her."

"It's nothing. She is a spirited little girl who I suspect will come into significant powers, and she will be able to teach our little Dmitry." He smiled benevolently, but Evie noted the smile didn't reach his eyes.

Kimbra swallowed hard and took a deep breath but said nothing.

Stanis allowed himself to savor the moment. The powerful Shadow leader was driven by only two things: control and power. He had every reason to expect that by marrying the wives of his enemies into his family, he would have an unending supply of both.

He clapped his hands together. "Enough with all this chatter. Let the ceremony begin."

25 A FATHER'S LOVE

Stanis took Kimbra by the arm as Niklas did the same with Evie and pulled them to a slightly raised area with a small pool behind it; under different circumstances, Evie could see how it would've been a magical location. Attendees who had been silently filing in to line the sides the room stepped forward and crowded around the raised area, elbowing each other for a better view.

A man came to stand before them, dressed in unrelieved black robes from head to toe. His hair was stark white, but his eyes were so dark they looked black. Evie wondered if he was even human – relatively speaking. He was probably one of the Shadow Fairies, or perhaps something even darker. He held his hands in the air and a red glow emanated from his fingertips. *Nope – definitely not human. What is he?* Then Evie felt cut in half by a vicious cramp and bent over. *Oh no, not now. Please don't choose now – you can't be born here.*

Stanis glared at her. "Stand up." He demanded. "This is a sacred ceremony. I would have you treat it as such." Lyrr's willful little brat was not going to spoil his plans. He would bring her to heel.

Niklas studied her with wide eyes and drawn eyebrows. He was obviously concerned yet conflicted; it hurt him to see Evie in pain, but he couldn't go against his father's wishes.

Stay calm. Take deep breaths. Kimbra's voice rang in Evie's head as clearly as if she had spoken aloud.

How can I hear you? Evie thought.

Oh thank the gods. I was hoping you would be able to hear me. Even Kimbra's mental voice sounded relieved. *It's a gift I possess, but it doesn't work with everyone. Since I couldn't communicate with Ari, I was afraid I wouldn't get through to you. Take deep cleansing breaths to keep the baby calm, and hopefully we can keep him right where he is until we can get home.* She sounded so sure; how could Evie not have faith what she was saying? Evie concentrated on slow and steady breathing but was unexpectedly hit with a contraction that almost dropped her to her knees.

"I'm warning you, child." Stanis glared.

Niklas took a step forward and helped Evie stand upright. "Father, I don't think she's doing it on purpose. I think she is entering labor."

"Nonsense. I created and wove that spell myself. They will not go into labor until tomorrow, long after we are already married. The children will belong to us as well as the mothers." He sneered. "Stop being such a weak, sniveling baby. Are you going to let this woman control your entire life?"

Evie wanted nothing more than to punch him in the face. Unfortunately she wasn't in any condition to fight him.

The guard Stanis had sent for Lyrr rushed back into the room. "My lord! Lyrr is gone from his cell! The bars have been ripped out of the wall." He panted.

"What do you mean, gone? He was there yesterday at the last check."

"I know, sir, but he's gone now." The guard braced himself for the consequences.

A dark red stain spread across Stanis' face. "Find. Him. Now!" He screamed.

"No need. I'm right here, Stanis." Lyrr stepped forward from among the attendants.

The crowd quickly dispersed to the edges of the cave, with many of them fleeing the room entirely. Aulis emerged from behind Lyrr, and Evie's knees went weak with relief.

"You will release my daughter and Kimbra immediately." Lyrr demanded quietly, almost conversationally, through impeccable self-control.

"Who are *you* to be making demands of *me*?" Stanis almost laughed. "You've been under my control for years; what makes you think things are different now?"

"Because he has a hell of a lot of backup." Ari and Oberon stalked out of the shadows. Kimbra greeted her husband with a brilliant smile.

"Guards!" Stanis cried.

Soldiers raced into the room, only to be dispatched by Ari and Aulis' men who had materialized from under cloaks in the crowd. Kimbra grabbed Evie by the hand and took off at a run; they made it only a few steps before Stanis grabbed Evie's other arm and wrenched her away from Kimbra. He whipped her backwards, causing Evie to crash to the stone floor.

"You stay *here*." He insisted, still expecting to exert control over the situation.

"Oh, no." Evie's voice shook as she realized her water had broken with her fall. The next contraction made her curl up on her side and scream.

"Get Evie and Kimbra home now!" Aulis roared. He dived for Stanis and fought with the strength of a man possessed. His fist smashed into Stanis' mouth, knocking out several teeth in the process; the next swing crushed Stanis' nose, sending blood in all directions. Ari jumped forward and grabbed Niklas by the throat. Oberon and Lyrr raced to Evie's side; Lyrr gathered her up in his arms while Oberon took a firm hold of Kimbra and quickly conjured a portal. In the barest instant, the four turned to mist and melted away from the cave.

"*No!*" Niklas cried as he watched Evie's form disappear. "I love her and she's in pain!"

"You should be far more concerned with your own fate." Ari growled while putting firmer pressure on Niklas' windpipe. The room shook with the power released by the portal's abrupt appearance and disappearance. Having dispatched the Shadow soldiers, the Tuatha guard turned to see that Aulis had Stanis pinned and was repeatedly slamming his head into the stone floor, his hands covered in Stanis' blood.

Niklas squirmed out of Ari's grasp and leapt for Stanis. "Father!" He screamed. He pushed Aulis away and knelt over Stanis, cradling the crushed skull. "Father, speak to me!" He begged as stalactites began to break from the ceiling and crashed around them. Ari dove across the room, hitting his brother in the chest; they rolled toward the cave wall in a ball of flailing arms and legs. Niklas turned from the twins and held tight to the lifeless body of his father as a sharp-edged, crystalline stalactite fell to impale them both.

Aulis stared at the gruesome scene before him. "Ari, you saved my life." He whispered.

"Of course I did. Life would be pretty boring without you around." Ari grinned. Aulis embraced his brother, painfully aware of how close he had come to sharing the same fate as Niklas and Stanis.

"Come on, Aulis. Taarmo and the rest of the men can finish up here; let's get you home and cleaned up before you miss the birth of your first son." Ari rose to his feet and extended a hand to his brother. Aulis leapt to his feet and immediately called forth a portal, and the two men jumped through. The moment their feet touched the familiar marble floors, they raced through the hallways straight to Aulis' suite, hoping to find everyone there. Aulis stopped just long enough to scrub the blood from his hands in a fountain before bursting through the heavy wooden door, gasping for air.

Evie lay in their massive bed, drenched in sweat, with Colleen and Winnie on one side and Kimbra on the other. Oberon was doing his best to contain Lyrr to the balcony just outside the room. Aulis flew to Evie's side and took her hand from Kimbra while Ari gathered his wife into his arms.

"I'm so sorry it took me so long, my love. You should never have to go through this alone." Aulis apologized.

"I'm just glad you're here now." Evie panted. "I wouldn't let him be born without you."

"We've been trying to get her to push, but she's so damn stubborn." Winnie grimaced.

"I'm here." He wrapped his free hand over their intertwined hands and raised to his lips. "Let's meet our new little man. What do you say?" Evie smiled through the pain of another contraction. "Together, then."

Winnie and Colleen raced to the end of the bed and prepared for the baby's arrival. Four pushes later, the room was filled with the newborn's strong cries. Colleen quickly cleared his eyes and mouth and wrapped him in a blanket before presenting him to his father.

"Aulis, meet your son." She said, smiling through her tears. Aulis cradled the baby in his arms and pulled back the blanket as his son looked directly at him. The baby's gaze was a perfect mirror image of his own, not to mention the thick shock of ebony hair gracing the top of his tiny head. Tears streamed down Aulis' face. He had never experienced such an unconditional love for something he had created.

He leaned over and placed the baby in Evie's arms before kissing her and dropping to his knees. "Thank you for giving me the most precious gift I ever could've imagined."

Evie burst into tears at the raw emotion on Aulis' face and the deep love she felt for her son.

After a few moments, Aulis rose to his feet and sat on the edge of the bed. "So what are we going to name this little guy? We never got to talk about it."

Evie blushed. "What about Riku?"

Aulis and Ari exchanged surprised looks. "That was our father's name." Aulis said quietly.

"I know. I think it fits him perfectly." She said softly.

Aulis embraced his wife and son together. "I love it. Riku it is." He stood up, and Evie placed Riku into his father's massive arms.

Ari leaned in close to smile into his nephew's face. "He's perfect, Aulis. But we'll have to get to know him later; looks like I have some work ahead of me as well." Aulis saw Ari was supporting Kimbra, who wore a stoic expression and a thin sheen of sweat on her brow.

"Are you kidding?" Aulis laughed.

"Nope, looks like our boys will share the same birthday." Ari grinned back.

"Go on, then, quick! I'll be there soon to check on you."

Kimbra hobbled forward and kissed her brother-in-law on the cheek. "Thank you, Aulis. Give Evie my love. You both did so well – Riku is beautiful."

Ari hurried Kimbra to the door as Aulis called, "Oberon, Lyrr, come meet Riku."

"Where are those two headed?" Oberon's brows drew together as the door closed behind the expecting couple.

"It's time to give Riku a playmate." Aulis smiled brilliantly.

"Oh my gosh!" Evie exclaimed. "Kimbra's in labor? She never said a word. I feel horrible." Evie wrung her hands together.

"Don't. I think it just started, so they may be a while. Winnie? Colleen? Would you ladies mind helping out?" Aulis asked. "Kimbra's mother passed away when she was very small; I know she would find your company very soothing. She's become quite attached to you both."

"Absolutely. We'll head over just as soon as we get things cleaned up here." Colleen insisted. "Evie, will you be OK for a while?"

Evie looked at her husband holding their newborn son. "I'm going to be just fine." She grinned.

Aulis turned to Lyrr. "Your Highness, it is my pleasure to introduce you to your grandson, Riku."

Lyrr took the small bundle and caressed the tiny hands with his finger; Riku wrapped his fist around his grandfather's finger as a single tear slipped down Lyrr's cheek. "Oberon, my brother, thank you for making sure I didn't miss this moment. I was robbed of my time to watch my Evie grow up, but I'll be present for every single second with my grandson."

Lyrr turned to Evie while Oberon admired the baby in Lyrr's arms. "You are everything I could've hoped for in a daughter, and this fine young man is simply the icing on the cake." He shifted Riku in one powerful arm and pulled Colleen against him with the other. "Thank you, my love, for everything – your strength and grace in watching over our precious little girl while I wasn't able to."

Colleen shook her head against his chest. "Lyrr, it's not like you abandoned us; you didn't *have* a choice. We're all together now, and we have all the time in the world." She tilted her head up and kissed him, then returned to setting the room to rights.

Lyrr passed the small bundle to Oberon, who kissed Riku on the head and smiled into the tiny face before handing the bundle to his mother.

"Come, my brother, let's go celebrate today's victories!" Oberon thumped Lyrr in the chest. "We can tell each other stories of our time apart, and then we'll make preparations for a banquet in the babies' honor, as well as yours. It will be a feast like Tuatha has never seen!" Wearing identical grins, the two men threw their arms around each other's shoulders and lumbered out the door.

Aulis took Riku so Colleen and Winnie could change Evie's clothes.

"Sweet girl, you did good." Winnie grinned. "I think you're going to find that a Tuatha pregnancy and birth have some added benefits. Now, we are going to go help Kimbra and Ari. We will see you two at dinner tonight." She and Colleen kissed the new family and rushed out.

Evie bit her lip and furrowed her brow. She was exhausted. Getting up and going to dinner was the last thing on her mind.

Aulis stroked her hair. "She's right. After a nap you are going to feel remarkably better. By tomorrow morning, you will feel like your old self."

"Are you kidding?" Evie exclaimed. "In my world, it would take *weeks* before things got back to normal. We'd better be careful or we'll end up with a dozen kids." She laughed.

"Can't say that sounds all that terrible." He chuckled, putting Riku back in his mother's arms.

Riku turned toward Evie and began rooting. Evie looked at him, mildly distressed. She understood the mechanics but had a serious fear of failure, and her mother and Winnie were gone. Things were simply going too perfectly; she hoped instinct would take over. She unbuttoned the top of her nightgown and lifted her son to her breast. He immediately latched on and suckled furiously.

Aulis was amazed that his wife managed to look so delectable after an ordeal like giving birth. He was grateful that she wouldn't be out of commission long. His wife affected him like no other woman.

"Would you stop looking at me like you're planning on joining Riku for his meal?" She laughed.

"It's an idea. I'll give you two days to recover, then I'm reclaiming you as my own." He waggled his eyebrows.

"Promise?" She ginned.

He climbed on the bed and embraced his wife and now-drowsing son. Evie leaned against Aulis and sighed contentedly before falling into a very peaceful sleep.

Evie awoke to the lusty cry of her son. "How long have I been asleep?" She scrambled to sit up.

Aulis had cradled his tiny son in his arms. "Sorry, I wanted you to sleep so I kept him entertained as long as possible. Unfortunately, I can't help with what he wants right now."

Evie grinned and held out her arms. "Let's see about getting him some dinner."

Once Riku had nursed his fill, Aulis reached out and gently lifted his sleeping son.

"Why don't you go get ready for dinner? I think you'll find your wardrobe options have opened up significantly." He winked.

Evie flipped back the covers and gasped. Her figure had almost returned to what it had been prior to being pregnant. She swung her legs over the side of the bed and allowed her feet to slide to the floor. She carefully stood up and realized she felt quite strong. She took one last look at Riku sleeping in Aulis' arms and strode into the bathroom for a much-desired shower. She came out of the bathroom wrapped in a towel and found Aulis hovering over Riku, trying to get him dressed in one of the outfits they had purchased in the human world. She couldn't help but smile at the picture the giant warrior made with their son. She crept into the closet, trying to keep from disturbing the father-and-son moment.

Feeling like a new person, she strolled out of the closet a few minutes later, dressed in a maxi dress with her hair hanging down her back.

"You look beautiful." Aulis breathed. "I've already packed a small bag of supplies for Riku. What do you say we pick up Ari and Kimbra and see how Lizzie likes her new little brother?"

Evie clapped her hands together. "Oh I would *love* to meet him. Can we go right now?"

"First tell me what you think of my handiwork. I've never done this before." He gestured to Riku, who was lying on the bed sleeping peacefully. He was wearing an infant gown in a soft blue and wrapped in the yellow and blue blanket covered in monkeys.

"He's perfect. Let's go introduce him to his aunt and uncle." Evie gathered up Riku as Aulis grabbed his bag and wrapped an arm around her waist.

The door to Ari's suite was almost identical to Aulis'. Aulis raised a fist and knocked.

"Come in." came a muffled voice.

Aulis opened the door, calling "Knock knock!" as he led Evie inside.

"Unca Owie! Come see my new baby!" Lizzie threw herself in Aulis' arms.

"My Lizzie girl." He gave her a quick hug. "I'll come see your baby if you give your new cousin a kiss first."

Lizzie squealed and peeked over his shoulder as Evie pulled the blanket back from Riku's face. Lizzie leaned over and placed a very gentle kiss on his tiny head. "Aunt Ebbie. He's bootyful. I love him. Come see our new baby too!" She grabbed Aulis by the hand and pulled him further into the suite.

Kimbra and Ari were sitting on a loveseat, where Kimbra cradled their son.

"Hey there." Ari jumped up and rushed toward Evie. "Hand over that nephew of mine."

Evie grinned. "I'll trade you, but only for a minute."

"Deal." Ari chuckled.

Kimbra stood up and handed her small bundle to Evie. "Evie, Aulis, meet Kari."

Evie's grin threatened to split her face. "I *love* it. It's a perfect combination of Ari and Kimbra!" She pulled the blanket back slightly and giggled. "I guess great minds think alike. I can't get over how much they resemble each other!"

Kari and Riku could've passed for twins; Kari had the same thick patch of ebony hair. There could be no doubt in anyone's mind who their fathers were. Kari was even wearing the yellow version of the same gown Riku was wearing and was wrapped in the identical blanket.

"It was too cute not to use, and the gowns make it *so* easy to change these little guys. You were brilliant to grab them while you were at home." Kimbra agreed.

Aulis cradled Kari's small head in his hand before handing him back to his mother. "Looks like you guys did a good job once again. He's definitely a good-looking kid." He turned and lifted Lizbeth high into the air. "What do you say, Lizzie? How about we go get some dinner? I'm *starving*!"

The families set out together for the dining hall, where they were immediately greeted by the thunderous cheers of their people. Lyrr and Oberon personally came to escort them in. They all settled down and thoroughly enjoyed their first meal with the whole family present. The babies were handed all around, and it appeared that Kari had been adopted by Winnie and Oberon as their very own grandson. Evie found that she wanted to eat far more than normal and chalked it up to nursing. Thankfully she got her metabolism from her father.

Lyrr leaned over and wrapped an arm around Evie. "My child, I want to talk to you about a promise your husband made to me."

"What promise?" Evie was utterly confused.

"He promised me that, once I was home, he would marry you all over again so I could give you away. Oberon and I talked, and we can have everything together day after tomorrow. There will be three weddings the same day."

"Three weddings?" Evie's eyes widened.

Lyrr beamed. "Yes. We will renew your wedding and then perform two additional weddings that should've happened years ago."

"You're kidding!" She squealed.

He shook his head. "I finally have the opportunity to marry your mother, and I'm not going to let it slip away again. I also have the chance to stand with my brother as he marries the love of his life."

Evie jumped up from the table and kissed her mother and Winnie on the cheek. "I'm so excited for you all!"

The room burst into deafening cheers when Oberon and Lyrr made the official announcements. The cheering woke the two babies, who immediately started crying. Kimbra and Evie gathered up the babies, said their goodbyes, and headed for their suites.

"I can't thank you enough for everything you've done for me over the past couple of weeks." Evie said fervently. "I don't think I could've done it alone."

Kimbra reached over and stroked the soft black fuzz covering Riku's head. "That's what family is for."

A laughing voice followed them. "Have you two already forgotten what happened the last time you wandered away from dinner together?"

The women turned to find Aulis and Ari striding down the hall with Lizbeth riding on her father's shoulders.

Evie shrugged. "We don't have to worry about things like that. Our husbands will always come to rescue us."

Ari grimaced, then broke into a grin. "Oh no – blind faith. We'll never get a day off."

Aulis leaned down and kissed his newborn son's forehead. "Some things are simply worth fighting for."

ABOUT THE AUTHOR

S.C. Wise attended the University of Texas at Arlington, where she met her husband. Her life did an about-face in January 2009 and the future of her career looked bleak. Her husband encouraged her to follow her dream and finally write the story which had been buzzing around in her head for a number of years, thus a writer was born.

These days she spends her time in Flower Mound, Texas with her husband, two children and a couple of crazy Jack Russell Terriers. When she's not writing she enjoys spending time watching her son play hockey or visiting her daughter at Oklahoma State University.

www.ingramcontent.com/pod-product-compliance
Lightning Source LLC
Chambersburg PA
CBHW051510260626
47162CB00008B/2900